Edward Marston was born and brought up in South Wales. A full-time writer for over thirty years, he has worked in radio, film, television and the theatre. A former chairman of the Crime Writers' Association, Edward lives in the Cotswolds with his wife, fellow author Judith Cutler.

www.edwardmarston.com

By Edward Marston

THE BRACEWELL MYSTERIES

The Queen's Head
The Merry Devils
The Trip to Jerusalem

THE CAPTAIN RAWSON SERIES

Soldier of Fortune
Drums of War
Fire and Sword
Under Siege
A Very Murdering Battle

THE RESTORATION SERIES

The King's Evil
The Amorous Nightingale
The Repentant Rake
The Frost Fair
The Parliament House
The Painted Lady

THE RAILWAY DETECTIVE SERIES

The Railway Detective
The Excursion Train
The Railway Viaduct
The Iron Horse
Murder on the Brighton Express
The Silver Locomotive Mystery
Railway to the Grave
Blood on the Line
The Stationmaster's Farewell

The Railway Detective Omnibus:
The Railway Detective - The Excursion Train - The Railway Viaduct

THE HOME FRONT DETECTIVE SERIES

A Bespoke Murder

The Queen's Head

An Elizabethan Mystery

EDWARD MARSTON

Allison & Busby Limited
12 Fitzroy Mews
London W1T 6DW
www.allisonandbusby.com

First published in Great Britain in 1988.
This paperback edition published by Allison & Busby in 2012.

A CIP catalogue record for this book is available from
the British Library.

10 9 8 7 6 5 4 3

ISBN 978-0-7490-1013-3

Typeset in 10.5/16 pt Sabon by
Allison & Busby Ltd.

The paper used for this Allison & Busby publication
has been produced from trees that have been legally sourced
from well-managed and credibly certified forests.

Printed and bound by
CPI Group (UK) Ltd, Croydon, CR0 4YY

TO THE ONLIE BEGETTER OF
THESE INSVING CHRONICLES
Mr. C.M. ALL HAPPINESSE
WISHETH
THE WELL-WISHING
ADVENTVRER IN
SETTING
FORTH

'Her head should have been cut off years ago.'
Queen Elizabeth I

Prologue

Fotheringhay Castle
February 1587

Death stalked her patiently throughout the whole of her imprisonment. Hardly a day passed when she did not hear or imagine its stealthy tread behind her, yet it stayed its hand for almost twenty years. When it finally struck, it did so with indecent haste.

'Tomorrow morning at eight o'clock.'

The Earl of Shrewsbury set the date and time of her execution in a faltering voice. He was part of the deputation which called on her after dinner in her mean apartments at the grim fortress. Mary was forced to get out of bed, dress and receive the men in her chamber. She was the Dowager Queen of France, the exiled Queen of Scotland and the heir to the English throne but she had to suffer the humiliations that were now borne in upon her.

Shrewsbury pronounced the sentence, then Beale, the clerk of the Council, read aloud the warrant from which the yellow wax Great Seal of England dangled so mesmerically. Everything was being done in strict accordance with the Act of Association.

Death had enlisted the aid of legal process.

Her captors gave her no crumbs of comfort to sustain her through her last hours. When she asked that her own chaplain be given access to her, in order to make ready her soul, the request was summarily denied. When she called for her papers and account books, she met with resistance again. The deputation was proof against all her entreaties.

Their licence extended beyond the grave. It was Mary's wish that her body might be interred in France either at St Denis or Rheims but they refused to countenance the idea. Queen Elizabeth had expressly ruled against it. Alive or dead, the prisoner was to have no freedom of movement.

All further appeals were turned down. The interview came to an end, the deputation withdrew and Mary was left to soothe her distraught servants and to contemplate the stark horror of her situation.

Tomorrow morning at eight o'clock!

In an impossibly brief span of time, she had to tie off all the loose ends of a life which, for some forty-four years now, had been shot through with moments of high passion and deeply scored by recurring tragedies. Twelve days would not have been long enough for her to prepare herself and she was given less than twelve hours. It was a cruelly abrupt departure.

Supper was quickly served so that Mary could begin the task of putting her affairs in order. She went through the contents of her wardrobe in detail and divided them up between friends, relations and members of her depleted household. When she had drawn up an elaborate testament, she asked for Requiem Masses to be held in France and made copious financial arrangements for the benefit of her servants. Even under such stress, she found time to make charitable bequests for the poor children and friars of Rheims.

Her spiritual welfare now took precedence and she composed a farewell letter to the chaplain, de Préau, asking him to spend the night in prayer for her. The faith which had sustained her for so long would now be put to the ultimate test.

It was two o'clock in the morning before her work was done. Her last missive, to her brother-in-law, King Henry of France, was thus dated Wednesday 8th February, 1587, the day of her execution.

Mary lay down on the bed without undressing while her ladies-in-waiting, already wearing their black garments of mourning, gathered around her in a sombre mood. One of them read from a Catholic bible. The queen listened to the story of the good thief as it moved to its climax on the cross then she made one wry observation.

'In truth, he was a great sinner,' she said, 'but not so great as I have been.'

She closed her eyes but there was no hope of sleep. The heavy boots of soldiers marched up and down outside her room to let her know that she was being guarded with the utmost care, and the sound of hammering came from the hall where the scaffold was being erected by busy carpenters. Time dragged slowly by to heighten the suspense and prolong her torment.

At six o'clock, well before light, she rose from her bed and went into the little oratory to pray alone. Kneeling in front of the crucifix for what seemed like an eternity, she tried to fit her mind for what lay ahead and to ignore the sharp pains that teased and tested her joints. The sheriff of Northampton eventually summoned her and the agony of the wait was over. The longest night of her life would now be followed by its shortest day.

Six of her servants were allowed to attend her. Mindful of her command that they should conduct themselves well, they drew strength from her evident composure and fortitude. Whatever the mistakes of her life, she was determined to end it with dignity.

Almost three hundred spectators had assembled in the great hall and they strained to catch a first glimpse of her as she came in, looking on with a mixture of hostility and awe. They knew that they were in the presence of a legend – Mary Queen of Scots, an erratic, imperious, impulsive woman who had lost two crowns and three husbands, was Catholic heir to a Protestant country and could, by her very existence, inspire rebellion while still under lock and key.

Her youthful charm might have vanished, her beauty might have faded, her face and body might have fleshed out, her shoulders might have rounded and her rheumatism might oblige her to lean on the arm of an officer as she walked along, but she was still a tall, gracious figure with the unmistakable aura of majesty about her and it had its due effect on her audience.

She was dressed in black satin, embroidered with black velvet and set with black acorn buttons of jet trimmed with pearl. Through the slashed sleeves of her dress could be seen inner sleeves of purple and although her shoes were black, her stockings were clocked and edged with silver. Her white, stiffened and peaked head-dress was edged with lace, and a long, white, lace-edged veil flowed down her back with bridal extravagance.

Mary held a crucifix and a prayer book in her hand, and two rosaries hung down from her waist. Round her neck was a pomander chain and an *Agnus Dei*. Her manner was calm and untroubled, and she wore an expression of serene resignation.

In the middle of the hall was the stage which had been built during the night. Some twelve feet square and two feet high, it was hung with black. As Mary was led up the three steps, her eye fell on the pile of straw which housed the executioner's instrument. Her rank entitled her to be despatched with the merciful swiftness of a sharp sword but she saw only the common headsman's axe. It was a crushing blow to her pride.

She listened with studied calm as the nervous Beale read out the commission for her execution. Mary was imperturbable. It was only when the Dean of Peterborough stepped forward to harangue her according to the rites of the Protestant religion that she betrayed the first sign of emotion.

'Mr Dean,' she said firmly, 'I am settled in the ancient Catholic Roman religion, and mind to spend my blood in defence of it.'

Resisting all exhortations to renounce her faith, she hurled defiance at her judges by holding her crucifix aloft and praying aloud in Latin and then in English. When she had attested her devotion to Catholicism, she was ready to submit to her fate.

The executioners and the two ladies-in-waiting helped her to undress. Above a red petticoat, she was wearing a red satin bodice that was trimmed with lace. Its neckline was cut appropriately low at the back. When she put on a pair of red sleeves, she was clothed all over in the colour of blood.

Her eyes were now bound with a white cloth embroidered in gold. The cloth was brought up over her head so that it covered her hair like a turban. Only her neck was left bare. She recited a psalm in Latin then felt for the block and laid her head gently upon it. The executioner's assistant put a hand on the body to steady it for the blow.

There was a rustle of straw as the axe was lifted up by strong hands, then it arched down murderously through the air. Missing her neck, it cut deep into the head, drenching the white cloth with blood and drawing involuntary groans from an audience that was watching with ghoulish fascination. The axe rose again to make a second glittering sweep, slicing through the neck this time but failing to sever the head from the body. With crude deliberation, the executioner hacked through the last few royal sinews.

The ceremony was not yet complete. Stooping down to grasp his trophy and exhibit it, the masked figure stood up and cried in a loud voice: 'Long live the Queen!' Gasps of horror mingled with shouts of disbelief. All that he was holding was an auburn wig.

The head parted from its elaborate covering, fell to the platform and rolled near the edge. From beneath her red skirts, a frightened lapdog came scurrying out to paddle in the blood that surrounded its mistress. Its pitiful whimpering was the only sound to be heard in the great hall.

Everyone was struck dumb. As they gazed at the small, shiny skull with its close-cropped grey hair, they saw something which made them shudder. The lips were still moving.

Chapter One

The Queen's head swung gently to and fro in the light breeze. It was an interesting sight. Wearing a coronet and pearls in red hair that was a mass of tight curls, she had a pale, distinguished face with a high forehead, fine nose and full lips. Her regal beauty had an ageless quality that was enhanced by a remarkable pair of eyes. Dark, shrewd and watchful, they managed to combine authority with femininity and – when the sun hit them at a certain angle – they even hinted at roguishness. Nobody who met her imperious gaze could fail to recognise her as Elizabeth Tudor, Queen of England.

Bright colours had been used on the inn sign. Enough of the neck and shoulders was included to show that she was dressed in the Spanish fashion, with a round, stiff-laced collar above a dark bodice fitted with satin sleeves which were richly decorated with ribbons, pearls and gems. A veritable waterfall of pearls flowed from her neck and threatened to cascade down from the timber on which they were painted. The same opulence shone with vivid effect on the reverse side of the sign. Royalty was at its most resplendent.

London was the biggest, busiest and most boisterous city in Europe, a thriving community which had grown up in the serpentine twists of the River Thames and which was already thrusting out beyond its boundary walls. Poverty and wealth, stench and sweetness, anarchy and order, misery and magnificence were all elements in the city's daily life. From her high eminence in Gracechurch Street, the queen's head saw and heard everything that was going on in her beloved capital.

'Ned, that gown will need a stitch or two.'

'Yes, master.'

'You can sweep the stage now, Thomas.'

'The broom is ready in my hand, Master Bracewell.'

'George, fetch the rushes.'

'Where are they?'

'Where you will find them, lad. About it straight.'

'Yes, master.'

'Peter!'

'It was not our fault, Nicholas.'

'We must speak about that funeral march.'

'Our cue was given too early.'

'That did not matter. It was the wrong music.'

Nicholas Bracewell stood in the courtyard of The Queen's Head and took charge of the proceedings. Noon had just brought the morning's rehearsal to a close. The afternoon performance now loomed large and it threw the whole company into the usual state of panic. While everyone else was bickering, complaining, memorising elusive lines, working on last minute repairs or dashing needlessly about, Nicholas was concentrating on the multifarious jobs that had to be done before the play could be offered to its audience. He was an island of calm in a sea of hysteria.

'I must protest most strongly!'

'It was only a rehearsal, Master Bartholomew.'

'But, Nicholas, my play was mangled!'

'I'm sure it will be far better in performance.'

'They ruined my poetry and cut my finest scene.'

'That is not quite true, Master Bartholomew.'

'It's an outrage!'

The book holder was an important member of any company but, in the case of Lord Westfield's Men, he had become absolutely crucial to the enterprise. Nicholas Bracewell was so able and resourceful at the job that it expanded all the time to include new responsibilities. Not only did he prompt and stage manage every performance from the one complete copy that existed of a play, he also supervised rehearsals, helped to train the apprentices, dealt with the musicians, cajoled the stagekeepers, advised on the making of costumes or properties, and negotiated for a play's licence with the Master of the Revels.

His easy politeness and diplomatic skills had earned him

another role – that of pacifying irate authors. They did not get any more irate than Master Roger Bartholomew.

'Did you hear me, Nicholas?'

'Yes, I did.'

'An outrage!'

'You did sell your play to the company.'

'That does not give Lord Westfield's Men the right to debase my work!' shrieked the other, quivering with indignation. 'In the last act, *your* voice was heard most often. I did not write those speeches to be spoken by a mere prompter!'

Nicholas forgave him the insult and replied with an understanding smile. Words uttered in the heat of the moment were normal fare in the world of theatre and he paid no heed to them. Putting a hand on the author's shoulder, he adopted a soothing tone.

'It's an excellent play, Master Bartholomew.'

'How are the spectators to *know* that?'

'It will all be very different this afternoon.'

'Ha!'

'Be patient.'

'I have been Patience itself,' retorted the aggrieved poet, 'but I'll be silent no longer. My error lay in believing that Lawrence Firethorn was a good actor.'

'He's a great actor,' said Nicholas loyally. 'He holds over fifty parts in his head.'

'The pity of it is that King Richard is not one of them!'

'Master Bartholomew—'

'I will speak with him presently.'

'That's not possible.'

'Take me to him, Nicholas.'

'Out of the question.'

'I wish to resolve this matter with him.'

'Later.'

'I *demand* it!'

But the howled demand went unsatisfied. Conscious of the disturbance that the author was creating, Nicholas decided to get him away from the courtyard. Before he knew what was happening, Roger Bartholomew was ushered firmly into a private room, lowered into a seat and served with a pint of sack. Nicholas, meanwhile, poured words of praise and consolation into his ear, slowly subduing him and deflecting him from his intended course of action.

Lawrence Firethorn was the manager, chief sharer and leading actor with Lord Westfield's Men. His book holder was not shielding him from an encounter with a disappointed author. Rather was he protecting the latter from an experience that would scar his soul and bring his career in the theatre to a premature conclusion. Roger Bartholomew might be seething with righteous anger but he was no match for the tempest that was Lawrence Firethorn. At all costs, he had to be spared that. Nicholas had seen much stronger characters destroyed by a man who could explode like a powder keg at the slightest criticism of his art. It was distressing to watch.

Allowances had to be made for the fact that Master Roger Bartholomew was a novice, lately come from Oxford, where his tutors held a high opinion of him and where his poetry had won many plaudits. He was clever, if arrogant, and sufficiently well-versed in the drama to be able to craft a play of some competence. *The Tragical History of Richard the Lionheart* had promise and even some technical merit. What it lacked in finesse, it made up for in simple integrity. It was over-written in some parts and under-written in others but it was somehow held together by its patriotic impulse.

London was hungry for new plays and the companies were always in search of them. Lawrence Firethorn had accepted the apprentice work because it offered him a superb central role that he could tailor to suit his unique talents. It might be a play that smouldered without ever bursting into flame but it could still entertain an audience for a couple of hours and it would not disgrace the growing reputation of Lord Westfield's Men.

'I expected so much more,' confided the author as the drink turned his fury into wistfulness. 'I had hopes, Nicholas.'

'They'll not be dashed.'

'I felt so betrayed as I sat there this morning.'

'Rehearsals often deceive.'

'Where is my play?'

It was a cry from the heart and Nicholas was touched. Like others before him, Roger Bartholomew was learning the awful truth that an author did not occupy the exalted position that he imagined. Lord Westfield's Men, in fact, consigned him to a fairly humble station. The young Oxford scholar had been paid five pounds for his play and he had seen King Richard make his first entrance in a cloak that cost ten times that amount. It was galling.

Nicholas softened the blow with kind words as best he could, but there was something that could not be concealed from the wilting author. Lawrence Firethorn never regarded a play as an expression of poetic genius. He viewed it merely as a scaffold on which he could shout and strut and dazzle his public. It was his conviction that an audience came solely to see him act and not to watch an author write.

'What am I to do, Nicholas?' pleaded Bartholomew.

'Bear with us.'

'I'll be mocked by everyone.'

'Have faith.'

After giving what reassurance he could, the book holder left him staring into the remains of his sack and wishing that he had never left the University. They had taken him seriously there. The groves of academe had nurtured a tender plant which could not survive in the scorching heat of the playhouse.

Nicholas, meanwhile, hurried back to the yard where the preparations continued apace. The stage was a rectangle of trestles that jutted out into the middle of the yard from one wall. Green rushes, mixed with aromatic herbs, had been strewn over the stage to do battle with the stink of horse dung from the nearby stables. When the audience pressed around the acting area, there would be the competing smells of bad breath, beer, tobacco, garlic, mould, tallow and stale sweat to keep at bay. Nicholas observed that servingmen were perfuming large ewers in the shadows so that spectators would have somewhere to relieve themselves during the performance.

As soon as he appeared, everyone converged on him for advice or instruction – Thomas Skillen, the stagekeeper, Hugh Wegges, the tireman, Will Fowler, one of the players, John Tallis, an apprentice, Matthew Lipton, the scrivener, and the distraught Peter Digby, leader of the musicians, who was still mortified that he had sent Richard the Lionheart to his grave with the wrong funeral march. Questions, complaints and requests bombarded the book holder but he coped with them all.

A tall, broad-shouldered man with long fair hair and a full beard, Nicholas Bracewell remained even-tempered as the stress began to tell on his colleagues. He asserted himself without having to raise his voice and his soft West Country accent was a balm to their ears. Ruffled feathers were smoothed, difficulties soon resolved. Then a familiar sound boomed out.

'Nick, dear heart! Come to me.'

Lawrence Firethorn had made a typically dramatic entrance before moving to his accustomed position at the centre of the stage. After almost three years with the company, Nicholas could still be taken aback by him. Firethorn had tremendous presence. A sturdy, barrel-chested man of medium height, he somehow grew in stature when he trod the boards. The face had a flashy handsomeness that was framed by wavy black hair set off by an exquisitely pointed beard. There was a true nobility in his bearing which belied the fact that he was the son of a village blacksmith.

'Where have you been, Nick?' he enquired.

'Talking with Master Bartholomew.'

'That scurvy knave!'

'It *is* his play,' reminded Nicholas.

'He's an unmannerly rogue!' insisted the actor. 'I could run him through as soon as look at him.'

'Why?'

'Why? *Why*, sir? Because that dog had the gall to scowl at me throughout the entire rehearsal. I'll not put up with it, Nick. I'll not permit scowls and frowns and black looks at *my* performance. Keep him away from me.'

'He sends his apologies,' said Nicholas tactfully.

'Hang him!'

Firethorn's rage was diverted by a sudden peal of bells from a neighbouring church. Since there were well over a hundred churches in the capital, there always seemed to be bells tolling somewhere and it was a constant menace to open air performance. The high galleries of the inn yard could muffle the pandemonium outside in Gracechurch Street but it could not keep out the chimes from an adjacent belfry. Firethorn thrust his sword arm up towards heaven.

'Give me a blade strong enough,' he declared, 'and I'll hack through every bell-rope in London!'

Struck by the absurdity of his own posture, he burst into laughter and Nicholas grinned. Working for Lawrence Firethorn could be an ordeal at times but there was an amiable warmth about him that excused many of his faults.

During their association, Nicholas had developed a cautious affection for him. The actor turned to practicalities and cocked an eye upwards.

'Well, Nick?'

'We might be lucky and we might not.'

'Be more exact,' pressed Firethorn. 'You're our seaman. You know how to read the sky. What does it tell you?'

Nicholas looked up at the rectangle of blue and grey above the thatched roof of the galleries. A bright May morning had given way to an uncertain afternoon. The wind had freshened and clouds were scudding across the sky. Fine weather was a vital factor in the performance as Firethorn knew to his cost.

'I have played in torrents of rain,' he announced, 'and I would willingly fight the Battle of Acre in a snowstorm this afternoon. I care not about myself, but about our patrons. And about our costumes.'

Nicholas nodded. The inn yard was not paved. Heavy rain would mire the ground and cause all kinds of problems. He was as anxious to give good news as Firethorn was to receive it. After studying the sky for a couple of minutes, he made his prediction.

'It will stay dry until we are finished.'

'By all, that's wonderful!' exclaimed the actor, slapping his thigh. 'I knew I chose the right man as book holder!'

The Tragical History of Richard the Lionheart was a moderate success. Playbills advertising the performance had been put up everywhere by the stagekeepers and they brought a large and excitable audience flocking to The Queen's Head. Gatherers on duty at the main gates charged a penny for admission. Many people jostled for standing room around the stage itself but the bulk of the audience paid a further penny or twopence to gain access to the galleries, which ran around the yard at three levels and turned it into a natural amphitheatre. The galleries offered greater comfort, a better view and protection against the elements. Private rooms at the rear were available for rest, recreation or impromptu assignations.

All sorts and conditions of men flooded in – lawyers, clerks, tinkers, tailors, yeomen, soldiers, sailors, carriers, apprentices, merchants, butchers, bakers, chapmen, silk-weavers, students from the Inns of Court, aspiring authors, unemployed actors, gaping countrymen, foreign visitors, playhouse gallants, old, young, lords and commoners. Thieves, cutpurses and confidence tricksters mingled with the crowd to ply their trade.

Ladies, wives, mistresses and young girls were fewer in number and, for the most part, masked or veiled. Gentlemen about town pushed and shoved in the galleries to obtain a seat near the women or to consort with the prostitutes who had come up from the Bankside stews in search of clients. Watching the play was only part of the entertainment and a hundred individual dramas were being acted out in the throng.

Some men wore shirts and breeches, others lounged in buff jerkins, others again sported doublet and hose of figured velvet, white ruffs, padded crescent-shaped epaulets, silk stockings, leather gloves, elaborate hats and short, patterned cloaks. Female attire also ranged from the simple to the extravagant with an emphasis on the latest fashions in the galleries, where stiffened bodices, full petticoats, farthingales, cambric or lawn ruffs, long gowns with hanging sleeves, delicate gloves, and tall, crowned hats or French hoods were the order of the day.

Wine, beer, bread, fruit and nuts were served throughout the afternoon and the cheerful hubbub rarely subsided. The trumpet sounded at two-thirty to announce the start of the play, then the Prologue appeared in his black cloak. The first and last performance of *The Tragical History of Richard the Lionheart* was under way.

Squeezed between two gallants in the middle gallery, Roger Bartholomew craned his neck to see over the feathered hats in front of him. The pint of sack had increased his anger yet rendered it impotent. All he could do was to writhe in agony. This was not *his* play but a grotesque version of it. Lines had been removed, scenes rearranged, battles, duels, sieges and gruesome deaths introduced. There was even a jig for comic effect. What pained the hapless author most was that the changes appealed to the audience.

Lawrence Firethorn held the whole thing together. He compelled attention whenever he was on stage and made the most banal verse soar like sublime poetry:

My name makes cowards flee and evil traitors start
For I am known as King Richard the Lionheart!

His gesture and movement were hypnotic but it was his voice that was his chief asset. It could subdue the spectators with a whisper or thrill them with a shout like the report of a cannon. In his own inimitable way, he made yet another play his personal property.

His finest moment came at the climax of the drama. King Richard was besieging the castle of Chalus and he strode up to its walls to assess any weaknesses. An arbalester came out on to the battlements – the balcony at the rear of the stage – and fired his crossbow. The bolt struck Richard between the neck and shoulder where his chain mail was unlaced.

For this vital part of the action, Firethorn used an effect that had been suggested by Nicholas Bracewell. The bolt was hidden up the actor's sleeve. As the crossbow twanged, he let out a yell of pain and brought both hands up to his neck with the bolt between them. The impact made him stagger across the stage. It was all done with such perfect timing that the audience was convinced they had actually seen the bolt fly through the air.

Richard now proceeded to expire with the aid of a twenty-line speech in halting verse. After writhing in agony on the ground, he died a soldier's death before being borne off – to the correct funeral music, on cue – by his men.

Thunderous applause greeted the cast when they came out to take their bow and a huge cheer went up when Lawrence Firethorn appeared. He basked in the acclaim for several minutes then gave one last, deep bow and took his leave. Once again he had wrested an extraordinary performance out of rather ordinary material.

Everyone went home happy. Except Roger Bartholomew.

Nicholas Bracewell had no chance to relax. Having controlled the play from his position in the tiring-house, he now had to take charge of the strike party. Costumes had to be collected, properties gathered up, the stage cleared and the trestles dismantled. Lord Westfield's Men would not be playing at The Queen's Head for another week and its yard was needed for its normal traffic of wagons and coaches. The debris left behind by almost a thousand people also had to be cleaned up. Rain added to the problems. Having held off until the audience departed, it now began to fall in earnest.

It was hours before Nicholas finally came to the end of a long day's work. He adjourned to the taproom for some bread and ale. Alexander Marwood came scurrying across to his table.

'How much was taken today, Master Bracewell?'

'I'm not sure.'

'There is the matter of my rent.'

'You'll be paid.'

'When?'

'Soon,' promised Nicholas with more confidence than he felt. He knew only too well the difficulty of prising any money out of Lawrence Firethorn and spent a lot of his time explaining away his employer's meanness. 'Very soon, Master Marwood.'

'My wife thinks that I should put the rent up.'

'Wives are like that.'

Marwood gave a hollow laugh. The landlord of The Queen's Head was a short, thin, balding man in his fifties with a nervous twitch. His eager pessimism had etched deep lines in his forehead and put dark pouches under his eyes. Anxiety informed everything that he did or said.

Nicholas always took pains to be pleasant to Marwood. Lord Westfield's Men were trying to persuade the landlord to let them use the inn on a permanent basis and there were sound financial reasons why he might convert his premises to a playhouse. But Marwood had several doubts about the project, not least the fact that a City regulation had been passed in 1574 to forbid the staging of plays at inns. He was terrified that the authorities would descend upon him at any moment. There was another consideration.

'We had more scuffles in the yard.'

'Good humoured fun, that's all,' said Nicholas. 'You always get that during a play.'

'One day it will be much worse,' feared Marwood. 'I don't want an affray at The Queen's Head. I don't want a riot. My whole livelihood could be at stake.' The nervous twitch got to work on his cheek. 'If I still have a livelihood, that is.'

'What do you mean, Master Marwood?'

'The Armada! It could be the end for us all.'

'Oh, I don't think so,' returned Nicholas easily.

'It's ready to set sail.'

'So is the English fleet.'

'But the Spaniards have bigger and better ships,' moaned the landlord. 'They completely outnumber us. Yes, and they have a great army in the Netherlands waiting to invade us.'

'We have an army, too.'

'Not strong enough to keep out the might of Spain.'

'Wait and see.'

'We'll all be murdered in our beds.' Armada fever had been sweeping the country and Marwood had succumbed willingly. He gave in before battle had even commenced. 'We should never have executed the Queen of Scots.'

'It's too late to change that,' reasoned Nicholas. 'Besides, you were happy enough about it at the time.'

'Me? *Happy?*'

'London celebrated for a week or more. You made a tidy profit out of the lady's death, Master Marwood.'

'I would give back every penny if it would save us from the Armada. The Queen of Scots was treated cruelly. It was wrong.'

'It was policy.'

'Policy!' croaked Marwood as the nervous twitch spread to his eyelid and made it flutter uncontrollably. 'Shall I tell you what policy has done to my family, sir? It has knocked us hither and yon.' He wiped sweaty palms down the front of his apron. 'When my grandfather first built this inn, it was called The Pope's Head, serving good ale and fine wines to needy travellers. Then King Henry fell out with the Catholic religion so down comes the sign and we became The King's Arms instead. When Queen Mary was on the throne, it was Protestants who went to the stake and

32

Catholics who held sway again. My father quickly hung the Pope back up in Gracechurch Street. No sooner had people got used to our old sign than we had a new queen and a new name.'

'It has lasted almost thirty years so far,' said Nicholas with an encouraging smile, 'and, by God's grace, it will last many more.'

'But the Spaniards are coming – thanks to policy!'

'The Spaniards will *attempt* to come.'

'We have no hope against them,' wailed Marwood. 'My wife thinks we should commission another sign in readiness. Henceforth, we will trade as The Armada Inn.'

'Save your money,' counselled Nicholas, 'and tell your wife to take heart. The Spaniards may have more ships but we have better seamen. Lord Howard of Effingham is a worthy Admiral and Sir John Hawkins has used all his experience to rebuild the fleet.'

'We are still so few against so many.'

'Adversity brings out true mettle.'

Marwood shook his head sadly and his brow furrowed even more. Nothing could still his apprehension. Seers had long ago chosen 1588 as a year of disaster and the portents on every side were consistently alarming. The landlord rushed to meet catastrophe with open arms.

'The Armada Inn! There's no help for it.'

Nicholas let him wallow in his dread. Like everyone else, he himself was much disturbed at the notion of a huge enemy fleet that was about to bear down on his country, but his fear was tempered by an innate belief in the superiority of the English navy. He had first-hand knowledge. Nicholas had sailed with Drake on his famous circumnavigation of the globe in the previous decade.

Those amazing three years had left an indelible impression upon him and he had disembarked from the *Golden Hind* with severe reservations about the character of the man whom the Spaniards called the Master Thief of the Unknown World. For all this, he still had immense respect for his old captain as a seaman. Whatever the odds, Sir Francis Drake would give a good account of himself in battle.

Darkness was falling when Nicholas left The Queen's Head to begin the walk home to his lodgings in Bankside. He glanced up at the inn sign to see how his sovereign was responding to the threat of invasion. Buffeted by the wind and lashed by the rain, Queen Elizabeth creaked back and forth on her hinges. But she was not dismayed. Through the gathering gloom, Nicholas Bracewell fancied that he caught a smile of defiance on her lips.

Chapter Two

Rumour was on the wing. It flew over the country like a giant bird of prey that swooped on its victims at will. Estimates of the size of the Armada increased daily. The Duke of Parma's army in the Netherlands was also swelled by report. A papal promise of a million crowns to reward a successful invasion became a guarantee of ten times that amount. Terror even invented a massive force of English Catholics, who would stream out of their hiding places to join forces with Spanish soldiers and to help them hack Protestantism to pieces. The satanic features of King Philip II appeared in many dreams.

England reacted with fortitude. An army of twenty thousand men was assembled at Tilbury under the Earl of Leicester. With the muster in the adjacent counties, it was a substantial force with the task of opposing any landing. A second army was formed at St James for the defence of the Queen's person. The martial activity at once reassured and unnerved the citizens of London. They watched armed bands doing their training at Mile End and they heard the gunners of the Tower in Artillery Yard, just outside Bishopsgate, having their weekly practise with their brass ordnance against a great butt of earth. Invasion had a frightening immediacy.

Queen Elizabeth herself did not hide away and pray. She reviewed her troops at Tilbury and fired them with stirring words. But the Armada would not be defeated with speeches and Rumour was still expanding its ranks and boasting about its dark, avenging purpose. On 12th July, the vast flotilla set sail from Corunna. The defence of Queen and country now became an imperative. King Philip of Spain was about to extend his empire.

A week later, the captain of a scout-boat sent news that some Spanish vessels were off the Scillies with their sails struck as they waited for stragglers. On the ebb tide that night, Lord Admiral Howard and Sir Francis Drake brought their ships out of Plymouth Sound, making use of warps, to anchor them in deep water and be ready for action. Howard commanded the *Ark Royal*, the imposing flagship of the English fleet. At dawn the next day, he took fifty-four ships to the leeward of the Eddystone Rock and sailed to the south in order to be able – by working to windward – to double back on the enemy.

Drake was in *Revenge*. That same evening, as he

positioned his eight ships for an attack on the Spanish rear, he caught his first glimpse of the Armada. It was a majestic sight. A hundred and thirty-two vessels, including several galleons and other first-line ships, were moving up the Channel in crescent formation. Their admiral, the Duke of Medina Sidonia, believed so totally in Spanish invincibility that he thought nothing could stop him reaching his support army in the Low Countries.

The English Fleet begged to differ. Staying to windward of the Armada, they hung upon it for nine days as it ran before a westerly wind up the Channel, pounding away with their long-range guns at the lumbering galleons, harrying, tormenting, inflicting constant damage, yet giving the Spaniards little chance to retaliate and no hope of grappling and boarding. The buccaneering skills of Drake and his like had free rein.

When the wind sank on 23rd July, both fleets lay becalmed off Portland Bill. There was a further engagement two days later off the Isle of Wight then Medina Sidonia made the fatal mistake of anchoring his demoralised fleet in Calais Roads.

The Queen's ships which had been stationed at the eastern end of the Channel now joined the main fleet in the Straits and the whole sea-power of England was combined. Because it was not possible to get safely within gunshot range of the enemy, Howard held a council of war on the *Ark Royal* and a plan of action was decided upon. Eight ships were speedily filled with pitch, tar, dry timber and anything that would easily burn. The guns were left aboard but were double-shotted so that they would explode from the intense heat.

Before midnight, the fire ships were lashed together and carried by the wind and a strong tide on their voyage. As the blazing vessels penetrated the cordon of fly-boats and pinnaces that guarded the galleons, the Spaniards flew into a panic and cut their cables. The pilotless ships wreaked havoc and the Armada was forced back out to the open sea where it was at the mercy of the English.

Soon after dawn, battle was joined in earnest and it went on for almost eight hours, a raging conflict at close quarters during which the English showed their superiority over their opponents in handling their ships in difficult water. The Armada was stricken. If the English fleet had not run out of ammunition, hardly a single Spanish vessel would have escaped. As it was, the shattered flotilla fled northwards to face the horrors of a long voyage home around Scotland and thence south past Ireland.

More than five hundred Spanish lives were lost on the return journey. Medina Sidonia limped home with less than half the fleet which had sailed out so proudly. The English had not lost a ship and scarcely a hundred men. The first invasion attempt for over five centuries had been gloriously repelled. Catholicism would never lay at anchor in the Thames.

Weeks passed before the news reached England. Rumour continued to flap its wings and cause sleepless nights. It also flew across to the Continent to spread guileful stories about a Spanish victory. Bells were rung in the Catholic cities of

Europe. Masses of thanksgiving were held in Rome and Venice and Paris. Rejoicing crowds lit bonfires in Madrid and Seville to celebrate the defeat of the heretic, Elizabeth, and the capture of the sea devil, Francis Drake.

Truth then caught up with Rumour and plucked its feathers. Shocked and shamed, the Spanish people went into mourning. Their king would speak to nobody but his confessor. England, by contrast, was delirious with joy. When the news was made public, there was a great upsurge of national pride. London prepared to welcome home its heroes and toast their bravery a thousand times over.

The Queen's Head got its share of the bounty.

'It's agreed then. Edmund is to begin work on the play at once.'

'I've not agreed,' said Barnaby Gill testily.

'Nor I,' added Edmund Hoode.

'We must seize the time, gentlemen,' urged Firethorn.

'You are rushing us into it,' complained Gill.

'Speed is of the essence, Barnaby.'

'Then find someone else to write it,' suggested Hoode. 'I'll not be hurried into this. Plays take much thought and many days, yet Lawrence wants it ready for tomorrow.'

'I'll settle for next Sunday,' said Firethorn with a ripe chuckle. 'Call upon your Muse, Edmund. Apply yourself.'

The three men were sitting downstairs in Firethorn's house in Shoreditch. Barnaby Gill was smoking his pipe, Edmund Hoode was drinking a cup of water and the host himself was reclining in his favourite high-backed oak chair. A meeting had been called to discuss future plans for Lord Westfield's Men. All three of them were sharers, ranked players who were named in the royal patent for the company and who took the major roles in any performance.

There were four other sharers but Lawrence Firethorn had found it expedient to limit decisions about the repertory to a triumvirate. Barnaby Gill had to be included. He was a short, stocky, pleasantly ugly man of forty with an insatiable appetite for foul-smelling tobacco and sweet-smelling boys. Morose and temperamental offstage, he was a gifted comedian once he stepped on to it and his facial expressions could reduce any audience to laughter. It was for his benefit that the comic jig had been inserted into the play about Richard the Lionheart.

Professional jealousy made the relationship between Gill and Firethorn a very uneasy one with regular threats to walk out being made by the former. However, the two men knew that they would never part. The dynamic between them onstage was a vital ingredient in the success of the company. For this reason, Firethorn was ready to make allowances for his colleague's outbursts and to overlook his indiscretions.

'I do not like the idea,' affirmed Gill.

'Then you've not fully understood it,' rejoined Firethorn.

'What is there to understand, Lawrence? England defeats the Armada. You seek a play to celebrate it – and every other company in London will be doing the same thing.'

'That is why we must be *first*, Barnaby.'

'I'm against it.'

'You always are.'

'Unfair, sir!'

'True, nonetheless.'

'Why must we ape everyone else?' demanded Gill, bristling. 'We should try to do something different.'

'My performance as Drake will be unique.'

'Yes, there you have it.'

'What?'

'I see no part in this new play for *me*.'

Edmund Hoode listened to the argument with the philosophical half-smile of someone who has heard it all before. As resident poet with the company, he was often caught between the rival claims of the two men. Each wished to outshine the other and Hoode usually ended up pleasing neither.

He was a tall, slim man in his early thirties with a round, clean-shaven face that still retained a vestige of youthful innocence. His curly brown hair and pale skin gave him an almost cherubic look. Hoode excelled in writing poems to the latest love in his life. What he found himself doing was producing hasty, if workmanlike, plays at a rate that moved him closer to nervous collapse each time. The one consolation was that he was always able to give himself a telling cameo role with romantic interest.

'How soon will you have something to show us, Edmund?'

'Christmas.'

'I'm serious about this.'

'So am I, Lawrence.'

'We ask you as a special favour,' purred Firethorn.

'You expect too much of me.'

'Only because you always deliver it, dear fellow.'

'He's wooing you,' warned Gill cynically.

'It will not serve,' said Hoode.

'I have your title,' explained Firethorn. 'It will leap off the playbills along with your name. *Gloriana Triumphant!*'

'An ill-favoured thing, to be sure,' noted Gill, wincing.

'Be quiet, sir!'

'I'm entitled to my opinion, Lawrence.'

'You're being peevish.'

'I simply wish to choose another play.'

'Yes,' agreed Hoode. 'Another play by another author.'

Lawrence Firethorn regarded them through narrowed eyes. He had anticipated opposition and he had the means to remove it at a stroke. His chuckle alerted them to the danger.

'The decision has already been taken, gentlemen.'

'By you?' challenged Gill.

'By Lord Westfield.'

There was nothing more to be said. The company owed its existence to its patron. Under the notorious Act for the Punishment of Vagabonds, the acting profession had been effectively outlawed. The only dramatic companies that were permitted were those which were authorised by one noble and two judicial dignitaries of the realm. All other players were deemed to be rogues, vagabonds and sturdy beggars, making them liable to arrest. Lord Westfield had saved Firethorn and his fellows from that indignity. The patron's word therefore carried enormous weight.

'Start work immediately, Edmund,' ordered his host.

'Very well,' sighed Hoode. 'Draw up the contract.'

'I have already done so.'

'You take too much upon yourself,' accused Gill.

'Someone has to, Barnaby.'

'We are sharers, too. We have rights.'

'So does Lord Westfield.'

Barnaby Gill summoned up his fiercest grimace. Not for the first time, he had been outwitted by Firethorn and it stoked his resentment even more. Edmund Hoode turned wearily to his new task.

'I must talk with Nicholas.'

'Do, do,' encouraged Firethorn. 'Use his knowledge of seamanship. Nicholas could be of great help to us here.'

'We lean on him too much,' said Gill irritably. 'Master Bracewell is only a hired man. We should treat him as such and not deal with him as an equal.'

'Our book holder has rare talents,' countered Firethorn. 'Accept that and be truly grateful.' He turned to Hoode. 'Make full use of Nicholas.'

'I always do,' answered the other. 'I often think that Nicholas Bracewell is the most important person in the company.'

Firethorn and Gill snorted in unison. Truth is no respector of inordinate pride.

London by night was the same seething, stinking, clamorous place that it was by day. As the two men made their way

43

down Gracechurch Street, there was pulsing life and pounding noise all around them. They were so accustomed to the turmoil of their city that they did not give it a second thought. Ignoring the constant brush of shoulders against their own, they inhaled the reek of fresh manure without complaint and somehow made their voices heard above the babble.

'Demand a higher wage from them, Nick.'

'It would never be granted.'

'But you deserve it, you bawcock.'

'Few men are used according to their deserts, Will.'

'Aye!' said his companion with feeling. 'Look at this damnable profession of ours. We are foully treated most of the time. They mock us, fear us, revile us, hound us, even imprison us, and when we actually please them with a play for two hours of their whoreson lives, they reward us with a few claps and a few coins before they start to rail at us again. How do we bear such a life?'

'On compulsion.'

'Compulsion?'

'It answers a need within us.'

'A fair fat wench can do that, Nick.'

'I talk of deeper needs, Will. Think on it.'

Nicholas Bracewell and Will Fowler were close friends as well as colleagues. The book holder had great respect and affection for the actor even though the latter caused him many problems. Will Fowler was a burly, boisterous character of medium height whose many sterling qualities were betrayed by a short temper and a readiness to trade

44

blows. Nicholas loved him for his ebullience, his wicked sense of humour and his generosity. Because he admired Fowler so much as an actor, he defended him and helped him time and again. It was Nicholas who kept Fowler in a job and it strengthened their bond.

'Without you, Westfield's Men would crumble into dust!'

'I doubt that, Will,' said Nicholas easily.

'We all depend upon you entirely.'

'More fool me, for bearing such an unfair load!'

'Seek more money. A labourer is worthy of his hire.'

'I am happy enough with my wage.'

'You are too modest, Nick!' chided the other.

'The same could not be said about you, I fear.'

Will Fowler broke into such irrepressible laughter that he scattered passers-by all around him. Slapping his friend between the shoulder blades, he turned a beaming visage upon him.

'I have tried to hide my light under a bushel,' he explained, 'but I have never been able to find a bushel big enough.'

'You're a born actor, Will. You seek an audience.'

'Applause is my meat and drink. I would starve to death if I was just another Nicholas Bracewell who looks for the shadows. An audience has to *know* that I am a good actor and so I tell them as loud and as often as I can. Why conceal my excellence?'

'Why indeed?'

Nicholas collected a second slap on the back.

They were crossing the bridge now and had to slow down as traffic thickened at its narrowest point. The massive huddle of houses and shops that made up London Bridge extended itself along the most important street in the city. The buildings stretched out over the river then lurched back in upon each other, closing the thoroughfare down to a width of barely twelve feet. A heavy cart trundled through the press. Nicholas reached forward to lift a young boy out of its path and earned a pale smile by way of thanks.

'You see?' continued Fowler. 'You cannot stop helping others.'

'The lad would have been hit by that wheel,' said Nicholas seriously. 'Too many people are crushed to death in the traffic here. I'm glad to be able to save one victim.'

'One victim? You save dozens every day.'

'Do I?'

'Yes!' urged Fowler. 'And they are not just careless lads on London Bridge. How many times have you plucked our apprentices from beneath the wheels of that sodden-headed, sheep-faced sharer called Barnaby Gill? That standing yard between his little legs will do far more damage than a heavy cart. You've saved Dick Honeydew and the others from being run down. You've saved Westfield's Men no end of times. Most of all, you save me.'

'From Master Gill?' teased Nicholas.

'What!' roared Fowler with jovial rage. 'Just let the fellow thrust his weapon at me. I'll saw it off like a log, so I will, and use it as a club to beat his scurvy head. I'd make him dance a jig, I warrant you!'

'Even *I* could not save you then, Will.'

They left the bridge, entered Southwark and swung right into Bankside. The Thames was a huge, rippling presence beside them. Nicholas had been invited to a tavern by Fowler in order to meet an old friend of the latter. From the way that his companion had been flattering him, Nicholas knew that he wanted a favour and it was not difficult to guess what that favour was.

'What is your friend's name, Will?'

'Samuel Ruff. As stout a fellow as you could find.'

'How long is it since you last saw him?'

'Too long. The years drift by so fast these days.' He gave a sigh. 'But they have been kinder to me than to Sam.'

'Does he know that I'm coming?' asked Nicholas.

'Not yet.'

'I've no wish to intrude upon an old friendship.'

'It's no intrusion. You're here to help Sam.'

'How?'

'You'll find a way, Nick. You always do.'

They strode on vigorously through the scuffling dark.

Even though it lay fairly close to his lodging, the Hope and Anchor was not one of Nicholas's regular haunts. There was something irremediably squalid about the place and its murky interior housed rogues, pimps, punks, thieves, pickpockets, gamblers, cheaters and all manner of masterless men. Ill-lit by a few stinking tallow candles, the tavern ran to rough wooden benches and tables, a settle and a cluster of low stools. Loamed walls were streaked with grime and the rushes on the stone-flagged floor were old and noisome. A dog snuffled for rats in one corner.

The Hope and Anchor was full and the noise deafening. An old sailor was trying to sing a sea shanty above the din. A card game broke up in a fierce argument. Two drunken watermen thumped on their table for service. Prostitutes laughed shrilly as they blandished their customers. A fug of tobacco and dark purpose filled the whole tavern.

Nicholas Bracewell and Will Fowler sat side by side on the settle and tried to carry on a conversation with Samuel Ruff, who was perched on a stool on the other side of the table. All three drank bottle-ale. It had a brackish taste.

Nicholas glanced around the place with candid surprise.

'You *lodge* here, Samuel?' he said.

'For my sins.'

'Can it be safe?'

'I sleep with one hand on my dagger.'

'And the other on your codpiece,' said Fowler with a grin. 'These drabs will give you the pox as soon as they breathe on you, then charge you for the privilege.'

'I've no money to waste on pleasure, Will,' added Ruff.

'What pleasure is there in a burning pizzle?' Fowler's grin became rueful. 'There be three things an actor fears – plague, Puritans and pox. I never know which is worse.'

'I can tell you.'

'Which one, Sam?'

'The fourth thing,' explained Ruff.

'And what is that?'

'The greatest fear of all. Being without employ.'

There was such sadness in his voice and such despair in his eyes that the garrulous Fowler was silenced for once. Nicholas had an upsurge of sympathy for Samuel Ruff. He knew what it was to fall on hard times himself and he had a special concern for those who fell by the wayside of a necessarily cruel profession. Ruff was not only evidently in need of work. He had to be helped to believe in himself again. Nicholas showed a genuine interest.

'How long have you been a player, Samuel?'

'For more years than I care to remember,' admitted Ruff with a half-smile. 'I began with Leicester's Men, then I toured with smaller companies.'

'At home or abroad?'

'Both, sir.'

'Where have you been on your travels?'

'My calling has taken me to Germany, Holland, Belgium, Denmark, even Poland. I've been hissed at in many languages.'

'And applauded in many more,' insisted Fowler loyally. 'Sam is a fine actor, Nick. Indeed, he is almost as good as myself.'

'No recommendation could be higher,' said Nicholas, smiling.

'We are old fellows, are we not, Sam?'

'We are, Will.'

'If memory serves me aright, we first played together in *The Three Sisters of Mantua* at Bristol. They were happy days.'

'Not for everyone,' recalled Ruff. 'How say you?'

'Have you forgotten, Will? You fetched the trumpeter such a box on the ear that he could not play his instrument properly for a week.'

'The knave deserved it!'

'If he'd not ducked in time, you'd have boxed his other ear and taken his breath away for a fortnight.'

'What was the man's offence?' wondered Nicholas.

'He blew a scurvy trumpet,' explained Will.

Fowler and Ruff shook with mirth at the shared recollection. As further memoirs were revealed by the former, the other seemed to relax and blossom, secure in the knowledge that there had been a time when his talent had been in demand. Samuel Ruff was older and greyer than Fowler but his build was similar. Nicholas noted the faded attire and the neglected air. He also studied the big, open face with its honest eyes and resolute jaw. There was an integrity about Ruff which had not been beaten out of him by his straitened circumstances, and his pride was intact as well. When Fowler offered him money, he was frankly wounded.

'Take it back, Will. I can pay my way.'

'I mean it as a loan and not as charity.'

'Either would be an insult to me.'

Fowler slipped the coins quickly back into his purse and revived some more memories of their time together. The laughter soon started again but it lacked its earlier warmth. Nicholas had taken a liking to Samuel Ruff but he could not see how he could help him in the immediate future. The number of hired men in the company was kept to a minimum by Firethorn in order to hold down costs. There was no call for a new player at the moment.

In any case, Ruff did not appear to be in search of a job. Months without work had taken their toll of his spirit and he was now talking of leaving the profession altogether. Will Fowler gasped with shock as he heard the news.

'What will you do, Sam?'

'Go back home to Norwich.'

'Norwich?'

'My brother has a small farm there. I can work for him.'

'Sam Ruff on a farm!' exclaimed Fowler with healthy disgust. 'Those hands were not made to feed pigs.'

'He keeps cows.'

'You're an *actor*. You belong on the stage.'

'The playhouse will manage very well without me.'

'This is treasonable talk, Sam!' urged Fowler. 'Actors never give up. They go on acting to the bitter end. Heavens, man, you're one of *us*!'

'Not any more, Will.'

'You will miss the playhouse mightily,' said Nicholas.

'Miss it?' echoed Fowler. 'It will be like having a limb hacked off. *Two* limbs. Yes, and two of something else as well, Sam. Will you surrender your manhood so easily? How can anyone exist without the theatre?'

'Cows have their own consolation,' suggested Ruff.

'Leave off this arrant nonsense about a farm!' ordered his friend with a peremptory wave of his arm. 'You'll not desert us. D'you know what Nick and I talked about as we walked here tonight? We spoke about the acting profession.

51

All its pain and setback and stabbing horror. Why do we put up with it?'

'Why, indeed?' said Ruff gloomily.

'Nick had the answer. On compulsion. It answers a need in us, Sam, and I've just realised what that need is.'

'Have you?'

'Danger.'

'Danger?'

'You've felt it every bit as much as I have, Sam,' said Fowler with eyes aglow. 'The danger of testing yourself in front of a live audience, of risking their displeasure, of taking chances, of being out there with nothing but a gaudy costume and a few lines of verse to hold them. That's why I do it, Sam, to have that feeling of dread coursing through my veins, to know that excitement, to face that danger! It makes it all worthwhile.'

'Only if you are employed, Will,' observed Ruff.

'Where will you get your *danger*, Sam?'

'A cow can give a man a nasty kick at times.'

'I'll give *you* a nasty kick if you persist like this!'

'My mind is made up, Will.'

Further argument was futile. No matter how hard he tried, Fowler could not deflect his friend from his purpose. Nicholas was brought in to add the weight of his persuasion but it was in vain. Samuel Ruff had decided to return to Norwich. It would be a hard life but he would have a softer lodging than the Hope and Anchor.

Nicholas watched the two men carefully. They were middle-aged actors in a profession which handled its members with callous indifference. Both had met the impossible demands made upon them for a number of years, but one had now been discarded. It was a sobering sight. Will Fowler's exuberance came in such sharp contrast to Ruff's quiet despair. Taken together, the two friends seemed to embody the essence of theatre with its blend of extremes and its death-grapple between love and hate.

There was something else that Nicholas observed and it made him feel sorry for his friend. Will Fowler had looked forward to the meeting with Samuel Ruff and placed a lot of importance upon it, but it was ending in disappointment. The man he had known in palmier days no longer existed. What was left was a pale reminder of his old friend, a few flashes of the real Samuel Ruff. An actor who had once shared his blind faith in the theatre had now become a heretic. It hurt Fowler and Nicholas shared that pain.

'Can *nothing* make you change your mind?' pleaded Fowler.

'Nothing, Will.'

'So be it.'

They finished their ale in a desultory way then Nicholas went across to the hostess to pay the reckoning. It was even more rowdy now and the air was charged with a dozen pungent odours. Couples groped their way up the narrow stairs to uncertain joy, raucous jeers rose from a game of dice and the old sailor, swaying like a mainmast in a gale, tried to sing a ballad about the defeat of the Armada. The dog barked and someone vomited in the hearth.

Nicholas was glad that they were about to leave. He

sensed trouble. The Hope and Anchor was a tinderbox that could ignite at any moment. Though more than able to take care of himself in a brawl, he did not look for a fight and it worried him that he had come to the tavern with someone who often did. A buoyant Fowler was problem enough but a jaded one was highly volatile. Nicholas paid the bill and turned to go.

But he was already too late.

'Away, sir!'

'Will you bandy words with me?'

'No, sir. I'll break your crown!'

'I have something here to split yours asunder!'

'Stand off!'

'Draw!'

Will Fowler was being challenged by a tall, hulking man with a red beard and a sword in his hand. The actor jumped up from the settle and grabbed his own blade. A space immediately cleared in the middle of the room as tables were pushed hurriedly away, then the two men circled each other. Before Nicholas could move, Samuel Ruff interceded.

'Put up your sword, Will,' he implored.

'Stand aside, Sam.'

'There is no occasion for this quarrel.'

'I mean to have blood here.'

Ruff swung around to confront the stranger. Unarmed but quite unafraid, he leapt between the two combatants and held out his arms, shielding his friend with his body.

'Let us settle this over a pint of ale, sir.'

'No!' snarled the other.

'Mend your differences,' advised Ruff.

The stranger was not deterred. He saw the chance to catch his adversary off guard and he took it. With a lightning thrust, his sword passed under Ruff's arm and went deep into Fowler's stomach. The fight was over.

'Will!' shouted Nicholas, darting forward.

'I'll . . . kill him,' threatened Fowler weakly.

Dropping his sword, he staggered a few steps then collapsed to the floor. Nicholas bent down to enfold him in his arms, shaken by the speed of it all. The hostess screamed, the card players yelled, the old sailor roared and the dog barked madly. In the general confusion, the stranger ran out through the door and vanished down the alley.

Everyone pressed in upon the fallen man.

'Stand back!' ordered Nicholas. 'Give him air.'

'What happened?' mumbled Fowler drowsily.

'It was my fault,' confessed Ruff, covered in remorse as he knelt beside the wounded man. 'I tried to stop him and he stabbed you under my arm.'

'Curse him!' groaned Fowler.

The hostess pushed through the crowd to view the hideous sight. Brawls were common enough in the tavern but they did not usually involve swordplay nor end with someone losing his life-blood all over the floor.

'Carry him to the surgeon!' she urged.

'He cannot be moved,' said Nicholas, doing what he could to stem the flow of blood. 'Bring the surgeon here. Tell him to hurry!'

The hostess despatched her boy with a curt command.

Nicholas was still cradling his friend in his arms and shuddering with disbelief. Will Fowler had been such a powerful and energetic man yet his life was now draining rapidly away in the miserable setting of a Bankside stew. The sense of waste was overwhelming.

'Who was he?' murmured Fowler.

'Save your strength, Will,' cautioned Nicholas.

'I want to know,' he said with a last show of spirit. 'Who *was* the rogue?'

He looked up questioningly but nobody had the answer.

Nicholas Bracewell was consumed with grief and anger. It was only now that he was about to lose Will Fowler that he realised how much the man's friendship had meant to him. The actor's warmth and effervescence would be sorely missed. Nicholas held the body more tightly to pull him back from death but he knew that it was all to no avail. Will Fowler was doomed.

Samuel Ruff was in tears, tormenting himself with the thought that he was to blame, muttering endless apologies to the prostrate figure. Nicholas saw the blank horror in his face then he noticed that Ruff's sleeve was dripping with blood that seeped from a wound of his own. The sword thrust had cut his arm before killing Will Fowler.

The dying man found enough breath to whisper.

'Nick . . .'

'I'm here, Will.'

'Find him . . . *please* . . . find the rogue!'

He clutched at his stomach as a new spasm of pain shot through him then his whole body went limp. A final hiss escaped his throat. Will Fowler had no need of a surgeon now.

Samuel Ruff buried his face in his hands. Nicholas felt his own tears come but his sorrow was edged with cold fury. A dear friend had been viciously cut down. In a flash of temper, a valuable life had been needlessly squandered. Will Fowler had begged him to track down the culprit and Nicholas now took this duty upon himself with iron determination.

'I'll find him, Will,' he promised.

Chapter Three

Bankside was not entirely given over to stews, gambling dens, taverns and ordinaries. Because it was outside the City's jurisdiction, this populous area of Southwark had its share of cockpits and bear gardens and bull-baiting rings to please the appetites of those who flocked to them, but it also had its shops, its places of work and its respectable dwellings. Lined with wharves and warehouses for much of the way, it commanded fine views across the river of St Paul's and the City.

Anne Hendrik had lived in Bankside for a number of years and she knew its labyrinthine streets well. Born of English stock, she married Jacob Hendrik while she was still in her teens. One of the many Dutch immigrants who poured into London, Jacob was a skilful hatmaker who found that the City Guilds had a vested interest in keeping him and his compatriots out of their exclusive brotherhoods. To make a living, therefore, he had to set up outside the City limits and Southwark was the obvious choice. Hard work and a willingness to adapt helped him to prosper. When he died after fifteen happy years of marriage, he left his widow with a good house, a flourishing business and moderate wealth. Other women might have moved away or married again but Anne Hendrik was committed to the house and its associations. Having no children, she lacked company and decided to take in a lodger. He soon became rather more than that.

'Is that you, Nicholas?' she called.

'Yes.'

'You're late.'

'There was no need for you to wait up.'

'I was worried about you.'

Anne came out to the front door as he closed it behind him. When she saw him by the light of the candles, her comely features were distorted with alarm.

'You're hurt!' she said, rushing to him.

'No, Anne.'

'But there's blood on your hands, and on your clothing.'

'It's not mine,' he soothed.

'Has there been trouble, Nick?'

He nodded. 'Will Fowler.'

'What happened?'

They adjourned to his chamber. Anne fetched him a bowl of water so that he could clean himself up and

60

Nicholas Bracewell told her what had occurred at the Hope and Anchor. He was still very shaken by it all. Anne was deeply distressed. Though she had only met Will Fowler a few times, she remembered him as a lively and loquacious man with a fund of amusing stories about the world of the playhouse. It seemed perverse that his life should be snuffed out so quickly and cheaply.

'Have you no idea who the man was?' she asked.

'None,' said Nicholas grimly. 'But I will catch up with the fellow one day.'

'What of this Master Ruff?'

'He was as stricken as I was, Anne. I helped him to find a new lodging for the night. He could not bear to stay in the place where Will had been murdered.'

'You should have brought him back here,' she offered.

Nicholas looked up at her and his affection for Anne Hendrik surged. Her oval face, so lovely and contented in repose, was now pitted with anxious frowns. Kindness and compassion oozed from her. In any crisis, her first instinct was always to give what practical help she could. It was a trait that Nicholas shared and it was one of the reasons that they bonded together.

'Thank you, Anne,' he said quietly.

'We could have found him something better than a room in some low tavern. Did you not think to invite him here?'

'He would not have come,' Nicholas replied. 'Samuel Ruff is a very proud and independent sort of man. His friendship with Will goes back many years and it was something that both of them treasured. Samuel wants to

61

keep his own counsel and mourn alone. I can respect that, Anne.'

While he dried his hands, she took away the clouded water. Nicholas was exhausted. It was hours past midnight and the events at the Hope and Anchor had taxed him. Officers had been sent for and the whole matter was now in the hands of a magistrate. The dead body had been removed and there was nothing that Nicholas could do until the morrow. Yet his mind would not let him rest.

Anne Hendrik came back. She was a tall, well-kept woman with graceful movements and a lightness of touch in all she did. Her tone was soft and concerned.

'You need your sleep, Nick. Can you manage?'

'I think so.'

'If you want anything, you have only to call me.'

'I know.'

She gazed fondly at him then a sudden thought made her reach out and clasp him to her bosom for a few moments. When she released him, she caressed his hair with long, delicate fingers.

'I'm sorry about Will Fowler,' she whispered, 'but it could so easily have been you who was killed. I could not have borne that.'

She kissed him tenderly on the forehead then went out.

It was typical of Lawrence Firethorn that he took the tragedy as a personal insult. Without a twinge of conscience, he turned the death of a hired man into a direct attack upon his reputation. On the following afternoon, Will Fowler was due to appear in the company's latest offering at The Queen's Head, playing the most important of the secondary roles. Since the other hired men were already doubling strenuously, it was impossible to replace him. The whole performance was threatened and Firethorn worked himself up into a fine frenzy as he contemplated it.

'Shameful!' he boomed. 'Utterly shameful!'

'Regrettable,' conceded Nicholas.

'Westfield's Men have never cancelled before. We would set a dreadful precedent. The audience would be robbed of a chance to see *me*! You must take some blame for this, Nicholas.'

'Why, master?'

'It was you who kept Will Fowler employed.'

'He was a good actor.'

'You stopped me tearing up his contract a dozen times.'

'Will was a valuable member of the company.'

'He was too quarrelsome. Sooner or later, he was bound to pick a fight with the wrong person. God's blood! If only I'd followed my own instincts and not yours!'

They were in the main bedchamber at Firethorn's house and the actor was rampaging in a white shirt. After a sleepless night, Nicholas had repaired to Shoreditch soon after dawn to break the sad news. His report was not well received.

'It's so unfair on *me*!' stressed Firethorn.

'My thoughts are with Will,' said Nicholas pointedly.

'One of my hired men stabbed in a tavern brawl – a pretty tale! It will stain the whole company. Did you not think of that when you took him to that vile place last night?'

'He took me.'

'It makes no difference. *I* am the one to suffer. Heavens, Nick, we take risks enough flouting the City regulations. The last thing we need is a brush with the authorities.'

'I've done all that is needful,' assured the other. 'You will not be involved at all.'

'I am involved in anything that touches Westfield's Men,' asserted Firethorn, striking a favourite pose. 'Besides, how are you to hold the book for us if you are hauled off to answer magistrates? Do you see how it all comes back on me? It will severely injure my reputation as a great actor.'

Nicholas Bracewell heaved a sigh. He was mourning the death of a friend but Firethorn was riding roughshod over his feelings. There were times when even he found it hard to accommodate his master's tantrums. He addressed the immediate problem.

'Let us consider *Love and Fortune*,' he suggested.

'Indeed, sir. An audience is expecting to see the play this very afternoon. It has always been popular with them.'

'And so it shall be again.'

'Without Will Fowler?'

'There is a solution.'

'There's no time to rewrite the piece,' said Firethorn dismissively. 'We could never unravel that plot at a morning's rehearsal. In any case, Edmund is in no condition to wrestle with such a task. The Armada play is putting him under great strain.'

'Edmund will not be needed.'

'Yet you say there is a solution?'

'Yes, master.'

'Will you raise Will Fowler from the dead, sir?'

'In a manner of speaking.'

'What riddle is this?'

'His name is Samuel Ruff.'

'Ruff!' bellowed Firethorn. 'That wretch who enticed you both into the Hope and Anchor?'

'He's an experienced player,' argued Nicholas. 'The equal of our own man in every way.'

'He could never learn the part in a couple of hours.'

'Samuel believes that he can. He is studying the role even now. I copied out the sides for him myself from the prompt book.'

'You take liberties, Nick,' warned Firethorn. *Love and Fortune* is our property. It is not for the eyes of strangers.'

'Do you wish the performance to take place today?'

'Of course!'

'Then this is the only remedy.'

'I will not hire a man I've never met.'

'With your permission, I'll invite him to the rehearsal. You'll soon be able to judge if he can carry the part. We'll not find a better man at such short notice.'

'But the fellow was injured last night.'

'A flesh wound in the left arm,' explained Nicholas. 'The surgeon dressed it for him and it's not serious. Lorenzo wears a cloak in every scene. It will hide the injury completely. As for the rest of the costume, Samuel is almost of Will's height and weight so no alterations will be necessary.'

'Stop thrusting the man at me!' protested Firethorn.

'He is anxious to help.'

'But for him, we would not need help.'

'Samuel accepts that. He feels guilty about what happened. That's why he wishes to make amends in some small way. Taking over his friend's role would mean so much to him.'

'The idea does not appeal.'

'Will Fowler would have approved.'

'*I* make the decisions in this company – not Will Fowler.'

'Maybe I should raise the matter with the other sharers,' said Nicholas artlessly. 'They might take a different view.'

'Mine is the view that matters!' snarled the actor.

Lawrence Firethorn prowled his lair like a tiger. When there was an explosion of boyish laughter from next door where the apprentices shared a room, he banged the wall and roared them to silence. When his wife sent word that breakfast was ready, he frightened the servant away simply by baring his fangs. At length, be began to come around.

'Experienced, you say?'

'Several years with good companies, Leicester's among them.'

'He can con lines quickly?'

'It was his trademark.'

'Is he quarrelsome?' demanded Firethorn. 'Like Will?'

'No, master. He's a very peaceful citizen.'

'And why does this worthy fellow lack work?'

'I don't know.'

'He must have some defects.'

'None that I could see. Will vouched for him.'

'Where did Ruff play last?'

'With Banbury's Men,' said Nicholas.

'Banbury's Men!'

Firethorn's exclamation rang through the whole house. His interest in Samuel Ruff had just come to an end. The Earl of Banbury and Lord Westfield were sworn enemies who lost no opportunity to score off each other. Their respective dramatic companies were major weapons in the feud and they regarded each other with cold hatred. Banbury's Men had been in the ascendant at first but they had now been displaced by Westfield's Men. In the shifting world of London theatre, it was Lawrence Firethorn and his company who now held the upper hand and they were not willing to relinquish it.

'Meet him, at least,' pressed Nicholas.

'He is not the man for us.'

'But he fell foul of Banbury's Men through no fault of his own. He was forced to leave.'

'I will not employ him, Nick. It's unthinkable.'

'Then we must cancel the performance as soon as may be.'

'Hold! I will not gallop into this.'

'The others will be shocked by your decision.'

'It has not been made yet.'

'Give Samuel a chance,' whispered Nicholas. 'He's the man for the hour.'

'Not with that pedigree.'

'Do you know why he left Banbury's Men?'

'I don't care,' snapped Firethorn.

'Shall I tell you what his crime was?'

'Forget him.'

'He spoke in praise of you.'

There was a pause that was just long enough for the first seed of interest to take root. Nicholas carefully watered it with a few details.

'Giles Randolph took exception to what was said.'

'Randolph is an amateur!'

'He's full of self-love. It's not enough for him to be the leading actor with the company. They have to fawn and flatter at every turn to suit his taste, and Samuel could not bring himself to do that. They were playing *Scipio Africanus*.'

'A miserable piece,' sneered Firethorn. 'Nothing but stale conceits and dribbling verse. I'd not soil my hands with it.'

'Giles Randolph was playing the hero. He had a scene with Samuel in the role of a tribune. It was—' Nicholas broke off abruptly and shrugged his shoulders. 'Ah, well. You've no wish to hear all this.'

'Go on, go on.'

'It may just be idle gossip.'

'What happened, Nick?'

Lawrence Firethorn was keen to know. He and Giles Randolph were deadly rivals, talented artistes who competed with each other every time they walked onto a stage. Anything that was to the detriment of Randolph would come as welcome news. Curiosity made Firethorn tap his book holder on the chest.

'Come on, sir. They had a scene together.'

'At an important point in the action.'

'Well?'

Nicholas had worked with actors long enough to learn some of their tricks. He delayed for a few seconds to heighten the tension then he plunged on.

'When Samuel gave of his best, Randolph complained that his performance was too strong. It stole the hero's thunder.'

'Ha! Some hero! Some thunder!'

'Samuel is a forthright man. He told the truth.'

'That Randolph is a babbling idiot!'

'That a leading actor should lead and not surround himself with poor players who would make him look all the better.'

'And me?' said Firethorn, intrigued. 'What of me?'

'Samuel used you as an example, master. You would outshine any company. The finer the players around you, the more you rise above them. They feed your inspiration.'

Firethorn beamed. No praise sweeter than that from a fellow actor. He judged Samuel Ruff to be very perceptive and began to forgive him for his association with Banbury's Men. Nicholas took advantage of his changed mood.

'Samuel is desperate to join us,' he continued. 'He feels it as a duty to Will Fowler. He is so eager to help us that he offered to do so without payment of any kind.'

'Indeed?' Firethorn's eye kindled.

'But I assured him that you were a man of honour, who would not conceive of employing someone without giving him fair reward.'

'Of course,' agreed the actor, hiding his disappointment.

'Then it's settled?'

Firethorn sat on the edge of the four-poster. Even in his night attire, he retained a crumpled dignity. He looked like a Roman senator brooding on affairs of state.

'Tell him to attend the rehearsal in one hour.'

Nicholas nodded then withdrew. It had worked out well. Confident of his powers of persuasion, he had already told Ruff at what time to present himself at The Queen's Head. The story of the hired man's departure from his previous company had not been entirely true but Nicholas had no qualms about embellishing the bare facts. A vain man like Lawrence Firethorn enjoyed seeing the vanity of others exposed. The main thing was that a crisis had been averted. The play would not be cancelled.

It was one small consolation after a horrendous night.

Samuel Ruff did not let them down. Though tired and grieving, he arrived at the rehearsal with a secure grasp on his lines and a real understanding of his character. When he was taken through his moves, he learned quickly and his evident respect for Firethorn was another telling factor. He was indeed the man for the hour.

The performance that afternoon delighted its audience. *Love and Fortune* was a romantic comedy about the perils of over-hasty passion and its use of mistaken identity was particularly endearing. Firethorn led the company with his usual verve, Edmund Hoode sparkled as a lovelorn gallant, and Barnaby Gill used all his comic skills to set the inn yard at a roar. With splendid wigs and costumes, the boy apprentices brought the female characters vivaciously to life.

Ruff himself was excellent in the testing role of Lorenzo. Not only did he carry his own part well, he improvised cleverly when, first, one of the actors missed an entrance, then another dried in the middle of a speech. Samuel Ruff was a veteran player, seasoned by long years in a demanding profession that had lately turned its callous back on him. In his ebullient performance, there was no hint of the dark sorrow that lay in his heart.

Love and Fortune proved the ideal play for the occasion. Will Fowler's death had shaken the whole company and there was a funereal air about the rehearsal. Once they began, however, the actors were swept along by the joyous romp and given no time to dwell on their sadness. Out of a deep tragedy, they had plucked forth a comic triumph.

Nicholas Bracewell was at the helm, marshalling the cast, cueing the action, making sure that the pace was maintained. Part of his job was to prepare a Plot of the drama, which gave details, scene by scene, of what was happening, who was involved and when they made their entrances and exits. Since they worked only from individual sides written out for them by the scrivener, the actors relied totally on the Plot that was hung up in the tiring-house and they had cause to be grateful for the legibility of Nicholas's hand and for his meticulousness. It was all there.

The book holder was thrilled at the way that Ruff was standing in for his old friend, and he saw the excitement in the man's face every time he came offstage. Here was no farm labourer, content to live out his days in rural anonymity. The playhouse was his true home. Like Will Fowler, he would never be happy away from it. Nicholas resolved to talk further with Firethorn.

The leading actor himself was in an affable mood, smiling upon all and sundry as he strode back into the tiring-house each time with applause at his heels. Before his next entrance, he would study himself carefully in a mirror and stroke his beard, fondle his locks or make slight adjustments to his hat and garments. It was not only the success of the play that was pleasing him, nor even the fact that Lord Westfield himself was there to witness it. Something else was putting that swagger into his walk. Barnaby Gill identified what it was.

'In the middle of the lower gallery,' he hissed.

'I thought so,' said Nicholas, flicking over a page of his prompt book. 'I recognised the signs.'

'He's directing every line at her.'

'Is he getting any response?'

'Response!' echoed Gill with spiteful relish. 'She keeps lowering her mask and favouring him with such ardent glances that he is almost smouldering. Mark my words, Nicholas, she knows how to tickle his epididymis.'

'Who is she?'

'Prepare yourself.'

'Why?'

'Lady Rosamund Varley.'

'Oh!'

Nicholas waved some of the actors into position to make their entrance. He did not dare to reflect on what he had just been told. A possible liaison between Lawrence Firethorn and Lady Rosamund Varley was far too disturbing to consider. He kept his mind on the job in hand and warned the lutenist to make himself ready. Gill's tone remained malicious.

'Love and fortune indeed!'

'Don't forget your costume change.'

'It's lust and misfortune!'

'Ben!' called Nicholas. 'Stand by.'

'Aye,' came the gruff reply from a thickset actor.

'His wife should geld him,' decided Gill. 'It's the only way to tame a stallion like that. Margery should geld him – with her teeth.'

Benjamin Creech went past with a tray of goblets. 'Remember to offer the first to Lorenzo,' said Nicholas.

'Aye.'

'Don't drink any yourself,' teased Gill wickedly.

'No,' grunted Creech.

When his cue came, he straightened his back and made his entrance. Nicholas turned over another page. Barnaby Gill rid himself of some more bilious comments then let his gaze wander until it settled on one of the apprentices. Richard Honeydew was standing in profile as he shook out his petticoats. His face was small and beautifully shaped with a youthful bloom on it that made his skin look like silk. Barnaby Gill watched him in wonderment.

'Lawrence is such a fool!' he murmured. 'Why bother with women when you can have the real thing?'

The afternoon had been a resounding success for Lawrence Firethorn. He had held a full audience spellbound, he had delighted his patron, and he had fallen in love. It was an intoxicating experience. He was so carried away that he even paid Marwood the rent that was outstanding. Spared the horrors of Spanish occupation, and now showered with money he never expected to get, the landlord almost contrived a smile. Firethorn slapped him on the back and sent him off. His next task was to take Samuel Ruff aside to put a proposition to him. The player was duly impressed.

'I take that as a great compliment.'

'Then you accept?'

'I fear not. My way lies towards a farm in Norwich.'

'A *farm*!' He invested the word with utter disgust.

'Yes, sir.'

'Buy why, man?'

'Because I'm minded to leave the profession altogether.'

'Actors do not leave,' announced Firethorn grandly. 'They act on to the very end of their days.'

'Not me,' said Ruff solemnly.

'Would you rather chase sheep in Norwich?'

'Cows. My brother has a dairy farm.'

'We must save you from that at all costs, dear fellow.

You'll be up to your waist in cow turds and surrounded by flies. That's no fit way for an actor to see out his full span.' He slipped an arm familiarly around the other's shoulder. 'When did you plan to travel?'

'Today, sir. But for that brawl in the tavern, I would have been well on my journey by now. As it is, I will stay in London until the funeral is over. I owe Will that.'

'You owe him something else as well,' argued Firethorn. 'To carry on in his footsteps. Can you betray him, sir?'

'I've already sent word to my brother.'

'Send again. Tell him he must milk his cows himself.'

Samuel Ruff was slowly being tempted. Firethorn took him across to a window that overlooked the inn yard. Down below was a mad bustle of activity as the trestles were cleared away by the stagekeepers and journeymen. It was an evocative scene and it had its effect on Ruff. He pulled away from the window.

'Nicholas Bracewell insists,' continued Firethorn. 'And I always listen to his advice. We need you.'

'I cannot stay, sir.'

'It would keep Will's memory alive for us.'

Ruff ran a hand through his grey hair and pondered. It was no easy decision for him to make. He had resigned himself to a course of action and he was not a man who lightly changed his mind. As the clamour went on outside, he tossed another glance towards the window. His old way of life beckoned seductively.

'How much were you paid with Banbury's Men?'

'Eight shillings a week.'

'Ah!' Firethorn was checked. He had been ready to offer a wage of seven shillings but something told him the man might be worth the extra money. 'Very well. I'll match that.'

'London has not been kind to me,' said Ruff quietly.

'Give it another chance.'

'I will think it over, sir.'

Firethorn smiled. He had himself a new hired man.

Murder caused only a temporary interruption at the Hope and Anchor. Everything was back to normal by the next evening. Fresh rushes hid those which had been stained by Will Fowler's blood. Beer and wine had already erased the memory from the minds of the regular patrons and they were preoccupied once again with their games, their banter and their vices. The low-ceilinged room was a throbbing cacophony.

Nicholas Bracewell coughed as he stepped into the smoky atmosphere. When he looked down at the spot where Will Fowler had lain, his heart missed a beat. He crossed quickly to the hostess, who was drawing a pint of sack from a barrel. She was a short, dark, plump woman in her forties with a pockmarked face that was heavily powdered and large, mobile, bloodshot eyes. Her dress was cut low to display an ample bosom and a mole did duty as a beauty spot on one breast.

She served the customer then turned to Nicholas.

'What's your pleasure, sir?' Her features clouded as she saw who it was. An already rough voice became even more rasping. 'You're not welcome here.'

'I need some help.'

'I told you all I know. So did my customers.'

'A man was killed here last night,' protested Nicholas.

'You think we don't know that?' she retorted vehemently. 'When the watch and the constables and goodness knows who else come running into the house. We like to keep out of harm's way down this alley. We don't want the law to pry into us.'

'Just answer one question,' said Nicholas patiently.

'Leave us alone, sir.'

'Look, I'll pay you.' He dropped coins on to the counter and they were immediately swept up by her flabby hand. 'That man with the red beard. Samuel Ruff says that he came downstairs.'

'He didn't lodge here,' she asserted. 'He was a stranger.'

'Then he was up there for another reason.'

The bloodshot eyes stared unblinkingly at him. Nicholas took more money from his purse and handed it over. She leaned forward to thrust her face close to his own.

'I want you out of here in five minutes.'

'You have my word.'

'For good.'

'For good,' he agreed. 'Now, who was she?'

'Joan. She has the end room on the first floor.'

Nicholas did not waste any of his meagre time. Bounding up the stairs, he found himself in a passage that was so narrow his shoulders brushed the walls. Crude sounds of love-making came from rooms where whores were busy earning their income. The stench made Nicholas cough again. Samuel Ruff's fortunes must have been at a very low ebb to drive him into such an unwholesome place.

He reached the end room and listened for a moment. No sound came from within. He tapped on the door with his knuckles. There was no answer and so he used more force.

'Come in,' said a frail voice.

He opened the door and looked into a tiny room that was lit by one guttering tallow. On the mattress that took up most of the floor space, a young woman was lying in heavy shadow. She seemed to be wearing a shift and was half-covered by a filthy blanket. He peered at her but could only see her in outline.

'Joan?' he asked.

'Did you want me?' she whispered.

'Yes.'

'Come in properly and close the door,' she invited in a girlish voice, sitting up. 'I like visitors.'

He stepped forward a pace and pulled the door shut. Joan reached for the tallow and held it so that its thin beam shone upon him. She gave a sigh of pleasure.

'What's your name, sir?'

'Nicholas.'

'You're a fine, upstanding man, Nicholas. Sit beside me.'

'I came to talk.'

'Of course,' she soothed. 'We'll talk all you want.'

'A man was up here with you last night, Joan.'

'Three, four, maybe five men. I can't remember.'

'This one was tall with a red beard.'

Joan stiffened and let out a cry. Putting the candle aside, she wrapped her arms around her body for protection and huddled against the wall. Her voice was trembling now.

'Go away!' she begged. 'Get out of here!'

'Did he give you his name?'

'There's nothing I can tell you.'

'It's very important.'

'Just go away,' she whimpered.

She broke down into frantic sobbing. When Nicholas bent over to comfort her, however, she pushed him away and drew herself into the very corner of the room. He watched the waif-like creature until her fear subsided a little then he spoke gently.

'I need to find him, Joan.'

'Leave me be, sir.'

'He killed a friend of mine. I want him.'

She curled herself up into a frightened ball and shook her head vigorously. Nicholas held out his purse to her.

'Keep your money!' she said.

'Listen to me!' he pressed. 'My friend was murdered last night by that man with the red beard. I'll find him no matter how long it takes. Please help me, Joan.'

She stayed in the shadows as she weighed him up, then she uncurled and sat up again. He crouched down beside her and tried once more to enlist her aid.

'There must be *something* you can tell me.'

'Oh yes!' she said ruefully.

'Had you seen him before?'

'Never! And I don't want to see him again.'

'Did he give you a name?'

'He gave me nothing but rough words, sir. But there is one thing I will always remember about him.' A shudder went through her. 'His back.'

'Why?'

'He told me not to touch it, and I didn't at first. But I like my arms around a man and I couldn't help it. When my fingers touched his back . . .'

'What was wrong with it?' he asked softly.

'Scars. Dozen of fresh scars all over it. Long, thick, raw wounds that made my flesh creep when I felt them.' A second shudder made her double up. 'He warned me. He did warn me.'

'What did he do to you, Joan?'

'This.'

She pulled the shift over her head and tossed it aside, then she lifted the tallow so that its pallid light fell on her. Nicholas blenched. He felt as if he had been kicked in the pit of the stomach. The slim, naked, girlish body was covered in hideous bruises. Thick powder was unable to disguise the swollen face, the split lip and the blackened eyes. There was a telltale lump across the bridge of her nose.

He understood her fear all too well now. She could scarcely be much more than sixteen. In a fit of rage, her client had beaten her senseless and put years on her. Joan would bear her own scars for the rest of her life.

Nicholas put the purse into her hands and closed her

fingers around it before leaving the room. He had learned something new and revolting about the killer with the red beard. It was not much but it was a start. There had been two victims the previous night. Will Fowler had been killed and Joan had been brutally assaulted. Both of them deserved to be avenged.

Chapter Four

Richard Honeydew was finding too much talent could be a disadvantage in the theatre. It excited envy. In the few months that he had been with Lord Westfield's Men, he had worked hard and shown exceptional promise but there was a high price to pay. The other three apprentices ganged up against him. Seeing him as a threat, they subjected him to all kinds of hostility, teasing and practical jokes. It was getting worse.

'Aouw!'

'That will cool you down, Dicky!' sneered John Tallis.

'Don't tell on us,' threatened Stephen Judd. 'Or it won't be water next time.'

'Unless it's our own!' added Tallis with a snigger.

The two boys scuttled away and left Richard shivering

with fright. As he came back from the privy, they had drenched him with a bucket of water. His blond hair was plastered to his head, his shirt was soaked and he was dripping all over the floor. It was as much as he could do to hold back tears.

Richard Honeydew was only eleven. He was small, thin and had the kind of exaggerated prettiness that made him an ideal choice for a female role. John Tallis and Stephen Judd were older, bigger, stronger and much more well-versed in the techniques of persecution. Hitherto, however, Richard had been fairly safe at a rehearsal because Nicholas Bracewell was usually on hand to take care of him. The book holder was his one real friend in the company and it was he who made life tolerable for the boy.

The apprentice's first instinct was to run straight to Nicholas but the warning from Stephen Judd still rang in his ears. He decided to clean himself up and say nothing. At the back of the tiring-house was a room that was used partly for storage and partly as a rest area where actors could sit out lengthy waits during a performance. Richard trotted along there and he was relieved to find it empty. Pulling off his shirt, he grabbed a piece of hessian and used it to dry his hair and body.

He did not hear Barnaby Gill. The actor stood in the doorway and marvelled at the pale torso with its delicate tracery of blue veins across the chest. There was something so natural and beautiful about the scene that his heart took flame. Stepping into the room, he closed the door behind him and caused Richard to spin around in alarm.

'Oh, it's you, Master Gill.'

'Don't be afeard, Dick. I won't harm you.'

'I was just drying myself.'

'I saw.'

Innocence is its own protection. As the actor moved stealthily towards him, Richard had no understanding of the danger he faced. He continued to work away with the hessian.

'That's too rough,' observed Gill. 'You need something softer for a body such as yours.'

'I've finished now.'

'But your breeches are wet as well. Slip them down and dry yourself properly.' As Richard hesitated, his voice coaxed on. 'Nobody will see you. Come, take them down. I'll help to rub you.'

The boy was still reluctant but he was at a disadvantage. Barnaby Gill was a leading member of the company with an influence upon its composition. He was not someone to antagonise. Besides, he had always been kind and considerate. Richard recalled gibes made about Gill by the other boys but he still could not fathom their meaning. As the avuncular smile got closer to him, he was ready to submit trustingly to the actor's touch. But it never came. Even as Gill reached out for him, the door opened and a voice spoke.

'Ah, there you are, Dick!'

'Hello, Master Ruff.'

'What do you want?' growled Barnaby Gill.

'I was looking for the lad,' explained the hired man

easily. 'Come, Dick. The best place for you is out in the hot sun. The yard is an Italian piazza today. We'll hang you up to dry with the washing.'

Before Gill could stop him, Samuel Ruff whisked up the shirt and led the boy out of the room. The sharer was left to fume alone. He reached for the hessian which Richard had used and he caressed its surface for a few seconds. Then he threw it violently aside and stalked back into the tiring-house.

Ruff, meanwhile, had taken the boy into the yard to watch some of the rehearsal. Without quite knowing how, Richard had the feeling that he had just been rescued.

'If that ever happens again,' said Ruff, 'you tell me.'

Richard nodded happily. He had found a new friend.

Patriotism is a powerful drug. In the wake of the victory against the Armada, it affected almost everyone. There was a surge of self-confidence and a thrill of pride that coursed through the veins of the entire nation. Master Roger Bartholomew also felt the insistent throb of patriotic impulse. He imbibed the details of the Spanish defeat, he listened to the sermons preached at St Paul's Cross and he attended many services of thanksgiving. In the faces all round him, he saw a new spirit, a greater buoyancy, a permissible arrogance. People were conscious as never before of the immense significance of being English.

The drug helped Bartholomew to forget all about his earlier setbacks and vows. Inspiration made him reach for his pen and a play seemed to fall ready-made from his fertile brain. It was a celebration of England's finest hour and it contained speeches which, he believed, in all modesty, would thunder down the centuries. The verse bounded from the page, the characters were moulded to stake their claim to immortality.

As he blotted the last line and sat back in his chair, Bartholomew allowed himself a smirk of congratulation. His first play was juvenilia. With *An Enemy Routed*, he had come of age in the most signal way. The success of the piece would wipe away any lingering memories of his disappointment and disillusion. Only one problem remained. Master Roger Bartholomew had to make the crucial decision as to which dramatic company he would favour with his masterpiece. He luxuriated in the possibilities.

Two weeks wrought many changes among Lord Westfield's Men. As soon as Will Fowler's funeral was over, the general gloom began to lift. Samuel Ruff was an able deputy for his friend and, in spite of occasional remarks about leaving for Norwich soon, he settled in very well. Richard Honeydew was glad to have someone else to look out for him and he revelled in the fatherly concern that the hired man showed him. Lawrence Firethorn moved about in a cloud of ecstasy. Each day, he was convinced, brought him closer to the promised tryst with Lady Rosamund Varley; each performance gave him a fresh opportunity to woo her from the stage. Barnaby Gill's acid comments on the romance were largely unheard and totally unregarded. The company was grateful to the lady. When Firethorn was in love, everyone stood to gain.

The punishing round of the book holder's life gave Nicholas Bracewell less time than he would have wished to pursue his investigation of Will Fowler's murder, but his resolve did not slacken. After a fortnight, the casual brutality of it all still rattled him. Time after time, he went over the events that had taken place at the Hope and Anchor that night.

'And Redbeard was carrying a bottle in his hand?'

'Yes, Nick,' said Samuel Ruff.

'You're sure of that?'

'Completely. When he got close, I could smell the ale on his breath. The man had taken too much and could not hold his drink.'

'Then what happened?'

Ruff had been through the details a score of times but he did not complain. He was just as committed to finding the man who had murdered his old friend.

'Redbeard lurched against the settle on which Will was sitting and pushed it a good foot backwards. Some of his ale was spilled over Will.'

'So he took exception?'

'The row flared up in a matter of seconds, Nicholas.'

The book holder sighed. Will Fowler's short temper had caught up with him at last. Nicholas saw the familiar image of his friend, roused in argument, eyes blazing, cheeks aglow, voice howling and brawny arms ready to exact stern punishment. When he was in such a choleric mood, Will

Fowler could not easily be calmed down. It had taken a cunning thrust from a sword to bleed all the rage out of him.

'I will never forgive myself,' said Ruff sadly.

'You tried to protect him.'

'I gave that ruffian his chance,' admitted the other. 'I would rather he had run *me* through than dear Will!'

'In some ways, I think he did,' observed Nicholas.

The two men had just come out of The Queen's Head at the end of another full day. Redbeard preyed on their minds. Nicholas reasoned that a man with a fondness for whores would not keep away from the brothels for long and he was visiting them all in turn. He was carrying a rough sketch of the stranger which Ruff had helped him to draw. They felt it was a good likeness of the man they sought but it had so far failed to jog any memories.

Samuel Ruff was eager to do his share of the work and he had taken the sketch around the stews in Eastcheap. Nicholas was concentrating on the more numerous brothels of Bankside, certain that their quarry would surface sooner or later.

'I think Redbeard is lying low,' said Ruff.

'He'll come out to play at night,' added Nicholas. 'The smell of a bawd will tempt him back.'

'I've been thinking about those wounds of his.'

'The scars on his back?'

'They might have cost Will his life.'

'In what way?'

'Redbeard must have taken a severe beating from

someone and his wounds still smarted. He wanted revenge. First of all, he attacks that poor girl and makes her pay for it, then he comes rolling downstairs in a drunken fury. Those scars were still on fire.'

'Did Will touch his back at all?'

'A glancing blow as he lashed out at the man. No wonder Redbeard drew his sword. He'd been caught on the raw.'

'That's no excuse for murder, Sam,' reminded Nicholas.

'Of course not, but you take my point? If that villain had not been given such a beating, Will might be alive today.'

Nicholas thought it through carefully before speaking.

'There's truth in what you say but I must disagree about those scars on his back. He was not given a beating.'

'Then what?'

'I think he was whipped through the streets.'

'A malefactor?' said Ruff in surprise.

'I will ask him when I finally catch up with him.'

Nicholas waved aside Ruff's offer of company on his search and set off into the night. His mind played endlessly with the possibilities as he walked over the Bridge and swung into Bankside. It was late but he had promised himself he would make three calls. The first two visits were fruitless but he was not dismayed. He went on to the third name on his list.

The Cardinal's Hat was situated in a narrow, twisting, fetid lane which had an open drain running down its middle. There was no declaration of papacy in the tavern's name. To advertise the wares of the house, the cardinal's hat on the sign outside had been painted with such lewd skill that its crown resembled in shape and colour the dimpled tip of the male sexual organ.

As Nicholas turned into the dark lane, a figure swung out of the shadows and bumped into him. After a grunted apology, the man tried to move off but Nicholas gripped him firmly by the throat. Slipping a hand into the man's jerkin, he retrieved his newly-stolen purse then flung the pickpocket against a wall. With groans and curses, the man limped off into the night.

The Cardinal's Hat was so grimy and sordid that it made the Hope and Anchor look like a church vestry. Bare-breasted whores lolled about, drink and tobacco stoked up an inferno of noise, and all the dregs of the London streets seemed to have fetched up within. Tables were jammed so close together that any movement across the room was almost impossible. The reek that greeted him was overwhelming.

Nicholas lowered his head to duck under the main beam and one of the prostitutes jumped up to plant a guzzling kiss on his lips. He eased her away and sought out the surly landlord. The man was small and sinewy, a watchful polecat with its claws at the ready. He gave Nicholas no help at all until the sketch was produced. Holding it up to the tallow, the landlord squinted at it then let out a yell of rage.

'That's him! I know the rogue!'

'He was here?'

'Last week. Monday. Tuesday, maybe.'

'You're certain he's the same man?'

'He's no man,' snarled the other, thrusting the sketch back at Nicholas. 'That's a vile beast you have there.'

'What did he do?'

'Alice would tell you if she was here – God help her!'

'Alice?'

'Yes!' hissed the landlord. 'When she took him up to her room, he was quiet as a lamb. Five minutes later, she's screaming for dear life and the scurvy knave is beating her black and blue. The poor drab is in the hospital with both arms broken. But that's not the end of it, sir.'

'What do you mean?'

'The dog smashed a window upstairs and leans out to hack at our sign with his sword.'

'The Cardinal's Hat?'

'He'd have cut it down if we hadn't chased him off.' The landlord cleared his throat and spat on the floor. 'It's the same man in the drawing. If ever he steps in here again, they'll have to carry him out in his coffin!'

Sympathy and excitement stirred inside Nicholas. He was sorry that another girl had been so grievously assaulted but he was elated to have picked up the trail at last.

Redbeard had broken cover. Nicholas would stay at his heels.

Anne Hendrik sat in her favourite chair and worked at her sewing by the light of a large candle. Her needle rose and fell with an easy rhythm. It did not pause for a second when the front door opened and her lodger returned. Anne kept her eyes and her mind on what she was doing, except that her needle now jabbed into the material with a touch of venom.

Nicholas Bracewell was puzzled. A warm smile and a welcome usually awaited him at the house. This time he had not even elicited a polite enquiry about how his day had gone. Anne sewed on.

'You have a visitor,' she said crisply.

'At this time of night?'

'The young woman insisted on seeing you.'

'Woman?' He was startled. 'Did she give her name?'

'No,' replied Anne tartly. 'Nor would she tell me what her business with you was. It was a private matter, she said. I showed her up to your chamber.' Her voice hardened as he took a conciliatory step towards her. 'Don't keep your visitor waiting, sir.'

He gestured his bafflement then went up to his bedchamber, tapping on the door before going in. The young woman leapt up from a chair and went over to him.

'Nicholas Bracewell?'

'Yes.'

'Thank heaven I've found you!'

She clasped his hands tightly and tears formed in blue eyes that looked as if they had cried their fill. The woman was short, neat, pleasantly attractive, no more than twenty and wearing a plain dress beneath a simple gown. Nicholas caught a whiff of the country. One glance told him why his landlady had been so offhand with him. The girl was clearly pregnant. Anne Hendrik had seen a distressed young woman in search of Nicholas and assumed that he was the father of the child.

He ushered her gently to a chair and knelt in front of her. The room was small but well-furnished and impeccably clean. She looked out of place in such comfortable surroundings.

'Who are you?' he asked.

'Susan Fowler.'

'Fowler? . . . Surely you are not his daughter?'

'No,' she replied in hurt tones. 'Will was my husband.'

Fresh tears trickled down her flushed cheeks and he took her in his arms to comfort her, letting her cry her fill before she spoke again. His head shook apologetically.

'I'm sorry. I had no idea that he was married.'

'It was almost two years ago.'

'Why did he say nothing?'

'He wanted it that way,' she whispered. 'Will said the theatre was a world of its own. He wanted somewhere to go to when he had to get away from it.'

Nicholas could sympathise with that desire but he still could not fit this attractive young housewife alongside the blunt and outspoken Will Fowler. There was a naive willingness about her that seemed unlikely to ensnare an actor, who, just like his fellows, had always taken his pleasures along the way with much more worldly creatures.

'Where do you live?' he asked.

'In St Albans. With my parents.'

'Two years ago, you say?'

'All but, sir.'

It began to make sense. Two years earlier, the company had toured in Hertfordshire and given a couple of performances at Lord Westfield's country house in St Albans. The relationship had somehow started there and, unaccountably, led to marriage. What now assailed Nicholas was a shaming guilt. They had laid Will Fowler in his grave without a thought for this helpless woman.

'How did you find out?' he wondered.

'I knew something had happened. He always sent word.'

'When did you come to London?'

'Today. Will had spoken about The Queen's Head.'

'You went there?'

She nodded. 'The landlord told me.'

Nicholas was mortified. Of all the people to report a husband's death to a vulnerable young wife, Alexander Marwood was the worst. He could make good news sound depressing. With a genuine tragedy to retail, he would be in his macabre element. Pain and embarrassment made Nicholas enfold Susan Fowler more tightly in his arms. He took the blame upon himself. Sensing this, she squeezed his arms gently.

'You weren't to know.'

'We thought he had no next of kin.'

'There'll be two of us come September.'

He released his grip and knelt back again. Susan Fowler had been told that he was the best person to explain the horrid circumstances of her husband's death. Nicholas was as discreet as he could be, playing down certain aspects of the tale and emphasising that Will Fowler had been an unwitting victim of a violent and dangerous man. She listened with remarkable calm until it was all over, then she fainted into his arms.

He lifted her on to the bed and made her comfortable, releasing her gown from her neck and undoing her collar. Pouring a cup of water from the jug on his table, he dipped a finger in it to bathe her forehead. When she began to stir, he helped her to sip some of the liquid. She began to rally.

'I'm sorry, sir.'

'There's no need. It's a trying time for you.'

'I miss Will so much.'

'Of course.'

'That man . . . at the tavern . . .'

'He'll be caught,' promised Nicholas.

Susan Fowler soon felt well enough to sit up with a pillow at her back. Now that her secret was out, she wanted to talk about it and did so compulsively. Nicholas was honoured that she felt able to entrust him with her confidences. It was a touching story. The unlikely romance between an ageing actor and a country girl had started with a chance meeting at St Albans and developed from there.

The picture that emerged of Will Fowler was very much at variance with the man Nicholas had known. His widow spoke of him as kind, gentle and tender. There was no mention of his abrasive temper which had led him into so much trouble and which had finally contributed to his death. Susan Fowler had been married to a paragon. Though the time they spent together was limited, it had been a blissful union.

Another surprise lay in store for Nicholas.

'We married in the village church.'

'Did you?'

'Will called it an act of faith.'

'All marriages are that,' he suggested.

'You don't understand,' she continued. 'Will had vowed that he'd never enter a Protestant church. He was a Catholic.'

Nicholas reeled as if from a blow. A man whom he thought he had known quite well was turning out to have a whole new side to his character. Religion was something with which the actor had always seemed cheerfully unconcerned. It did not accord too well with the freebooting life of a hired man.

'He gave it up,' she said with pride. 'For me.'

'Are you quite certain of all this?'

'Oh, yes.'

'Will, of the old religion?'

'He was very devout.'

'You talked about it?'

'All the time. He showed me his Bible and his crucifix.'

'Did he say how long he'd followed Rome?'

'For years.'

Astonishment gave way to speculation. Nicholas began to wonder if the actor's ebullient manner was a kind of disguise, a wall behind which he hid himself so that nobody could get too close. If he could conceal his religion and his marriage so effectively, it was possible that he had other secrets.

Susan Fowler was now patently exhausted. The shock of it all was draining her strength and her eyelids were drooping. He told her to stay exactly where she was and went quickly downstairs. Anne Hendrik was waiting for him, schooling herself to be calm yet evidently upset by the situation. She continued to ply her needle and avert her eyes from him.

'An apology is due,' he began.

'Do not bother, sir,' she answered.

'The girl will have to pass the night in my chamber.'

'Oh, no!' said Anne, looking up at him. 'I make objection to that, Nicholas. This is not a tavern with rooms to let for any doxy who happens to pass by.'

'Susan Fowler is no doxy.'

'Take her out of my house, if you please!'

'You hear what I say?'

'I care not what her name is.'

'Susan *Fowler*,' he repeated.

'She will not pass the night under my roof, sir.'

'The girl is Will Fowler's widow.'

Realisation dawned on her and her jaw dropped. It was the last thing she had expected and filled her instantly with remorse. She looked upwards then put her sewing aside and rose from her chair. Her natural compassion flowed freely.

'Oh, the poor lass! Of course, she must stay – for as long as she wishes. The girl should not be travelling alone in that condition.' She turned to Nicholas. 'Why did you not tell me that Will Fowler was married?'

'Because I only found out about it myself just now.' He

flashed her a warm grin. 'Does this alter the case?'

A brief smile lit up her face and she leaned forward to kiss him on the cheek. Duties intruded.

'If she is to sleep in that chamber, I must take up some clean bedding. And she may need help undressing.' Her hand went up to her mouth. 'Oh dear! What must she think of me, giving her such a frosty welcome when she came to my door?'

'She did not even notice it, Anne.'

'It was unpardonable.'

'Susan Fowler is concerned with weightier matters.'

'How long has she known?'

'Today.'

'No wonder the girl is in such distress. I'd better go up to her at once and see what I can do to help her.'

'She will be very grateful.'

Anne went bustling across the room then stopped in her tracks as a thought struck her. She swung round on her heel.

'If the girl is going to be in *your* bed . . .'

'Yes?'

'Where will you sleep?'

His grin broadened and she replied with a knowing smile. It would give her the chance to show him how sorry she was.

Chapter Five

Edmund Hoode laboured long and hard over *Gloriana Triumphant*, and it underwent several sea changes. The first decision he made was to set it in the remote past. Censorship of new plays was strict and Sir Edmund Tilney, the Master of the Revels, was especially vigilant for any political implications in a piece. A drama featuring the real characters and issues involved in the defeat of the Armada would be far too contentious to allow even if it were a paean of praise.

The principals had to be disguised in some way and a shift in time was the easiest solution. Elizabeth therefore became the fabled Gloriana, Queen of an ancient land called Albion. Drake, Hawkins, Howard, Frobisher and the other seadogs all appeared under very different names. Spain was transmuted into an imperial power known as Iberia.

Creation came easily to some authors but Edmund Hoode was not one of them. He needed to correct and improve and polish his work all the time. It made for delays and heightened frustration.

'When *will* it be finished?' demanded Firethorn.

'Give me time,' said Hoode.

'You've been saying that for weeks.'

'It's taking shape, but slowly.'

'We need to have it in rehearsal soon,' reminded the other. 'It will first see the light of day at The Curtain next month.'

'That's what worries me, Lawrence.'

'Pah!'

The Curtain was one of the very few custom-built outdoor playhouses in London and Firethorn was delighted that *Gloriana Triumphant* would have its premiere there. Apart from the fact that the theatre was close to his own home in Shoreditch, it offered far better facilities and a far larger audience than The Queen's Head. It was also patronised more extensively by nobility – Lady Rosamund Varley among them – and this added to its lustre. Edmund Hoode still had qualms.

'I do not like The Curtain.'

'It is ideal for our purposes.'

'The audience is too unruly.'

'Not when *I* am on stage,' boasted Firethorn.

'All they want are jigs and displays of combat.'

'Then they will be satisfied, sir. You give them a jig, two

galliards and a coranto. What more can they ask? As for combat, they will watch the greatest sea battle in history.'

'I'm still not sure that it will work.'

'Leave it to Nicholas. He'll make it work.'

'But I have never put ships on stage before.'

'It is a brilliant device. When the cannons go off, the audience will believe they see the Armada itself sink below the waves.' Firethorn caressed his beard. 'There is just one small thing, Edmund.'

'What?' sighed the author. 'Your small things always turn out to be a complete rewrite of the play.'

'Not this time. A few lines here and there will suffice.'

'To what end?'

'We need more romance somehow.'

'Romance?'

'Yes,' explained Firethorn, slapping the table for effect. 'I am portrayed as a famous hero and rightly so, but there must be another side to my character. Show me as a great lover!'

'During a sea battle?'

'Insert a scene on land. Perhaps two.'

It was yet another example of the influence that Lady Rosamund Varley was having upon him. Since she had taken an interest in him, he went out of his way to present himself in the most attractive light. To play a love scene on stage was a means of rehearsing a dalliance with the lady herself. Firethorn was ready to distort the drama with incongruous material so that he could convey a message to one person in the audience.

'We already have romance,' argued Hoode.

'Between whom?'

'The seamen and their ships. The subjects and their queen. The people and their country. It is all love in one form or another.'

'Give me real passion!' insisted Firethorn.

'Passion?'

'Between a man and a woman.'

'But there's no reason for it.'

'Invent one.'

They were sitting in the room at Hoode's lodgings where the author had spent so many interminable nights struggling with the play. He looked down at the sheaf of papers that made up *Gloriana Triumphant*. To contrive a love affair would mean radical alterations to the whole structure but he knew that he had to comply. Firethorn was relentless in his persistence.

Hoode's mind wandered back to an earlier humiliation.

'I played my first important role at The Curtain.'

'Were you well-received?'

'They threw apple cores at me.'

'Ungrateful dolts!'

'It was an omen,' said the author gloomily. 'The Curtain has never been a happy place for me.'

'We will change all that with *Gloriana Triumphant*.'

Edmund Hoode did not share his optimism. Like most men who took their precarious living from the playhouse, he was racked by superstition. Those apple cores still hurt.

* * *

Being married to one of the finest actors in England was an experience which would have cowed most wives but Margery Firethorn rose to the challenge splendidly. She was a woman of strong character with a Junoesque figure, an aggressive beauty and a bellicose charm. There were four apprentices to look after as well as two small children of her own and occasional lodgers from the company, and she ran the household with a firm hand and a fearless tongue.

She enjoyed a tempestuous relationship with her husband and they shuttled at will between loathing and love, so much so that the two extremes sometimes became interchangeable. It made the house in Shoreditch a lively place.

'Who is she, Barnaby?'

'I have no idea what you are talking about.'

'Lawrence is smitten again.'

'Only with you, Margery,' he said with mock innocence.

'I feel it in my bones.'

'Marriage has many ailments.'

'How would you know?'

He rolled his eyes and gave her a disarming smirk. It was Sunday and Barnaby Gill had called at the house, ostensibly to pay his respects, but chiefly to feed her suspicions about the existence of a new *amour* in her husband's life. When she pressed him further, he deployed innuendo and denial with such skill that he confirmed all she had guessed at. Smug satisfaction warmed him. It was always pleasing to spread marital disharmony.

The performance of plays was forbidden on the Sabbath and not even the reckless Firethorn was ready to flout that ruling within the City walls. Lord Westfield's Men had a nominal day of rest though it rarely worked out like that.

Barnaby Gill glanced around and tried to sound casual. 'Is young Dick Honeydew at home?'

'Why do you ask?'

'I wanted a word with the lad.'

'Indeed?'

Margery Firethorn had got his measure the first time that she had ever met him. Though she liked him and found him amusing company at times, she never forgot the more sinister aspect of Barnaby Gill and it brought out her protective instinct.

'Is he here?'

'I don't think so. He was going to sword practise.'

'Oh.'

'Nicholas promised to instruct him.'

'The boy should have come to me. I'd have taught him to thrust and parry. Where is this instruction taking place?'

'I cannot tell you.'

'Would any of the other lads know?'

'They are not here, Barnaby.'

'I see,' said the other, angry at being baulked. 'Nicholas Bracewell is getting above himself. Dick is apprenticed to Edmund Hoode and it's he who should bear the responsibility for the boy's training. It should not be left to a menial like a book holder.'

'Nicholas is much more than that,' she replied with

spirit. 'You do him a grave disservice. As for Edmund, he's so busy with this latest play of his that he has no time to spend with the child and is grateful for any help.'

Though she was kept very much on the fringe of events, Margery Firethorn could see how much the book holder contributed to the running of the company, but that was not the only reason why she rushed to his defence. She was particularly fond of him. In a profession with more than its share of self-importance and affectation, he stood out as a modest soul and a true gentleman.

'I will bid you farewell,' said Gill.

'Good day, Barnaby.'

'And remember what I told you.'

'About Lawrence?'

'There is no other lady in his life.'

His tone made it quite clear that there was. Having assured Firethorn of a stormy reception when next he came home, Barnaby Gill took his leave. As he walked abroad through the streets of Shoreditch, he thought about the pleasures there might be in instructing Richard Honeydew how to use a sword and dagger. An opportunity would surely come one day.

Margery, meanwhile, turned to her household duties. She was in the middle of upbraiding the servant girl when there was a loud banging at the front door. A breathless George Dart was admitted. Margery glared down at him and the diminutive stagekeeper cowered in fear.

'Why do you make such noise at my door?' she demanded.

'Master Bracewell sent me,' he said between gulps for air.

'For what purpose?'

'To fetch Dick Honeydew.'

'He's already gone.'

'Are you sure, mistress? He has not turned up for sword practise. Master Bracewell has waited over an hour.'

'The boy left the house around ten.'

'Did you *see* him leave?'

'No, but I heard him go with the others.'

A frown settled on her forehead as she tried to puzzle it out, then she grabbed George Dart by the arm and dragged him towards the stairs.

'We'll soon sort this out,' she promised.

'Dick is never late as a rule.'

'There has to be an explanation.'

Having reached the first landing, she went along to another small flight of stairs. When Richard Honeydew had first moved in, he had slept in the same room as the other apprentices and suffered nightly torments. Margery had moved him up to an attic room on his own, and it was to this that she now hurried.

'Dicky!'

She flung open the door but the room was empty.

'Dicky!' she called again.

'Where can he be, mistress?'

'Not here, as you see. Dicky!'

Her third shout produced a response. There was a muffled thumping from somewhere nearby. Dart's elfin face puckered.

'Did you hear that?'

'Listen!'

'There was a—'

'Shhhh!'

They waited in silence until more thumping came. Margery went out into the passageway and soon tracked it down. There was a small cupboard under the eaves and its rough wooden door was vibrating with each sound. George Dart was terrified but Margery plunged on, seizing the handle and throwing open the door with a flourish.

'Dick!' she cried.

'God in heaven!' exclaimed the stagekeeper.

Richard Honeydew was not able to answer them. Completely naked, he was lying bound and gagged on the bedding that was stored in the cupboard. His eyes were pools of horror and his cheeks were puce with embarrassment. Both his heels were bruised from their contact with the timber.

Margery Firethorn plucked him to her bosom and held him in a maternal embrace. As her mind began to devise a punishment for this latest prank of the other apprentices, something else flitted across it to make her catch her breath.

What if Barnaby Gill had been the one to find him?

Alexander Marwood was unrepentant. As landlord of a busy inn, he had countless duties to attend to and he was always working under intense pressure, not to mention the dictates of a nagging spouse. He saw it as no part of his job to be tactful in passing on bad news. When Susan Fowler

109

came to him, he simply delivered a plain message in a plain way.

'What was wrong with that?' he asked.

'Common decency should tell you,' replied Nicholas.

'The man's dead, isn't he? No helping that.'

'Perhaps not but there's a way of helping his widow.'

'I told her the truth.'

'You *hit* her with it.'

'Who says so?'

'I do,' accused Nicholas.

Marwood's face was in its usual state of wrinkled anxiety but there was no hint of apology in its folds and twitches. It was useless to take him to task about the way that he had met Susan Fowler's enquiry. Here was a man who gravitated towards misery and positively rejoiced in being the bearer of bad tidings.

After a final word of reproach, Nicholas Bracewell turned on his heel and walked across the taproom. He did not get very far. A familiar figure was obstructing his path.

'Good morning, Master Bartholomew.'

'Hello, Nicholas.'

'I did not think to see you at The Queen's Head again.'

'Times have changed,' admitted the poet. 'I have a favour to ask of you. I know that you will oblige me.'

'I will do my best, sir.'

Roger Bartholomew pulled out the manuscript that was tucked under his arm. He handled it with the reverence that is only accorded to holy writ. Pride and pain jostled for supremacy in his expression and Nicholas could see just how much effort it had cost him to return to the scene of his earlier dejection. The young scholar inhaled deeply before blurting out his request.

'I wanted you to show this to Master Firethorn.'

'A new play?'

'It is a vast improvement upon the last one.'

'Even so.'

'If you could persuade him to read it, I'm sure that he will discern its quality.'

'We are not looking for a new play at the moment.'

'You will be unable to refuse *An Enemy Routed*.'

'But we do not purchase much new work,' explained Nicholas. 'Most of our pieces come from stock. Westfield's Men only stage six or seven new plays a year.'

'Ask him to read it,' urged Bartholomew, handing the precious manuscript to him. 'It tells of the Spanish Armada.'

'Ah.'

'It is a celebration of a supreme achievement.'

'That may be so, Master Bartholomew, but . . .' Nicholas searched for a way to let him down lightly. 'It is a popular subject these days. Many authors have been inspired to write dramas that deal with our triumphs at sea. As it happens, Edmund Hoode is writing a play for us on that selfsame theme.'

'Mine is the better,' asserted Bartholomew.

'Possibly, sir, but *Gloriana Triumphant* has been contracted.'

'It has a base title.'

'Have you thought of offering your play to another company?'

'I bring it to you first.'

'It may get a fairer hearing elsewhere.'

'The leading role was written with Lawrence Firethorn in mind,' said the poet. 'It's the part of a lifetime for him.'

'Why not try the Queen's Men?' suggested Nicholas. 'They commission more new plays than we can afford. So do Worcester's. Of course, the most appropriate company would be the Admiral's Men.'

Roger Bartholomew's face fell. He had learned much about Greek, Latin, Poesy and Rhetoric at Oxford but nothing whatsoever about the art of dissembling. His countenance was an open book in which Nicholas read the pathetic truth. *An Enemy Routed* had been taken around every dramatic company in London and rejected by them all, including the children's companies. Far from being at the top of the list, Westfield's Men were essentially a last resort, a final, desperate bid by a young poet with a burning conviction of the merit of his work.

Nicholas knew that there was not even the slightest possibility that the company would take the play, but he had too much compassion to crush the author's hopes there and then.

'I will see what I can do, Master Bartholomew.'

'Thank you, thank you!'

'I make no promises, mark you.'

'I understand that. Just put my work into his hand.'

'It may be some little while before he reads it.'

112

'I can wait.'

Bartholomew squeezed his arm in gratitude then headed quickly for the exit. Nicholas glanced down at the manuscript and saw the list of *dramatis personae*. Those names alone told him that the piece was unactable in its present form. It might be a kindness to protect the author from the kind of searing comments that Firethorn was likely to offer, but Nicholas had given his word and he would hold to it.

He went through into the yard to make sure that everything was in order for the morning rehearsal. The stagekeepers broke off from their chat when they saw him and busied themselves at once. Samuel Ruff was talking in a corner to Benjamin Creech, another of the hired men. Nicholas waved Ruff over to him. Since his visit from Susan Fowler, he had had no chance to speak to the other alone. When he described what had happened, Ruff was as amazed as he had been. There was a tide of regret in his voice.

'Will Fowler married? I can't believe it.'

'Neither could I.'

'He said nothing.'

'Not even a hint between old friends?'

'No,' replied Ruff. 'And we drifted apart for so long. Will Fowler! I'd never have thought him serious-minded enough to take a wife. And such a young, untried girl at that.'

'It has been an ordeal for her.'

'Is she still at your lodging, Nick?'

'She travels back to St Albans today,' explained the

113

other. 'Susan is in good hands. A close friend of mine will see her safely on her journey.'

Anne Hendrik had treated the girl like a daughter and helped her through the first difficult days of mourning. A widow herself, she knew at first hand the deep pain and the numbing sense of loss that Susan felt, though she could only guess at how much worse it must be to have a husband violently cut down in a brawl. Nicholas had been touched to see how Anne had opened her heart to their young guest and it had deepened his affection for his landlady. Susan's visit had also given him paternal feelings that surprised him.

'Do you know where the girl lives?' asked Ruff.

'Why?'

'I would like to know. One day, I might just find myself in that part of the country. If I stay in this verminous profession, anything can happen.' A grim smile brushed his lips. 'The truth is that I'm curious to meet her. Anyone who can take Will Fowler as a husband must have rare qualities.'

'Oh, she does.'

'He was not the easiest man to live with.'

'No. Did Will ever talk to you about his faith?'

'Only to curse it now and again in his cups.'

'He was of the Church of Rome.'

'What?' Ruff was thunderstruck. 'That is impossible.'

'So was his marriage.'

'But he never showed any inclination that way.'

'He was an actor, Sam. I think he had been giving us all a very clever performance for some time.'

'But the Romish persuasion . . .'

He shook his head in wonder. Life in the theatre was likely to turn a man to anything but religion, still less to an exiled faith for which its martyrs were still dying the death of traitors. Samuel Ruff was dazed. Having enjoyed a friendship with someone for many years, he was now learning that it was founded on deceit. It hurt him to think that he had been hoodwinked.

'Nicholas,' he whispered.

'Yes?'

'Who *was* he?'

'I will let you know when I find out.'

There was only one thing worse than the extended agony of writing *Gloriana Triumphant* and that was waiting for Lawrence Firethorn to read it and pass judgement. He did not mince his words if he had criticisms and Edmund Hoode had suffered many times at his hands. As he waited for his colleague to dine with him at The Queen's Head, he sipped a glass of malmsey to fortify himself. He was of a different cast from Roger Bartholomew. The latter was an inexperienced playwright who believed that everything he wrote was superb; Hoode was an author of proven worth who became more uncertain of his talent with each play he wrote.

Firethorn made an entrance and posed in the doorway. His brow was troubled and his eyes malevolent. Fearing the inevitable, Hoode drained his cup of malmsey in one urgent gulp.

'Sorry to keep you waiting, Edmund,' muttered Firethorn

as he took his seat at the table. 'I was delayed.'

'I've not been here long.'

'It has been a devilish day. I need a drink.'

Hoode sat there in silence while the wine was ordered, served and drunk. His companion was in such a foul mood over the play that he wondered if anything about it had given pleasure. Though he had been forced into developing a romance, it had actually enriched the drama and become an integral part of it. He had at least expected Firethorn to approve of that.

'Are you in love, Edmund?' growled the other.

'In love?' The question caught him off guard.

'With a woman.'

'I have been. Many times.'

'Have you ever considered marriage?'

'Often.'

'Never do so again!' warned Firethorn, using his hand like a grappling iron on the other's wrist. 'It's a state of continual degradation for a man. The bridal bed is nothing but purgatory with pillows!'

Hoode understood. Margery had found him out.

'What has your wife said, Lawrence?'

'What has she not? She called me names that would burn the ears off a master mariner and issued threats that would daunt a regiment of soldiers.' He brought both hands up to his face. 'Dear God! It is like lying with a she-tiger!'

More wine helped Firethorn to recover from his wife's accusations and molestations. The irony was that nothing had so far happened between him and Lady Rosamund

Varley apart from an exchange of glances during his performance on stage. The actor was being drawn and quartered for an offence that had not yet been committed but which, in view of Margery's venomous attack, he would now advance to the earliest possible moment.

'I will need you to write some verse for me, Edmund.'

'Verse?'

'A dozen lines or so. Perhaps a sonnet.'

'To your wife?' teased Hoode.

'You may compose a funeral dirge for that harridan!'

Food was ordered. Firethorn was ready for the business of the day. His wife had been the cause of the scowling fury which he had brought into the room. Hoode was relieved. He decided to grasp the nettle boldly.

'Have you read the play, Lawrence?'

'Enough of it,' grunted his companion.

'Oh.'

'A few scenes, sir. That was all I could stomach.'

'You did not like it?' asked Hoode tentatively.

'I thought it the most damnable and detestable piece ever penned! Dull, stale and meandering without a touch of wit or poetry to redeem it. I tell you, Edmund, had there been a taper nearby, I'd have set fire to the thing!'

'I felt it had some things to recommend it.'

'They eluded me, sir. It is one thing to praise the victory over the Armada but you have to sail through the narrow straits of the Revels Office first. That play would founder on the rocks. It would never be allowed through.'

'It was truly as bad as that?' said the demoralised author.

'What can you expect from a scribbler like Bartholomew?'

'Bartholomew?'

'Who but he would choose a title like *An Enemy Routed*? That little rogue is the enemy, sir. The enemy of good theatre. He must be routed! I don't know why Nicholas gave me his miserable play. It was an abomination in rhyming couplets!'

Edmund Hoode had been saved for the second time. Margery Firethorn and Roger Bartholomew had borne the brunt of an attack which he had thought was aimed at him. He did not wish to press his luck again. Patience was his strong suit. He waited until Firethorn had poured further bile upon the Oxford scholar.

The meal was served, they began to eat, then the verdict was at last pronounced. Firethorn held up his fork like a sceptre and beamed with royal condescension.

'It's magnificent, Edmund!'

'You think so?' stuttered Hoode.

'Your best work without a shadow of a doubt.'

'That is very heartening, Lawrence.'

'The action drives on, the poetry soars, the love scenes are divinely pretty. If Nicholas can devise a way to bring those ships on and off the stage, we will be the talk of London!'

They fell to discussing the finer points of the drama and an hour sneaked past without their noticing its departure. Firethorn suggested a few alterations but they were so minor that Hoode was glad to agree to them. Long days and even longer nights had gone into the creation of *Gloriana*

Triumphant but the comments it was now receiving made all the suffering worth it.

'There is just one small thing . . .'

Edmund Hoode tensed as the familiar phrase sounded. Was there to be a total reworking of the play, after all? His fears proved groundless.

'Who will play the part of Gloriana?'

'I assumed that it would be Martin Yeo.'

'So did I until I read it.'

'Martin has the maturity for the role.'

'I am wondering if that is enough, Edmund,' said Firethorn. 'He is our senior apprentice, yes, and brings a wealth of experience but . . . well, he does have a hardness of feature that is more suited to an older woman.'

'Gloriana is in her fifties,' reminded Hoode.

'Only in your play. Not when she sits upon the throne of England.' An affectionate chuckle came. 'All women are the same, Edmund. They try to defy time. In her heart, Elizabeth is still the young woman she was when she was first crowned.'

'What are you saying, Lawrence?'

'I think we should alter her age. Let her shed some twenty or thirty years. A Virgin Queen with the glow of youth still hanging upon her. It will strengthen the role immeasurably and make her love scenes with me much more convincing.'

'You have a point. It might work to our advantage.'

'It will, sir.'

'In that case, we must cast John Tallis in the part.'

'Indeed we must not.'

'But he has such presence.'

'So does that unfortunate jaw of his,' returned Firethorn with a low moan. 'John has talent but it is seen at its best when he is a witch or a lady-in-waiting. We cannot have a queen with a lantern jaw.'

'That leaves Stephen Judd. I would settle for him.'

'You're forgetting someone, Edmund.'

'Am I?' He sat up in surprise. 'Dick Honeydew?'

'Why not?'

'The boy has not been with us long enough. He still has much to learn. And he is so young.'

'That is exactly why I would choose him. He has a quality of frail innocence that is perfect. It enlists the audience's sympathy at once. They will not see a termagant queen who flings the gauntlet down to her enemies. They will have a vulnerable young woman who will touch the heart.' He snorted aloud. 'If John Tallis addresses the troops at Tilbury with his lantern jaw, he will look like a recruiting sergeant in female attire.'

'We have not talked about Stephen Judd.'

'He always has that knowing look. It was ideal for *Love and Fortune* but not here. I go for Dick.'

'You really believe he could bring it off?'

'I do. It may be the title role but it does not involve many speeches. Gloriana exists largely as a symbol. It is her grizzly sea captains like myself who carry the burden of the dialogue.'

Edmund Hoode tapped his fingers on the table and pondered.

120

'The other boys will not like this, Lawrence.'

'I don't care two hoots about them!' said Firethorn. 'It will put them in their place. They've been hounding poor Dick on the sly since he came here. If he lands the title role over them, they will be duly chastised.' He pushed his chair back so that he could stretch himself out. 'Well? What do you think, Edmund?'

'I'm not entirely persuaded.'

'He'll not let us down – I'm certain of it.'

'We'd have to spend a lot of time on him.'

'As much as you wish. You agree, then?'

'I agree.'

'Dick Honeydew as Gloriana!'

The two men lifted their cups in toast.

Chapter Six

When Nicholas got back to the house late that night, Anne Hendrik was waiting for him with a smile of welcome. Her pleasure at seeing him home again was mingled with relief that he had come to no harm. Nicholas had been working his way through the Bankside stews once more and she feared for his safety in an area that swarmed with low life. His task was fraught with dangers because it took him to some of the most notorious criminal dens in London.

'How did you fare?' she asked.

'Not well,' he admitted. 'Someone at the Antelope remembered a tall man with a red beard but he was not sure if our sketch bore any likeness to him. The hostess at the Dog and Doublet thought she recognised the face in the drawing but she insists that his beard was black.'

'Did you call at the Cardinal's Hat?'

'Yes,' he said, rallying, 'and there was better news. Alice will be discharged from the hospital soon. She's recovered well and got her wits back, by all accounts. I have great hopes that she will be able to give me more details about Redbeard.'

'What of Samuel Ruff?'

'He continues to search as diligently as me,' he said. 'We will run our man to earth in the end.'

Apprehension flitted across her face and she stepped in close to give him a brief hug. Her eagerness to see the killer brought to justice was tempered by a natural anxiety.

'If you *do* find him, Nicholas . . .'

'No question but that we will.'

'You will have the utmost care?' she pleaded.

'Have no fear, Anne,' he soothed. 'I go armed. Redbeard will not have the chance to stab me unawares.'

He took her in his arms and gave her a reassuring kiss.

Susan Fowler was no longer staying in his room but he still did not return to it. He and Anne went upstairs together to her bedchamber at the front of the house. It was a large, low room with solid pieces of furniture, tasteful hangings and a small carpet over the shining oak floorboards. Paintings of Dutch interiors hung on the walls as a memento of her late husband's homeland. Like all parts of the house, it was kept spotlessly clean.

The four-poster was soft and comfortable, and they made love with a languid tenderness under its linen. Afterwards, they lay in the dark with their arms entwined. Nicholas Bracewell and Anne did not share a bed often. Neither of them was ready to commit themselves to any full or permanent relationship. He was far too independent and she was still wedded to memories of a happy marriage with Jacob Hendrik. It suited them both to drift in and out of their moments of intimacy, and to see them as occasional delights rather than as a routine habit. The magic was thus retained.

'Nick . . .'

'Mm?'

'Are you asleep?'

'Yes.'

They both laughed. She dug him playfully in the ribs.

'I was thinking about Will Fowler,' she continued.

'So was I.'

'Maybe that is the reason he was drawn to the theatre.'

'Reason?'

'It's a kind of refuge,' she argued. 'Actors have to be seen but only as somebody else. Do you understand me? Will Fowler went into the theatre to hide. Just like you.'

'Is that what I did?' he asked with amusement.

'You tell me, sir.'

But she knew that he would not. Anne Hendrik had enquired about his past life many times but he had yielded only the barest details. Born and bred in the West Country, he was the son of a well-to-do merchant who ensured that Nicholas had a sound education then took him into the business. It gave him the chance to travel and he made many voyages to Europe.

Suddenly, he broke with his family and took service with Drake on his voyage around the world. The experience changed his whole attitude to life and left him a more philosophical man. When he came back to England, his days as a sailor were over. Eventually, he moved to London and began to work in the theatre.

'What exactly did you do, Nick?' she wondered.

'When?'

'In those years between coming home to your own country and joining Lord Westfield's Men. You must have done *something*.'

'I did. I survived.'

'How?'

He kissed her by way of reply. The missing years in his life had left their mark on him but he would never disclose why. Anne would have to accept him as he was, a quiet, strong-willed person whose self-effacing manner was a form of mask. She might not know everything about him but there was enough to make him very lovable.

'Speak to me,' she whispered.

'What shall I say?'

'Do you agree with me? About Will Fowler?'

'Perhaps.'

'And what about Nicholas Bracewell?'

'Perhaps not.'

'Oh, Nick!' she sighed, as she tightened her grip on him. 'I love this closeness but there are times when I wonder who the man I am holding really is.'

'I wonder that myself,' he confessed.

He kissed her softly on the lips and began to stroke her dark, lustrous hair. Nestling into his chest, she felt at once soothed and aroused. It was several minutes before she broke the silence.

'What are you thinking?' she said.

'It doesn't matter, Anne.' There was a shrug in his voice.

'Please. Tell me.'

'It was not very cheering.'

'I still want to know.'

'Very well,' he explained. 'I was thinking about failure.'

'Failure?'

'High hopes that end in chaos. Noble ambitions that crumble.'

'Is that what happened to your hopes and ambitions?'

'You keep on trying,' he said with a little laugh, then he became more serious. 'No, I was thinking about Susan Fowler, poor creature. Her plans have fallen apart. Then there is Samuel Ruff. Failure brought him low as well. Even now there is still a deep sadness in the man that I cannot fathom.'

There was a long pause. Her voice was a murmur in the pillow.

'Nick . . .'

'I know what you're going to say.'

'You might go back to your own room tomorrow.'

'I will, Anne.'

But she was his for some luscious hours yet. His need made him tighten his grip on her and it did not slacken until he at last fell asleep from a lapping fatigue.

* * *

127

Richard Honeydew was overwhelmed at the news that he was to be cast in the title role of the new play. Performing for the first time at The Curtain would have been thrill enough for him, but to make his debut there as Gloriana, Queen of England, filled him with a blend of excitement and terror. They evidently had great faith in him and that thought helped to steady his nerves and still his self-doubts.

The other apprentices were outraged and Firethorn had to slap down their complaints ruthlessly. Martin Yeo was wounded the most. A tall, slim, assured boy of fourteen, he had played most of the leading female roles for the company over the past couple of years, and he had come to look upon them as his by right. To be deprived of an outstanding part by a novice was more than his pride could take, and he withdrew into a sullen, watchful silence.

John Tallis and Stephen Judd did the same. If they had disliked Richard before, they now hated him with vengeful intensity. Every morning, as they sat around the table with him for breakfast, they glared their anger at Richard and were only restrained from attacking him by the vigilance of Margery Firethorn. As a punishment for the way they had tied their victim up, she had put the three of them on reduced rations, so that they had half-empty bellies while the youngest of their number ate from a full plate. In every way, Richard Honeydew was getting more than them.

'I could have killed him!' asserted John Tallis.

'Yes,' added Stephen Judd. 'The worst thing is the way he tries to be friendly with us – as if we could ever be friends with him now!'

'It's not fair,' said Martin Yeo simply.

They had gone back up to their room and they fell easily into a conspiratorial chat. The three boys often had differences among themselves but they had now been united against a common enemy. Tallis was livid, Judd was aching with envy, and Yeo took it as a personal insult. They came together in a solid lump of resentment.

Some companies actually paid their apprentices a wage, but Lord Westfield's Men did not. In return for their commitment to the company, the boys were given board, lodging, clothing and regular training in all the arts of the playhouse. The arrangement had been satisfactory until Richard Honeydew appeared. He had unwittingly upset the balance of power within the Firethorn household, and within the company, and he had to pay for it.

'What are we going to do about it?' asked Tallis.

'There's nothing much we can do,' admitted Judd. 'He's got Samuel Ruff and Nick Bracewell on his side now.'

'He'll need more than them,' warned Yeo.

'You should have that part, Martin,' said Tallis.

'I know – and I will.'

'How?' asked Judd eagerly.

'We'll have to work that out.'

'Can we get rid of him altogether?' urged Tallis.

'Why not?' said Yeo.

The conspirators shared a cosy snigger. Richard Honeydew

was riding high at the moment but they would bring him down with a bump when he least expected it. All that they had to do was to devise a plan.

Back in his own room, Nicholas Bracewell reached under the bed and pulled out a large battered leather chest. As well as being the book holder he was, literally, the book keeper. It was his function to keep the books of all the plays that the company used, new, old or renovated. The play chest was an invaluable item that had to be kept safe at all times. With so much piracy of plays going on, it behoved every company to guard its property with the utmost care.

Nicholas unlocked the chest with a key then lifted up the lid to reveal a confused welter of parchment and scrolls. The history of his involvement with Lord Westfield's Men was all there, written out in various hands then annotated by himself. As he ran his eye over the myriad prompt copies, a hundred memories came surging back at him from his past. He quickly reached for the manuscripts that lay on the very top of the pile then closed the lid firmly. When the chest had been locked, he pushed it back to its home beneath the bed.

After taking his leave of Anne, he walked across to the nearby wharf to be ferried by boat across the river. The Thames was thronged by craft of all sizes and they zigzagged their way across the busiest and oldest thoroughfare in London. Nicholas loved the exuberance of it all, the hectic bustle, the flapping sails, the surging colour, the distinctive tang and the continuous din that was punctuated by cries of 'Westward Ho!' and 'Eastward Ho!' from vociferous boatmen advertising their routes.

He had seen many astonishing sights in his travels but he could still be impressed anew by the single bridge that spanned the Thames. Supported by twenty arches, it was a miniature city in itself, a glorious jumble of timber-framed buildings that jutted out perilously over the river below. A huge water wheel of Dutch construction stood beneath the first arch, harnessing the fierce current that raced through the narrow opening and pumping water to nearby dwellings.

On the Bridge itself, it was Nonesuch House that dominated, a vast, ornate and highly expensive wooden building which had been shipped from Holland and reassembled on its stone foundations. A more grisly feature could be seen above the gatehouse tower where the heads of executed traitors were displayed on poles. Nicholas counted almost twenty of them, rotting in the morning sun as scavenger kites wheeled down to peck hungrily at the mouldering flesh. London Bridge was truly one of the sights of Europe but it embodied warning as well as wonder.

When he alighted on the other bank, Nicholas paid and tipped his boatman then made his way to the teeming Gracechurch Street. Roger Bartholomew was waiting for him outside The Queen's Head in a state of high anxiety.

'I got your message, Nicholas.'

'Good.'

'Did he read my play?'

'Yes, Master Bartholomew. So did I.'

'Well?' The poet was on tenterhooks.

'It's a fine piece,' praised Nicholas, trying to find something positive to say that would cushion the disappointment. 'It has memorable speeches and stirring moments. The account of the battle itself is very striking.'

'Thank you. But what of Lawrence Firethorn?'

Everything hung on the decision. For Roger Bartholomew, it was the last hope of a career as a playwright. Acceptance would nourish him and rejection would destroy. Nicholas hated to be the one to deal the blow. What he could do was to conceal the virulence of Firethorn's attack on the play.

'I believe that he . . . saw its promise as well.'

'And the leading role?' pressed Bartholomew. 'Did it captivate him as I foretold?'

'To a degree, sir. He recognised the extent of your talent.'

'Then he wishes to present it?' asked the poet with a wild laugh. 'Lord Westfield's Men will offer me another contract?'

'Unhappily, no.'

'Why not?'

'Because it does not fit in with our plans, sir.'

Roger Bartholomew was stunned. *An Enemy Routed* had become his obsession and he thought of nothing but the day when it would first be staged. He had put his whole being into the play. If his work was rejected then he himself was being cast aside as well.

'Are you sure that he *read* it?' he demanded.

'I can vouch for it.'

'Make him reconsider.'

'He will not, sir.'

'But he must!'

'There's no point, Master Bartholomew.'

'There's every point!' howled the other. 'He does not realise what is at stake here. My play is a work of art. It's his sacred duty to bring it before the public.'

Nicholas reached into the leather bag he was carrying. Taking out one of the manuscripts that lay inside, he held it out to the scholar.

'I'm sorry,' he said firmly. 'Thank you for offering it to us but I've been told to return it herewith.'

'Let *me* see Master Firethorn.'

'That would not be wise.'

'Is the man hiding from me?'

'Indeed not, sir.'

'Then I'll hear this from his own lips.'

'I strongly advise against it.'

'You'll not get in my way this time,' insisted Bartholomew. 'Make an appointment for me. I mean to have this out with him in person and nothing will stop me.'

Nicholas felt the truth would halt him. His attempt to protect the other from it had failed. It was time for plain speaking.

'Master Firethorn does not like the play at all, sir.'

'That cannot be!' protested the author.

'His comments were not kind.'

'I won't believe this, Nicholas!'

'He could only bring himself to read a few scenes and he found them without interest. He was especially critical of your rhyming. You may talk with him if you wish, but he will only tell you the same thing in much rounder terms.'

Roger Bartholomew was dazed. Rejection was torment enough but an outright condemnation of him and his work was far worse. His face was ashen and his lip was trembling. He snatched his play back then turned all the venom he could muster upon Nicholas.

'You lied to me, sir!'

'I thought to spare you some pain.'

'You led me astray.'

'There was never a chance of your play being accepted.'

'Not while I have friends like you to thank!'

'We already have a drama about the Armada,' said Nicholas, indicating his leather bag. 'I did warn you of that.'

'You will all suffer for this,' threatened Bartholomew, lashing out blindly with words. 'I'll not be treated this way by *anybody*, no, not by you, nor Master Firethorn, nor anyone in your vile profession. I want satisfaction for this and, by heaven, sir, I mean to get it!'

Vibrating with fury, he clutched his play to his chest then pushed past Nicholas to rush off at speed. The book holder watched him go then looked down at the leather bag that contained a copy of *Gloriana Triumphant*. Two plays on the same subject had brought different rewards to their authors.

Once again, he was profoundly grateful that he was not a playwright in such a treacherous world as that of the theatre.

Barnaby Gill had been unhappy at first about the decision to promote Richard Honeydew to the title role of the new play. He had a high opinion of Martin Yeo's talent and felt that the older boy would bring more regal authority to the part of Gloriana. At the same time, he was ready to recognise the claims of Stephen Judd, who had improved his technique markedly in recent months and who had been an undoubted success in *Love and Fortune* as a wanton young wife. The lantern jaw of John Tallis put him out of reckoning but the other two were powerful contenders.

Apprenticeship was bound by no formal rules and practises varied with each company, but Barnaby Gill accepted the general principle of seniority. On that count alone, Richard Honeydew had to be excluded. The other three boys had earned the right to be considered before him, and Gill put this point forcefully at a meeting with his colleagues.

Lawrence Firethorn spiked his guns. Edmund Hoode and the other sharers had already been talked around by the wily Firethorn so the decision stood. All that Gill could do was to register his protest and predict that they would rue their mistake. Richard Honeydew was over-parted.

* * *

'Well done, Dick.'

'Thank you, sir.'

'You have natural grace.'

'I simply wish to please, sir.'

'Oh, you do that, boy,' said Gill. 'You may prove me wrong yet.'

The more he watched Richard, the more he came to see his unusual gifts as a performer. His voice was clear, his deportment good and his use of gesture effective. With a dancer's eye, Gill admired his sense of balance, his timing and the easy fluency of movement. Most important of all, the boy had now learned to wear female apparel as if he were himself female and this was a special accomplishment. Richard Honeydew might turn out to be the best choice as Gloriana, after all, and Gill did not in the least mind admitting it.

Lord Westfield's Men had rented a large room at The Queen's Head for early rehearsals. Barnaby Gill contrived a word alone with the boy during a break for refreshment.

'How are you enjoying it, Dick?'

'Very much, sir.'

'Have you ever played a queen before?'

'Never, Master Gill. It's a great honour.'

'Who knows?' he teased softly. 'You may even outshine our own Gloriana.'

'Oh, no,' replied the boy seriously. 'Nobody could do that, sir. I think that our Queen is the most wonderful person in the world.'

Gill saw a chance to impress the boy and he took it.

'Yes,' he said casually. 'Her Majesty has been gracious to admire my playing on more than one occasion.'

Richard gaped. 'You've *met* her?'

'I've performed at court a number of times.'

There had, in fact, been only two appearances at the royal palace and they had been some years ago, but Gill disguised all this. He also concealed his true feelings about Queen Elizabeth. Most women filled him with mild distaste but the royal personage had done rather more than that.

Richard Honeydew might worship her along with the rest of her subjects but the fastidious, observant actor had got close enough to her to see her as no more than a middle-aged woman with a ginger wig, black teeth and a habit of using thick raddle on any part of her skin that could not be covered by clothing. Queen Elizabeth was a walking wardrobe. Beneath the flamboyant attire was a mass of wires, stays and struts, which supported the stiff exterior. Gill acknowledged that she had given a striking performance but the ravaged beauty had not won his heart.

'Will the company play at court again?' asked Richard.

'We hope so. It wants but an invitation.'

'It must be inspiring to play before Her Majesty.'

'Oh, it is. I was transported, Dick.'

'Did you dance your jig, Master Gill?'

'Twice. The Queen insisted that I repeat it.' He took a step closer to the boy. 'I would teach you the steps one day if we could find time together.'

'I would appreciate that, sir.'

'Swordplay, too,' continued Gill. 'I was instructed by a

Master of Fence. I know far more about it than Nicholas Bracewell. You would do well to seek my help with a sword in the future.'

'Nicholas has taught me so much, though.'

'I will teach you a lot more, Dick. Would you like that?'

The boy hesitated. The avuncular smile was worrying him again. Besides, his first loyalty was to Nicholas. He tried to speak but the actor stopped him with a raised palm.

'Come to me this evening,' he wooed. 'We'll have a bout then.'

'That will not be possible, Master Gill,' said a voice.

'Who asked *you*, sir?' rejoined the actor.

'Dick will be with me this evening. I am to instruct him in the use of the rapier.'

Richard was surprised to hear this but grateful for the interruption. Samuel Ruff had come to his aid once again. The boy's relief was not shared by Barnaby Gill.

'Why must you meddle, sir?' he snapped.

'The boy and I have an arrangement.'

'Is this true, Dick?'

'Yes, I think so . . .'

'Well, I do not think so.' He rounded on the hired man. 'And I do not believe that you have ever carried a rapier.'

'You do me wrong, Master Gill.'

'Ah!' mocked the other. 'Have you been hiding your light under a bushel all this time? Are you a Master of Fence?'

'No, sir. But I have borne a sword.'

'Let us see how much you remember.'

Ruff's intercession had annoyed Gill intensely and he wanted to teach the man a lesson. There would be the additional bonus of being able to show off in front of Richard. Crossing to a table, Gill snatched up two rehearsal foils and offered one of the bell-like handles to Ruff.

'Not a rapier, sir, but it will serve.'

'I do not wish to have a bout with you, Master Gill.'

'Are you afeard, then?'

'No, sir. But it would not be wise.'

'Who asks for wisdom out of swordplay?'

'Somebody might get hurt,' explained Ruff. 'Even with a button on, a foil can cause injury.'

'Oh, I forgot,' teased Gill. 'You have wounds enough already.'

'My arm is mended, sir. That is not the reason.'

'Then what is?'

'Common sense.'

'Common sense or cowardice?'

Samuel Ruff was stung by the gibe. He had no wish to fence with Gill but the insult could not be ignored. Slipping off his jerkin, he handed it to Richard and accepted the foil from his adversary. The latter gave him an oily grin. He was going to enjoy humiliating this troublesome hired man and would not even bother to remove his doublet to do so.

Others in the room quickly came over to watch the bout. Benjamin Creech shouted words of encouragement to Ruff but the general feeling was that he had little chance. The three older apprentices lent their support to

Barnaby Gill. They wanted to see Richard Honeydew's friend humbled.

'Instruct him, Master Gill,' urged Martin Yeo.

'I'll wager a penny you have the first hit,' said Stephen Judd. 'Tuppence. Will you back your man, Dick?'

'I have no money, Stephen.'

'Owe it to me. The wager stands.'

Barnaby Gill held the tight, slender foil and swished it through the air a few times before taking up his stance. His opponent held his weapon ready. The hired man was bigger and sturdier but Gill was much lighter on his feet.

'Come, Samuel,' he invited. 'Let me trim your ruff!'

The three apprentices sniggered but Richard was frightened, sensing that his friend was in real danger. Gill had been involved in a sword fight on stage during the play about Richard the Lionheart and had shown himself to be an expert. The boy quailed. Anxious for the duel to be prevented, his spirits rose when the book holder came striding into the room.

'Stop them, Master Bracewell!' he begged.

'What is going on?' asked Nicholas.

'Keep out of this!' ordered Gill.

'Is this a quarrel?'

'Stand off, Nick,' said Ruff. 'It is only in play.'

Before Nicholas could make any move, the duel had begun. The foils clashed in a brief passage of thrust, parry and counter-thrust. They started again. Barnaby Gill forced the pace of the bout, keeping his opponent under constant attack, lunging with vicious intent and using all his tricks to entertain the audience. Ruff could do little but defend and he went through all eight parries time and again. Gill circled him, first one way and then the other, baiting him like a dog with a bull.

Yet somehow he could not score a hit to appease his burning resentment of the man. Remise, reprise and flanconade were used but Ruff somehow held him at bay. Gill speeded up his attack and found an opening to slash at his opponent's left arm. The hired man was quick enough to elude injury but the button opened up the sleeve of his shirt and a bandage showed through.

'A hit!' cried Stephen. 'You owe me tuppence, Dick!'

'No hit,' insisted Ruff. 'A touch.'

Gill cackled. 'Here comes your wager, Stephen.'

He attacked again with his wrists flashing, thrusting in quarte and tierce, setting up another opening for himself. Crouching low as he lunged towards his adversary's stomach, he was astonished when his foil was deftly twisted out of his hand and sent spinning through the air. Unable to save himself, Barnaby Gill ended up flat on his back with the point of Ruff's weapon under his chin. It was the hired man's turn to use the well-tried pun.

'You have a Ruff at your throat now, sir.'

A tense silence ensued. The apprentices were nonplussed, Creech and his fellows were astounded, and Nicholas Bracewell was delighted. Barnaby Gill was seething. Instead of humiliating Samuel Ruff, he had been chastened in public himself and his pride had taken a powerful blow. He would not forget or forgive.

It was left to Richard Honeydew to speak first.

'I will claim my wager now, Stephen.'

The cardinal's hat presented a sorry sight to the morning sun. Long splinters of wood had been hacked away and much of the paint had been scored. On one side of the tavern sign at least, the hat was very much the worse for wear. No wind disturbed Bankside. The cardinal's hat hung limp and forlorn.

Nicholas Bracewell looked up to assess the damage that Redbeard had caused. There was a window adjacent to the sign and he supposed that it was in the room belonging to Alice. He was soon given confirmation of this.

'She is upstairs now, sir.'

'May I see her?'

The landlord looked even more like a polecat in daylight. His narrowed eyes went to his visitor's purse. Nicholas produced a few coins and tossed them on to the counter.

'Follow me, sir.'

'Is the girl fully recovered now?' said Nicholas, as he went up the winding staircase with the man.

'Alice? No, sir. Not yet.'

'What are her injuries?'

'Nothing much,' replied the landlord callously. 'One of her arms must stay bound up for a week or more and she still limps badly.'

They reached the first landing and walked along a dingy passageway. Nicholas glanced around with misgivings.

'Will the girl get proper rest here?'

'Rest!' The polecat drew back his teeth in a harsh laugh. 'Alice came back to work, sir, not to rest. She was as busy as ever in the service last night.'

The sleeping figure of an old man now blocked their way. Kicking him awake with the toe of his shoe, the landlord stepped over him and went on to a door. He banged hard on it.

'Alice!'

There was no sound from within so he peered through the keyhole. He used his fist to beat a tattoo on the timber.

'Are you alone in there, Alice?'

With a shrug of his shoulders, he grabbed the latch of the door and lifted it. Nicholas was led into a small, filthy, cobwebbed room with peeling walls and a rising stench that hit his nostrils. A mattress lay on the floor with a ragged blanket over it. Under the blanket was a small head that the landlord nudged with his foot.

'Wake up, girl. You've a visitor.'

'Perhaps this was not a good time to call,' suggested Nicholas. 'She plainly needs her sleep.'

'I'll rouse her, sir, have no fear,' said the landlord.

After shaking her roughly by the shoulder, he took hold of the blanket and pulled it right away from her. The sight which met them made Nicholas quake. Lying on the mattress at a distorted angle was the naked body of a young woman in her early twenties. One arm was heavily strapped, one ankle covered with a grimy bandage. Eyes stared sightlessly up at the ceiling. The mouth was wide

143

open to issue a silent scream for mercy.

Alice would not be able to tell Nicholas Bracewell anything. Her throat had been cut and the blood had gushed in a torrent down her body. The stink of death was already upon her.

Chapter Seven

Lawrence Firethorn slowly began to make headway against his domestic oppression. His wife continued to watch him like a hawk and abuse him at every turn but he bore it all with Stoic mien and never struck back. Even the nightly horror of the bedchamber failed to break him. His studied patience at last had its effect. Margery listened to – if she did not believe – his protestations. She permitted his little acts of kindness and concern. She allowed herself to think of him once more as her husband.

Her suspicions did not vanish but they were gradually smothered beneath the pillow of his subtlety. Firethorn smiled, flattered, promised and pretended until he had insinuated his way back into the outer suburbs of her affections. With a skill born of long practise, he chose his moment carefully.

'Lawrence!'

'Open it, my sweet.'

'But why have you bought me a present, sir?'

'Why else, my angel? To show you that I love you.'

Margery Firethorn could not contain her almost girlish curiosity and excitement. She opened the little box and let out a gasp of wonder. Her husband had just given her a pendant that hung from a gold chain.

'This is for *me*?'

'I had been saving it for your birthday, my dove,' he lied, 'but it seemed a more appropriate moment. I wanted you to know how deep my feelings are for you in spite of your cruelty to me.'

Remorse surfaced. 'Have I been cruel?' she asked.

'Unbearably so.'

'Have I been unjust?'

'With regularity.'

'I felt I had cause, Lawrence.'

'Show it me.'

'There were . . . indications.'

'Produce them against me,' he challenged. 'No, I have been maligned here. Someone turned you against me. I have been a model of fidelity to you and that gift shows it.'

She bestowed a kiss of gratitude on his lips then looked into the box once more and marvelled. The pendant was small, oval and studded with semi-precious stones. Sunshine was slanting in through the chamber window to make them dance and sparkle.

'May I try it on, sir?'

'I will hold it for you, Margery.'

'It will go best with my taffeta dress,' she decided.

'It will become you whatever you wear,' he said, then collected a second kiss. 'Hold still now.'

Margery Firethorn stood in front of the mirror while he dangled the pendant around her neck. She was thrilled with the present, all the more so because it was so unexpected and – she now began to imagine – completely undeserved. A husband who had been reviled as much as hers had of late could only buy her an expensive present like that if he was besotted with her.

He nestled into her back and rubbed his beard against her hair. His eyes met hers in the mirror.

'Will it suit, madam?'

'It will suit, sir.'

'It is only a trifle,' he apologised. 'If I was a richer man, it would have been edged with pearls and encrusted with diamonds.' He squeezed her again. 'Are you pleased?'

'I will treasure it for ever.'

The third kiss was longer and more ardent. It gave him time to rehearse an excuse for the fact that he would not be able to leave the gift with her because it would be worn around the neck of Gloriana, Queen of Albion, in the forthcoming play.

'Fix the catch, Lawrence. I will wear it now.'

'You cannot, I fear.'

'Why not?'

'The catch is faulty. It will need to be repaired by the jeweller. No matter,' he said, whisking the pendant away and replacing it in its box. 'I will take it to his shop this very morning and set the fellow to work on it.'

'I am loathe to part with it.'

'It will be but a short absence.'

'Take the chain, sir. Let me keep the pendant at least.'

'Alas!' he replied, snapping the lid of the box shut. 'That is not possible. The pendant is attached to the chain for safety's sake. It cannot be removed.'

A last small cloud of suspicion drifted across her mind.

'Lawrence . . .'

'My love?'

'You did buy that gift for *me*?'

He looked so stricken at the very suggestion that she immediately took back the question and showered him with apologies. In a marriage as crazily erratic as theirs, reconciliation was always the most prized moment. It was an hour before he was able to get dressed and take his leave. The gift of the pendant had been a happy inspiration. He had been keeping it by him for just such an emergency.

Margery waved him off and addressed herself to the management of the household with increased vigour. After the storm came the blissful calm. She had been through a period of turmoil, only to emerge with a new and devoted husband.

The old and wandering husband, meanwhile, went straight to Edmund Hoode's lodging to see if another gift for a lady was ready yet. He studied the fourteen lines with rapt attention.

'It seemed to work better as a sonnet,' said Hoode.

'You've surpassed yourself, Edmund.'

'Have I?'

'This will wing its way to her heart.'

The sonnet was in praise of Lady Rosamund Varley and it punned on the words 'lady' and 'rose' with bewitching skill. Lawrence Firethorn did not believe in the lone pursuit of his prey. He cheerfully enlisted the aid of those around him. Hoode had provided the sonnet and the message now needed a bearer.

'I must find Nicholas Bracewell at once.'

The Curtain was situated to the south of Holywell Lane, off Shoreditch, on land that had once been part of Holywell Priory. To the Puritans, who railed against the playhouses for their filth and lewdness, the Curtain was an act of sacrilege on what had once been consecrated ground. To Nicholas Bracewell, who took a more philosophical view, it was a pleasing amalgam of the sacred and the profane, in short, the stuff of theatre.

On a rare afternoon of freedom, Nicholas had come along to The Curtain to watch a performance by the Earl of Banbury's Men. He was not so much interested in the rival company as in the new play they were giving, *God Speed the Fleet*. This was yet another eulogy of the English navy, thinly disguised by a time shift to the previous century and a geographical shift to Venice. Nicholas was keen to see how they mounted their sea battle, hoping that he might glean some ideas that could be used when his own company staged *Gloriana Triumphant*.

Fine weather brought a full house to The Curtain and they were crammed into the pit and the galleries. The playhouse was a tall, circular structure of timber which resembled a bull-ring. Three storeys of seating galleries projected into the circle from the outer walls and this perimeter area was roofed with thatch, leaving the central arena open to the sky.

The stage projected out like an apron into the pit. It was high, rectangular and contained a large trap door. Over part of the acting area was a large canopy, supported on heavy pillars that descended to and through the stage. A flat wall behind the stage broke through the smooth inner curve of the arena. At each end of the wall was a door through which entrances and exits could be made. The tiring-house was directly behind the wall.

Halfway up the tiring-house wall was a recess, showing some more galleries. This space was curtained over for use as an acting area and Nicholas guessed rightly that it would be used as the deck of a warship. At the top of the tiring-house were the huts, pitched-roof gabled attic rooms, where the musicians sat. Above these was a small balcony from which the trumpeter would start the performances and run up the flag to signal it was under way.

After the makeshift facilities of The Queen's Head, it was good to be in a real playhouse again and Nicholas felt his heart lift. He paid twopence for an uncushioned seat in the second gallery and settled down to enjoy the performance. Food and drink were being sold by noisy, ubiquitous vendors. The standees in the pit were already restive. The whole place was bubbling with an anticipatory delight.

Nicholas noted that the Earl of Banbury was present. Surrounded by his entourage of gallants and ladies, he occupied one of the lords' rooms closest to the stage. The Earl was a venal old lecher with a florid complexion and a tufted beard that sorted well with his goatish inclinations. A self-styled dandy, he had been heavily-corseted then dressed in doublet and hose of the most arresting colours. His tall crowned hat was festooned with feathers that were held in place by jewels. His gloved hand held a silver-topped cane which he used for pointing or prodding as the spirit moved him.

God Speed the Fleet was not deathless drama. It was full of good ideas that had been badly strung together and the overriding impression was one of wanton prodigality. Banbury's Men played it with plenty of attack but rowdiness was developing in the pit before the end of the first act. Only the duels and dances held their interest.

Giles Randolph dominated the proceedings with effortless ease. He was a tall, slim, moodily handsome man with a commanding presence and a voice that was just a little too conscious of its own beauty. His attire was magnificent and worthy to compete with that worn by his patron in the gallery, but he did not entirely convince as an English sea captain under the Venetian flag.

There was something faintly sinister about Giles Randolph. It may have been to do with his Italianate cast of feature or it may have emanated from his sly lope, but it robbed him of true heroic status. Wicked cardinals and duplicitous politicians were his forte. As a beard-stroking revenger in a recent play, he had been supreme. Today, it was different. While he had the barked authority of a sea dog, he looked as if he would be more adept at poisoning his enemies with a drugged chalice than bombarding them with broadsides.

The ladies in the audience, however, clearly adored him. Those in Banbury's entourage were particularly struck with his brooding magnificence and they almost swooned when he directed one of his soliloquies up at them. Nicholas Bracewell was less persuaded. He felt that Randolph was miscast. The actor had none of Lawrence Firethorn's storming passion and that is what the part required.

The sea battle almost worked. Controlled by the book holder with real skill, it involved a small army of stagekeepers and journeymen. Giles Randolph stood on the poop deck – the balcony above the stage – with a telescope to his eye, so that he could give a commentary on the engagement in which his fleet was involved. The stage itself was used as the gun deck and a small cannon was brought into play.

Alarums and excursions went on indefinitely as drums were banged, cymbals struck, trumpets were blown, explosions were set off and fireworks were used. The mariners on the gun deck were thrown to and fro as their vessel pitched in the swell and absorbed the broadsides of its adversaries. Barrels of water swished offstage to suggest a turbulent sea and someone pounded on stout timber with a blacksmith's hammer.

Nicholas liked the three final touches. Cannon balls were rolled on stage with thunderous effect as if they had just come hurtling through the rigging. The small mast which was held up by a beefy journeyman at the front of the acting area suddenly collapsed and pinned a few groaning sailors to the deck. Then – to the loudest cheer of the afternoon – the cannon itself was fired to deafen the audience and bring the battle to a close.

There was warm applause as Randolph led out his company for their bow but several catcalls emerged from the pit. The mixed reception did not disconcert the leading actor, who waved grandly in acknowledgement, but some of the players looked very uncomfortable as they viewed the grumbling standees around them. *God Speed the Fleet* would not be retained in the repertory of Banbury's Men.

It took a long time for the big audience to disperse and Nicholas lingered to avoid the crush of bodies. As he sat on a now deserted bench, he gazed down at the stage and went through the battle again in his mind, listing the effects and making a note to incorporate the trap door into his own version of the defeat of the Armada.

His attention was then seized by something below and the play was forgotten. Stagekeepers were busy clearing away the debris of battle and sweeping the boards. One of them was chatting with a thickset member of the audience in a way that showed they were old friends. Nicholas recognised the standee at once. It was Benjamin Creech from Lord Westfield's Men.

What had released Nicholas to see the play was the fact that the afternoon was given over to a costume fitting at The Queen's Head. Visual splendour was an imperative in every stage presentation and care was taken to produce costumes that would enthral the groundlings and combat those worn by the gallants. In the forthcoming production, Creech was due to wear three costumes, two of which at least would require a lot of work. His presence at The Queen's Head was thus very necessary.

Nicholas was surprised and dismayed to realise that the actor must have ignored his appointment. It was not the first time that Creech had given cause for complaint. His fondness for the alehouse was a standing joke among his fellow actors, and he had more than once been late for rehearsal because he was sleeping off a night of indulgence. Nicholas had to fine him now and again for his unpunctuality and it had not endeared him to the actor.

The hired men of any company tended to come and go at will but Nicholas had persuaded Firethorn to build up a small knot of actors with a fairly permanent contract. It made for company loyalty and stability. The nucleus of regulars could always be augmented for individual plays if a larger cast was required. Firethorn had seen the value of it all. A handful of semi-permanent hired men would commit themselves to a company that offered them a more long-term future, and – the clinching argument for

Firethorn – they might accept a lower wage in return for security.

Benjamin Creech was part of the nucleus. He was a big, solid character with a rather surly temperament, but he was an actor of some range with two additional recommendations. He had a fine singing voice and he could play almost any stringed instrument. An actor-musician was a valuable asset, especially on tour when the size of a company would be restricted to the bare essentials. Creech more than earned his keep, which was why Nicholas was sometimes lenient about the man's drinking habits.

The pit was almost empty now and the book holder with Banbury's Men came out on the stage to see how his minions were getting along. When he spotted Creech, he went across and shook him warmly by the hand. They fell into animated conversation. Some joke passed between them and the actor pushed the other man playfully away. It was only a small moment but it triggered off a memory at the back of Nicholas Bracewell's mind.

The last time he had seen Creech push someone away like that it had not been in fun. A fight had erupted and Nicholas had had to jump in and separate the two men. The memory came back to him now with a new significance.

Benjamin Creech had exchanged blows with Will Fowler.

Lady Rosamund Varley draped herself in a window seat and read the sonnet yet again. It was agreeably fulsome and its witty wordplay was very pleasing. The poem was unsigned but the phrase 'Love and Friendship' had been written underneath it in a bold hand. Because the letters *L* and *F* had been enlarged and embossed, she had no difficulty in identifying the sender as Lawrence Firethorn. She gave a brittle laugh.

Fortune had smiled on her. A rich and doting husband had made light of a thirty-year age gap for a short while, then he had obligingly succumbed to gout, impetigo and waning desire. Lady Rosamund was free to seek her pleasures elsewhere. She did so without compunction and turned herself into a practised coquette. Her beauty and charm could ensnare any man and she toyed with them unmercifully. A whisper of scandal hung upon her at all times.

The court supplied most of her admirers – earls, lords, knights, even foreign ambassadors on occasion – but she had a special fondness for actors. Their way of life intrigued her. It combined danger and excess to a high degree. They were commoners who could be kings for an afternoon, men of great courage who could strut proudly on a stage for a couple of hours and blaze their way into the hearts of all around them. Lady Rosamund was captivated by the tawdry glamour of the theatre.

She glanced down at the sonnet again. Not for a moment did she imagine that Firethorn had actually composed it himself, but that did not matter. In commissioning and sending it, he had made it his own and she was flattered by the compliment. He was an extraordinary man who was adding to his reputation with each new performance. No role was beyond him, not even the one that she was about to assign to him.

Crossing the chamber to a small table, she opened a drawer in it and put the poem inside. It took its place alongside many other poems, letters, gifts and keepsakes. Lawrence Firethorn was in exalted company.

Lady Rosamund returned to the window to gaze down at the Thames. Her sumptuous abode stood on the stretch of river bank called the Strand. Before the dissolution of the monasteries, it had been the town house of a bishop, and she often imagined how he would have reacted if he saw some of the antics that took place in his former bedchamber. Her impish spirit was such that she felt she was helping to purge the place of Catholicism.

A gentle tap on her door disturbed her reverie.

'Come in,' she called.

The maidservant entered and halted with a token curtsey.

'Your dressmaker is below, Lady Varley.'

'Send him up at once!' she ordered.

He had come at exactly the right time. Lady Rosamund wanted to give an order for a very special outfit. She was confident that it would secure Lawrence Firethorn for her without any difficulty.

Richard Honeydew was too inexperienced to sense what was coming. When the other apprentices started to be more pleasant to him, he took it as a sign of real friendship rather than as a device to lure him off guard. Notwithstanding all the things they had done to him, he was anxious to get along with them and to put the past behind him. Achieving the signal honour of a role like Gloriana had not made him arrogant or boastful. He was far too conscious of his shortcomings and would have sought the advice of his fellow apprentices if he were on better terms with them. That time looked as if it might soon come. They were making efforts.

'Goodnight, Dick.'

'Goodnight, Martin.'

'Would you like to borrow my candle to light you up the stairs?' offered the older boy.

'No, thank you. I can manage.'

'Sleep well, then.'

'I will.'

'You have another busy day ahead tomorrow.'

Richard went off to say goodnight to Margery Firethorn, who was sitting in her rocking chair beside the open hearth and thinking fondly about her pendant. As soon as the boy had gone, Martin Yeo looked across at the others. John Tallis lowered his lantern jaw in an open-mouthed grin while Stephen Judd gave a knowing wink. They were happy accomplices.

'Are you sure it will work?' asked Tallis.

'Of course,' said Yeo. 'The beauty of it is that no finger will be pointed at us. We will all be sitting here together when it happens.'

'All but me,' added Judd.

'Oh, you were right here all the time,' insisted Yeo.

'Yes, Stephen,' corroborated Tallis.

'We both saw you.'

'We'll swear to it!'

'I've always wanted to be in two places at once.'

'Then so you will be,' promised Yeo.

They fell silent as they heard the tread of Richard's light feet up on the stairs, then they smirked as he creaked his way up to perdition. It was only a question of time now.

Oblivious to their plan, Richard Honeydew went up to his attic room by the light of the moonbeams that peeped in through the windows. Every other night, his first job had been to bolt the door behind him to keep outrage at bay. Lulled into a mood of trust by the others, he did not do so now. He felt safe.

The chill of the night air made him shiver and he got undressed quickly before jumping into bed. Through the narrow window above his head, the moon was drawing intricate patterns on the opposite wall. Richard was able to watch them for only a few minutes before he dozed off to sleep but his slumber was soon disturbed. There was a rustling sound in the thatch and his eyes opened in fear. It would not be the first rat he had heard up in the attic.

He sat up quickly and was just in the nick of time. Something came crashing down on his pillow in a cloud of loam, cobwebs and filth. Richard coughed as the dust got into his throat then he turned around to see what had happened.

The dormer window was set in the steeply pitched roof and small, solid beams formed a rectangle around the frame to keep the thatch away. Richard had often noticed how loose the lower beam was. All four of them had just come falling down with a vengeance. He sat there transfixed by it all.

'What is it, lad! What happened?'

Margery Firethorn was galloping up the stairs to the attic in her nightgown. Her voice preceded her with ease.

'Are you there, Dick? What's amiss?'

Seconds later, she came bursting into the room with a candle in her hand. It illumined a scene of debris. She let out a shriek of horror then clutched Richard to her for safety.

'Lord save us! You might have been killed!'

Martin Yeo, John Tallis and Stephen Judd now came charging up to the attic to see what had caused the thunderous bang.

'What is it!'

'Has something fallen?'

'Are you all right, Dick?'

The three of them raced into the room and came to a halt. When they saw the extent of the damage, they were all astonished. They looked quickly at Richard to see if he had been hurt.

'Is this *your* doing?' accused Margery.

'No, mistress!' replied Yeo.

'That beam has always been loose,' added Tallis.

'We will sort this out later,' she warned. 'Meanwhile, I must find this poor creature another place to lay his head. Come, Dick. It is all over now.'

She led the young apprentice out with grave concern.

As soon as the two of them had gone, Martin Yeo bent down to untie the cord that was bound around the lower beam. Fed through a gap in the floorboards, the cord had come down to their own room so that they could create the accident with a sudden jerk. But they had only expected to dislodge the lower beam. A blow on the head from that would have been sufficiently disabling to put Richard out of the play. They had planned nothing more serious.

Stephen Judd examined the dormer with care.

'Those other beams were quite secure earlier on,' he said. 'Someone must have loosened them. They would never have come down otherwise.'

'Who would do such a thing?' wondered Tallis.

'I don't know,' said Yeo uneasily. 'But if Dick had been underneath it when it all came down, he might never have appeared in a play again.'

The three apprentices were completely unnerved.

They stood amid the rubble and tried to puzzle it out. A small accident which they engineered had been turned into something far more dangerous by an unknown hand.

Evidently, someone knew of their plan.

Susan Fowler went to London as a frightened young wife in search of a husband and returned to St Albans as a desolate widow with her life in ruins. The passage of time did not seem to make her loss any easier to bear. It was like a huge bruise which had not yet fully come out and which yielded new areas of ache and blemish each day.

Her mother provided a wealth of sympathy, her elder sister sat with her for hours and kind neighbours were always attentive to her plight, but none of it managed to assuage her pain. Not even the parish priest could bring her comfort. Susan kept being reminded of the day that he had married her to Will Fowler.

Grief inevitably followed her to the bedroom and worked most potently by night. It was a continuous ordeal.

'Good morning, father.'

'Heavens, girl! Are you up at this hour?'

'I could not sleep.'

'Go back to your bed, Susan. You need the rest.'

'There is no rest for me, father.'

'Think of the baby, girl.'

She had risen early after another night of torture and come downstairs in the little cottage that she shared with her parents and her sister. Her father was a wheelwright and had to be up early himself. A wagon had overturned in a banked field the previous day and one of its wheels was shattered beyond repair. The wheelwright had promised to make it his first task of the day because the wagon was needed urgently for harvesting.

After a hurried breakfast of bread and milk, he made another vain attempt to send his daughter back to bed. Susan shook her head and adjusted her position in the old wooden chair. The baby was more of a presence now and she often felt it move.

Her father crossed the undulating paving stones to the door and pulled back the thick, iron bolt. He glanced back at Susan and offered her a look of encouragement that went unseen. He could delay no longer. The wagon was waiting for him outside his workshop.

When he opened the door, however, something barred his way and he all but tripped over it.

'What's this!' he exclaimed.

Susan looked up with only the mildest curiosity.

'Bless my soul!'

He regarded the object with a countryman's suspicion. It might be a gift from the devil or the work of some benign force. It was some time before he overcame his superstitions enough to pick the object up and bring it into the cottage. He set it down on the table in front of his daughter.

It was a crib. Small, plain and carved out of solid oak, it rocked gently to and fro on its curved base. Susan Fowler stared at it blankly for a few moments then a tiny smile came.

'It's a present for the baby,' she said.

Chapter Eight

Nicholas Bracewell confronted him first thing the next morning.

'You must be mistaken,' said Creech bluntly.

'No, Ben.'

'I did not go to The Curtain yesterday.'

'But I saw you with my own eyes.'

'You saw someone who *looked* like me.'

'Stop lying.'

'I'm not lying,' maintained the actor hotly. 'I was nowhere near Shoreditch yesterday afternoon.'

'Then where were you?'

Creech withdrew into a defiant silence. His mouth was closed tight and his jaw was set. Nicholas pressed him further.

'You were supposed to be *here*, Ben.'

'Nobody told me that,' argued the other.

'I told you myself – in front of witnesses, too – so you can't pretend that that never happened either. The tiremen were expecting you and you failed to turn up.'

'I . . . couldn't get here yesterday.'

'I know – you were at The Curtain instead.'

'No!' denied Creech. 'I was . . .' He glowered at Nicholas then gabbled his story. 'I was at the Lamb and Flag. I only went in for one drink at noon but I met some old friends. We started talking and had some more ale. The time just flew past. Before I knew what was happening, I fell asleep in my seat.'

'I don't believe a word of it,' said Nicholas firmly.

'That is your privilege, sir!'

'We'll have to fine you for this, Ben.'

'Do so,' challenged the hired man.

'One shilling.'

Creech's defiance turned to shock. One shilling was a steep fine to a person whose weekly wage was only seven times that amount. He had many debts and could not afford to lose such a sum. Nicholas read his thoughts but felt no regret.

'You've brought this upon yourself,' he stressed. 'When will you learn? I've covered for you in the past, Ben, but it has to stop. You simply must be more responsible. There are dozens of players to be had for hire. If this goes on, one of them may be taking over your place.'

'It's not up to you, Nicholas,' muttered Creech.

166

'Would you rather discuss it with Master Firethorn?'

'No,' he said after a pause.

'He would have kicked you out months ago.'

'I earn my money!'

'Yes, when you're here,' agreed Nicholas. 'Not when you're lying in a drunken stupor somewhere or sneaking off to The Curtain.'

'That was not me!'

'I'm not blind, Ben.'

Creech bunched his fists and he breathed heavily through his nose. Discretion slowly got the better of him. The book holder might seem quiet but he would not be intimidated. If the occasion demanded it, Nicholas Bracewell could fight as well as the next man and his physique was daunting. Nothing would be served by throwing a punch.

'One shilling, Ben.'

'As you wish.'

'And no more of your nonsense, sir.'

Benjamin Creech risked one more glare then he withdrew to the other side of the tiring-house. The talk had sobered him in every sense. Samuel Ruff had watched the exchange from the other side of the room and he now came across to the book holder.

'What was all that about, Nick?'

'The usual.'

'Too much ale?'

'And too little honesty, Samuel. I saw the fellow at The Curtain yesterday in broad daylight – yet he denies it!'

'He may have good cause.'

'In what way?'

'Where did you see him, Nick?'

'Talking with a couple of the hired men.'

'There's your answer. He does not wish to admit it.'

'Admit what?'

'I never thought to mention this because I assumed that you knew. Obviously you do not,' Ruff looked across at the man. 'Ben Creech was with Banbury's Men for a time.'

'Is this true?' asked Nicholas in astonishment.

'Oh, yes. I was there with him.'

While the future of one hired man was being discussed in the tiring-house, the future of another was under dire threat in an upstairs room. No rehearsal period of Westfield's Men was complete without a fit of pique from Barnaby Gill and he was supplying one of his best. Edmund Hoode bore it with equanimity but Lawrence Firethorn was becoming progressively more irritated. Pacing the room madly, the anguished sharer worked up a real froth.

'He is not fit to belong to Lord Westfield's Men!'

'Why not?' asked Hoode.

'Because I say so, sir!'

'We need more than that, Barnaby.'

'The man has the wrong attitude.'

'I disagree,' said Hoode. 'Samuel Ruff is probably the only hired man we have with the right attitude. He takes his work seriously and fits in well with the company.'

'Not with me, Edmund.'

'He's an experienced actor.'

'London is full of experienced players.'

'Not all of them are as reliable as Ruff.'

'He must leave us.'

'On what pretext?'

'I do not *like* the man!'

'He will be relieved to hear that,' said Firethorn with a wicked chuckle. 'Come, Barnaby, this is too small a matter to waste any more breath on.'

'I want him dismissed,' said Gill, holding firm.

'This is a mere whim.'

'I mean it, Lawrence. He has crossed me and he must suffer.'

'Why not challenge him to a duel?' suggested Hoode.

Gill cut short their mirth by lifting a chair and banging it down hard on the floor. His nostrils were flaring now and his eyes were rolling like those of a mare caught in a stable fire.

'I would remind you of just how much this company owes to me,' he began. 'In the face of constant temptation, I have remained faithful to Lord Westfield's Men. Others have approached me with lucrative offers many times but I always refused them, believing – in error, it now seems – that I was needed and appreciated here.'

'We have heard this speech before,' said Firethorn petulantly, 'and it does not grow more palatable.'

'I am serious, Lawrence! He has to go.'

'Why? Because he mastered you in a bout with foils?'

'Because he unsettles me.'

'We all do that to you, Barnaby,' joked Hoode. 'Are we to be put out as well?'

'Do not mock, sir. This is in earnest.'

'Then let me be in earnest as well,' decided Firethorn, putting his hands on his hips as he confronted the smaller man. 'We both know what lies behind all this. Young Dicky Honeydew.'

'Have care, Lawrence.'

'I do – for the boy.' He wagged a warning finger. 'I am not one to pry into a man's private affairs. Live and let live, say I. But there is one rule that must always hold in this company, Barnaby, and you know it as well as I do. You understand me?'

'Yes.'

'*Not* with the apprentices.'

'This has nothing to do with the matter, Lawrence.'

'I have said my piece, sir.'

'And I must support it,' said Hoode. 'As for Samuel Ruff, you are out on your own. Everyone else is happy with the fellow. We have fared much worse with our hired men.'

Barnaby Gill was profoundly offended. He walked slowly to the door, opened it, drew himself up to his full height, and put every ounce of disdain into his tone.

'I will contend no further!'

'Then what have you been doing all this while?' asked Firethorn. 'You have argued for argument's sake.'

'The choice is simple, gentlemen,' said Gill.

'Choice?'

'Either *he* goes – or I do!'

He slammed the door behind him with dramatic force.

George Dart was much given to reflections upon the misery of his lot. As the youngest and smallest of the stagekeepers, he was always saddled with the most menial jobs, and everyone in the company had authority over him. One of the tasks he hated most was being sent out with a sheaf of playbills to put up around the City. It was exhausting work. He would be chased by dogs, jeered at by children, jostled by pedestrians, harangued by tradesmen, frowned on by Puritans, menaced by thieves, solicited by punks and generally made to feel that he was at the mercy of others.

His latest errand introduced him to a new indignity. With the playbills of *Gloriana Triumphant* fresh from the printers, he set off on a tortuous route through Cheapside, using every post and fence he could find along the way as a place of advertisement. With the market sprawled all around him, he had to push almost every inch of the way and his size was a real disadvantage. Hours of persistence, however, finally paid off as he posted up his last playbill outside the Maid and Magpie.

George Dart slowly began to retrace his short steps, wondering, as he did so, if anyone led such a pitiable existence as he did. They were always sending him somewhere. He was continually on the move, shuttling between this place and that, for ever heading towards or away from somewhere, never settling, never being allowed to dwell at the centre of action. He was one of nature's intercessaries. Every arrival was a departure, every halt was merely to pick up instructions for the next journey. He was nothing but a carrier pigeon, doomed to fly in perpetuity.

His reverie was rudely checked when he turned a corner and walked along a street where he had put up a number of his playbills. Most of them had gone and those that remained had been defaced. He shuddered at the prospect of having to report the outrage. They would send him out again with fresh bills to endure fresh torments.

When he looked around the crowded street, he saw dozens of suspects. Any one of them could have ruined his work. As he studied a playbill that had been scribbled upon, he decided that it was the work of a drunken ruffian who wanted a morning's sport.

George Dart wept copiously. Watching him from a shop doorway on the opposite side of the street was a young man with a complacent smile. It was Roger Bartholomew.

The apprentices were still mystified. They had no idea who could have loosened the other beams in the attic chamber, nor could they understand the motive that lay behind it all. Was it some malign joke? Had the intention been to cripple Richard Honeydew permanently? Or were they themselves the target? Could someone have tried to implicate them in a much more serious business than the one they devised? If the apprentice had been badly injured – even killed – suspicion would naturally have fallen on them.

As it was, the luck which had saved Richard worked to

their advantage as well. Margery Firethorn railed at them but they were able to swear, with the light of truth in their eyes, that they had not been responsible for loosening the beams around the dormer. Martin Yeo, John Tallis and Stephen Judd were off the hook but one fact remained. Richard Honeydew would still play Gloriana.

Shedding their fears about the person who had exploited their first plan, they set about concocting another. This one was foolproof. It would be put into operation the next day and the venue was the yard at The Queen's Head.

'Here's a fine chestnut,' admired Yeo, leaning over the stable door. 'Come and see, Dick.'

'Yes,' agreed Richard, looking at the horse. 'He is a fine animal. See how his coat shines!'

'Would you like to ride him? asked Tallis.

'I'd love to, John, but I am no horseman. Who owns him?'

'We have no notion,' said Tallis with an artful glance at Yeo. 'He must have arrived last night.'

They had come into the yard when the stage had been taken down to make way for a coach and a couple of wagons. The horses had been stabled. Knowing Richard's fondness for the animals, Yeo and Tallis had invited him over to inspect them all, casually stopping at the last of the loose boxes to inspect the chestnut stallion. It was a mettlesome beast some seventeen hands high, and Yeo had watched it trot into the yard the previous afternoon. He had also overheard the instructions which the rider had given to the ostler.

A second trap had been set. Stationed in the window of the rehearsal room was Stephen Judd. He waved a hand to confirm that both Nicholas Bracewell and Samuel Ruff were fully occupied. Richard was now shorn of his guardians.

'He looks hungry,' noted Yeo.

'I've an apple he can have,' decided Tallis, pulling it out from his pocket. 'Here, Dick. You give it to him.'

'Not me, Stephen.'

'He won't bite you, lad,' said Yeo. 'Hold it on the palm of your hand like this.' He demonstrated with the apple. 'Go on.'

'I'm afraid to, Martin.'

'Horses love apples. Feed him.'

They cajoled the boy together until he eventually agreed. Opening the stable door, Yeo went in a yard or so with Richard. The chestnut was at the rear of the box, tethered to an empty manger and presenting its side to them.

Richard held the apple on the flat of his hand and approached with hesitant steps. The chestnut shifted its feet slightly and the straw rustled. Richard did not see Yeo move back through the door before closing it. He was now alone in the loose box with the towering animal.

'Give it to him, Dick,' urged Yeo.

'Hold it under his nose,' added Tallis.

'Hurry up, lad.'

As Richard slowly extended his hand, the horse suddenly reared his head, showed the whites of his eyes, laid his ears back, then swung sideways with a loud neigh. His gleaming flank caught the boy hard enough to send him somersaulting into the straw. When the animal bucked wildly and lashed out with his powerful hind quarters, Richard was only inches away from the flashing hooves.

Martin Yeo was disappointed but Stephen Judd was having second thoughts about it all. Keen as he was for his friend to succeed to the part of Gloriana, he did not want Richard to be kicked to death by a horse.

'Hey!' yelled an ostler as he came running.

'Dick tried to give him an apple,' said Yeo.

Throwing open the stable door, the ostler grabbed Richard and dragged him to safety. Then he lifted the boy up and shook him soundly.

'What did you do that for, you fool!' he shouted. 'That horse will only let his master feed him. Do you want to be killed?'

Richard Honeydew turned crimson and fainted.

Lady Rosamund Varley expected the impossible and she was never satisfied until she got it. When she had given her dressmaker his orders, the man protested that he needed more time than he was allotted but she had been firm with him. If he wished to retain her custom, he had to obey her instructions. The impossible was once more accomplished, and the dressmaker arrived on time with his assistant at Varley House. She was duly delighted with their work but she had learned never to over-praise her minions. Instead, she found fault.

'I ordered three-inch ribbons.'

'Four, Lady Varley,' he corrected deferentially. 'But we can shorten them, of course.'

'I wanted a lawn ruff.'

'Cambric, Lady Varley. But we can change that.'

'The gown is cut too full.'

'My needlewomen are standing by, Lady Varley.'

The dressmaker was a tall, almost debonair man who made himself look much smaller and meaner by his compulsion to bend and bow. His unctuous manner was further supplemented by a nervous washing of his hands. He absorbed all her criticisms and promised that the mistakes would be rectified.

'I will try it on first,' she announced.

'When it falls short of your wishes, Lady Varley.'

'Wait here.'

She retired to her bedchamber with two of her women, who first undressed her then helped their mistress into her new attire. Over her linen chemise, they put on a whalebone corset and a farthingale, which was fastened round the waist to hold the gown out in a becoming semi-circle at the back. Over this came several petticoats, worn beneath a striking bodice of royal blue velvet with gold figure-work. A gown of the same material, slightly darker for contrast, had hanging sleeves of cambric.

In the fashion of the day, Lady Rosamund's hair was curled, frizzed and lightened to a golden-red. It was piled high above the forehead and swept away from the sides of her face. A stiff lace cartwheel ruff framed and set off her pale-skinned loveliness. Jewellery, perfume, a hat, gloves, and shoes were added to complete a picture of devastating beauty. Everything fitted perfectly.

Full-length mirrors allowed her to view herself from all angles. She called for a few adjustments to be made then she was content. As she paraded around the room, the former owner of the house popped back into her mind.

'Not even a bishop would be safe from me in this!'

Sweeping back downstairs, she let the dressmaker and his assistant cluck their praises at her then she clapped her hands to dismiss them.

'Leave your account.'

'Yes, Lady Varley.'

'My husband will pay you when he has a mind to.'

Alone again, she headed for the nearest mirror. The dress was a sartorial triumph. She could not wait to put it on display at The Curtain for the benefit of Lawrence Firethorn.

Edmund Hoode stood at the window of the rehearsal room and gazed moodily out at the inn yard. The effort of writing the new play had left him with the usual exhaustion and depression nudged at him. *Gloriana Triumphant* was an excellent piece of drama but it was also designed as a vehicle in which Lawrence Firethorn could both extend his reputation and further his love life. All that Hoode was left with was some effusive thanks and a small but telling role in the fourth act.

In such moods as this, he always felt used. His talent had

been manipulated for the use of others. The best sonnet that he had written for years had been appropriated by someone else and it pained him. He spoke the lines softly to himself, and wished that the poem could instigate a romance for him. It dawned on him that he had not been in love for months. He missed the sweet sorrow of it. His soul was withering.

For Edmund Hoode, the thrill of the chase was everything. He was a true idealist who liked nothing better than to commit himself wholeheartedly to a woman and to draw his pleasure from the simple act of being in love. Lawrence Firethorn was very different. To a seasoned voluptuary like him, conquest was all and his standards were high. Hoode was ready to compromise. He would take someone far less grand than Lady Rosamund Varley. In his present despondency, he would take almost anyone.

Even as he brooded, something came into his field of vision that made him start. It was the landlord's daughter, tripping lightly across the inn yard with her dark hair streaming behind her. Hoode had noticed her several times before and always with pleasure. No more than twenty, she was happily free from the slightest resemblance to her father and her buxom openness was very refreshing.

As he watched her now, he discerned qualities that had eluded him before. She was lithe, graceful, vivacious. She was less like a landlord's daughter than a princess brought up by a woodcutter. Hoode gasped with joy as he realised something else about her.

Her name was Rose Marwood.

He began to recite his sonnet over again.

Nicholas Bracewell's earlier visit to The Curtain had been well-spent and he had devised some clever ideas for the staging of *Gloriana Triumphant*. He was anxious to have the chance to put them to the test. The luxury of a full day's rehearsal at the theatre gave him all the opportunity he needed. Some of his notions had to be scrapped, but the majority – including those for the climactic sea battle – were ingeniously workable. It enabled him to relax. Given the mastery of its technical problems, the play could now take flight. He was confident that there would be no shuffling of feet in the pit this time.

Though acutely busy throughout the day, he tried to keep an eye on Richard Honeydew. The incident with the horse had rocked him and he was convinced that it had been set up by the other apprentices. They had been in disgrace ever since and no further attacks had been made on Richard. With the supportive vigilance of Samuel Ruff and Margery Firethorn, Nicholas felt he could keep the boy from harm.

'Let us try the end of the battle scene!' ordered Firethorn.

'Positions!' called Nicholas.

'We will not fire our cannon,' decided the actor. 'We will keep our powder dry.'

'And the sail, master?'

'Oh, we must have that.'

Where Banbury's Men had simply used a thick pole to

suggest a mast, the other company had constructed a much more elaborate property with a full sail that could be raised and lowered. It was set into a circular wooden base which was self-standing. As the wind picked up, however, the sail began to billow.

'Hold it, Ben!' directed Nicholas.

'Aye.'

'Stand beside him just in case, Gregory.'

'Yes, Master Bracewell,' said a strapping journeyman, the author of *God Speed the Fleet*. Where the earlier play had spent itself in the naval engagement, *Gloriana Triumphant* ended with a scene on the deck of the flagship which brought together all the main characters in the drama. The Queen of Albion herself came on board and, with a spontaneous gesture of gratitude, she borrowed a sword to knight her magnificent sea dog.

Everyone took up their positions then Nicholas cued the musicians. Peter Digby led his men in a stately march as the royal personage came on to the vessel. With back erect and voice expressive, Richard Honeydew delivered his longest speech of the play, trying to ignore the flapping havoc that the wind was now causing to his costume. Firethorn went down on one knee to accept his knighthood then kissed the hand of his monarch and went into his monologue.

He was not destined to reach the end of it. A sudden gust of wind hit the sail and wrenched it out of Benjamin Creech's grasp. Before Gregory could grab it, the whole mast keeled over across the middle of the stage.

'Look out!'

'Help!'

'Jump, Dick!'

The Queen of Albion had only a split second to take the advice that Samuel Ruff bawled out. As the mast lunged down at him, Nicholas leapt instinctively off the stage altogether. There was a tremendous crash as the timber hit the deck but at least it had not hit anyone. The cast were in a state of shock but nobody seemed to be hurt.

'Aouw!'

'Are you hurt, Dick?'

'I think so.'

'Stay there!' advised Nicholas.

He bounded across the stage and leaped down beside the prone figure of the young apprentice. Richard was in pain. Landing awkwardly after his own jump, he had twisted his ankle so badly that he could put no weight on it. When Nicholas examined the injury, the joint was already beginning to swell.

The miracle was that the boy had eluded the falling mast. If he had been hampered by his costume, he would never have got out of the way in time and the extravagant finery of the Queen of Albion would now be lying crushed beneath the heavy timber. As it was, Richard had leaped from the deck of the flagship for good. He would never be able to perform next day.

It was ironic. The other three boys had tried to disable him and failed. Chance contrived what design could not. A gust of wind had just recast the part of Gloriana.

Nicholas Bracewell lifted the boy up in his arms and turned back to the stage. Looking down at them was Benjamin Creech, who had been holding the mast when it fell. The hired man was impassive but his eyes were slits of pleasure.

Chapter Nine

Rejection had wrought deep changes in Master Roger Bartholomew. He felt defiled. When he saw his play about Richard the Lionheart performed at The Queen's Head, he thought that he had finished with the theatre for ever but his Muse had other ideas. Directed back to the playhouse, he had now suffered such comprehensive rejection that it turned his brain. He discovered a vengeful streak in himself that he had never even suspected before. They had hurt him; he wanted to strike back.

Lord Westfield's Men became the target for his obsessive hatred. Other companies had turned him down but Lawrence Firethorn had done far worse than that. He had ruined one play by the young poet then reviled another. To make matters worse, he was playing the leading role in a new drama on exactly the same subject as *An Enemy Routed*. In his feverish state, Bartholomew wondered if his play had been plundered to fill out the other. It would not be the first time that an author's work had been pillaged.

As he stood outside The Curtain, he could hear the voices booming away inside during the rehearsal. He could not make out the words or identify the speakers, but he knew one thing. *Gloriana Triumphant* had dispossessed him. He reached out to snatch another playbill from its post. If talent and justice meant anything in the theatre, it was *his* play that should be advertised all over London, and his words that should now be ringing out behind the high walls of the playhouse.

Bartholomew stood above all things for the primacy of the word, for the natural ascendancy of the poet. Firethorn and his company worked to other rules. They promoted the actor as the central figure in the theatre. A play to them was just a fine garment that they could wear once or twice for effect before discarding. *An Enemy Routed* had been discarded before it was even worn. No consideration at all had been shown for its author's feelings.

Lord Westfield's Men deserved to be punished for their arrogance. He elected himself to administer that punishment. All that he had to decide was its exact nature.

Adversity was a rope that bound them more tightly together. In the face of their setbacks, Westfield's Men responded with speedy resolution. The injured apprentice was taken home and his deputy, Martin Yeo, started to rehearse at once. Even as he was working out on stage, the tiremen were altering Gloriana's costume to fit him and redressing the red wig that he was to wear. Yeo had already learned the role in readiness and so the eleventh hour substitution was less of a problem than it might have been, but there were still movements to master, entrances and exits to memorise, due note to be taken of the performances of those around the Queen so that he could play off them.

Nicholas Bracewell, meanwhile, had taken steps to stabilise the mast and sail. When it was set up now, a series of ropes led down from its top to different parts of the stage and tied off on hooks or cleats. The mast was so solid that it was possible for someone to climb it. Ever the opportunist, Firethorn cast the smallest of the journeymen as a ship boy and told him to shin up the mast. It would be a good effect in performance.

A bewildering variety of chores kept George Dart on the move throughout the play. At Nicholas's suggestion, he was given another job as well. Because they could not guarantee that a wind would blow the next afternoon, Dart was handed a long piece of rope that was attached to the heart of the sail. Concealed on the balcony above the stage, he was to tug violently on cue to give the impression that the ship was being blown along by a gale. It was the first time in his young career that he had ever taken on the role of the west wind.

Even Barnaby Gill pitched in to help with the emergency. He suspended his ultimatum about Samuel Ruff until after the performance, and did what he could to keep

185

up everyone's spirit. Against all the odds, the play began to come together. Frantic rewriting by Edmund Hoode eliminated the part that Martin Yeo had played before and smoothed out one or two other lumps. Morale was high at the end of an interminable rehearsal.

'Well, Nick. What do you think?'

'I think we'll get through.'

'We'll do more than that, dear heart. Dicky may have gone but there are still many other sublime performances. I wager that we'll hold them in the palm of our hands.'

'It never does to tempt fate,' warned Nicholas.

They were standing together on the now almost empty stage at The Curtain, reviewing the day and its vicissitudes. Firethorn suddenly declaimed his first speech, aiming it at the galleries and taking up various positions to do so. Nicholas soon realised what he was doing. The actor was trying to work out precisely where Lady Rosamund Varley would be sitting.

'We'll show 'em, Nick.'

'Who, master?'

'Giles Randolph and his ilk.'

'Ah.'

'You saw the fellow here last. How did he fare?'

'Indifferently. It was a poor play.'

'A poor play with a poor player. I will act him off the stage, sir!'

'You are without compare,' said Nicholas tactfully.

'Tomorrow is an important day for us,' continued the other. 'We must prove ourselves once and for all. Our dear patron will rely on us to increase his lustre. We must use this new play to stake our claim to the highest honour – an invitation to play at court.'

'It's long overdue.'

Firethorn made a deep bow to acknowledge non-existent applause that reverberated in his ears. He was already at court, performing before the Queen and her entourage, receiving royal favour, achieving yet another success in the auditorium of his mind. Nicholas saw that his ambition had another side to it than mere glory. Performance at court would be in front of a small, exclusive, private audience that would include Lady Rosamund Varley. She ruled on the throne of his heart at the moment.

'I would be in Elysium,' confided Firethorn.

'It will come.'

'Let us ensure it, Nick.'

When everything had been cleared away and locked up ready for the morrow, they all departed. There was sadness for Richard Honeydew that he had been robbed of his first taste of stardom but the performance had to continue and everyone had bent themselves to that end. Company rivalry was paramount. Banbury's Men had done themselves less than credit at The Curtain. Lawrence Firethorn and his fellows could dazzle by comparison.

It was a long, lonely walk back to Bishopsgate and Nicholas still had more than a mile to go when he entered the City. But he was too preoccupied to notice the extent of his journey or the stiff breeze that swept through the dark night. Will Fowler still haunted him as did the actor's young widow. Two battered prostitutes, one of whom had been subsequently murdered, also had a strong claim on his sympathy. He feared for Samuel Ruff whose place with the company was now in jeopardy. He worried for Richard Honeydew. There was even a vestigial concern for Roger Bartholomew, who had been ousted from the theatre almost before he had got into it. The book holder puzzled over the ruined playbills that George Dart had reported with such trepidation. They had enemies enough without that.

What kept pushing itself to the forefront of his mind, however, was the surly face of Benjamin Creech. Why had the man denied being at The Curtain and concealed his old association with Banbury's Men? What had been the real cause of his fight with Will Fowler? Had the injury to Richard Honeydew really been an accident? Did Nicholas truly see a glint of relish in Creech's eyes or had he imagined it?

Speculation and recrimination carried him all the way back to Bankside. He was almost home when the trouble came. Turning into a side-street, he suddenly had the feeling that he was being followed. His years at sea had helped him to develop a sixth sense for self-preservation and his hand stole quickly to his dagger. He listened for a footfall behind him but heard none. When he spun around, there was nobody there. He continued on his way, ready to dismiss it as a trick of his imagination, when a tall, hulking figure stepped out of an alley ahead of him to block his way. The man was some fifteen yards away and seen only in hazy outline through the gloom, but Nicholas knew at once who he was. They had met before at the Hope and Anchor when a friend had been murdered. There had been more evidence of his handiwork at The Cardinal's Hat.

Pulling out his dagger, Nicholas bunched himself to charge but he did not get far. Before he had moved a yard or so, something hard and solid struck him on the back of the head and sent him down into a black whirlpool of pain. The last thing he remembered was the sound of footsteps running away over the cobblestones. The rest was cold void.

Lawrence Firethorn was at his best in a crisis. The threat of resignation by Barnaby Gill and the sudden loss of Richard Honeydew had imposed pressure which he had surmounted with bravery. Pulling the company together in its hour of need, he fired them with the possibilities of the morrow and infected them with his unassailable self-confidence. The play would be another afternoon of glory for him and it would be followed – in time – by a whole night of magic. *Gloriana Triumphant* and fourteen lines of poetry would win him the favours of Lady Rosamund Varley.

After all the setbacks of the day, therefore, he returned home with a light step to receive a kiss of welcome from his trusting wife. But the kiss did not come and the trust seemed to have gone. Frost had settled on Margery's ample brow.

'What ails you, my love?' he asked blithely.

'I've been talking with Dicky.'

189

'Poor lad! Where is he?'

'He has gone to bed to rest that swollen ankle.'

'It was a dreadful accident,' said Firethorn. 'We must thank God that no serious injury resulted.'

'There *is* a more serious injury,' she added grimly.

'What's that you say, my sweet?'

'Sit down, Lawrence.'

'Why?'

'Sit down!'

The force of her request could not be denied and he sank into a chair. Margery Firethorn stood directly in front of him so that there was no possibility of escape. Her anger was banked down but ready to blaze up at any moment.

'The boy is heart-broken,' she began.

'Who would not be? It is his first leading role – and such a role at that! All his hard work has gone for nothing.'

'He talked about you, Lawrence.'

'Did he?'

'He told me how wonderful it was to play opposite such a superb actor as you.' She waited as he gave a dismissive laugh. 'The boy worships you.'

'Every apprentice should choose a good model.'

'Oh, I am sure that you are an excellent model, sir,' she said crisply. 'As an actor, that is. As a husband, of course, you have your faults and it is not so wonderful to play opposite them.'

'Margery . . .' he soothed.

'Spare me your ruses, Lawrence.'

'What ruse?'

'I spent hours listening to Dick Honeydew,' she said. 'That accident at the playhouse cost him dear. It cost me dear as well.'

'You, my angel?'

'He lost a role in a play but I have lost far more.'

'I do not understand you, sweeting.'

'Then let me speak more plain, sir,' she asserted with a crackle of menace. 'Dicky told me everything. He talked of his speeches and dances and magnificent costumes. He also mentioned the jewellery he was to have worn as Gloriana – including a beautiful pendant which had nothing at all wrong with its catch . . .'

Lawrence Firethorn had been caught out. The mast which had fallen on the stage of The Curtain now landed squarely on him. Margery had learned the unkind truth. Far from being a gift that was bought specifically for her, the pendant was a theatrical prop that had been used to mollify her. Reconciliation was now only a distant memory in their marriage. Instead of coming home to a loving wife, he was staring into the eyes of Medusa.

Margery guessed at once what lay behind the subterfuge. Reining in her fury, she spoke with an elaborate sweetness.

'What is her name, Lawrence?'

'Hold still now,' said Anne Hendrik. 'Let me bathe it properly.'

'I'm fine now. Tie the bandage.'

'This wound needs a surgeon.'

'I have no time to stay.'

'Let me send for one, Nick.'

'The pain is easing now,' he lied.

They were at the house in Bankside and Nicholas Brace-well was sitting on a chair while his landlady dressed the gash on the back of his head. As soon as he had recovered consciousness in the street, he had dragged himself up from the ground and staggered on as far as his front door. His hat was sodden with blood, his mind blurred and his whole body was one pounding ache.

When the servant answered his knock on the door, she let out a scream of fright at the condition he was in. Anne Hendrik had rushed out and the two women had carried Nicholas to a chair. Left alone with him, Anne now tended his wound with the utmost care and sympathy. She was almost overwhelmed by apprehension.

'You believe it was the same man?' she asked.

'I know it was.'

'It was dark, Nick. How can you be certain?'

'I would recognise him anywhere. It was Redbeard.'

'A murderous villain, lying in wait for you!' she said with trembling anxiety. 'It does not bear thinking about!'

'I survived, Anne,' he reminded her.

'Only by the grace of God! You are lucky to be alive!'

'They were not after me,' decided Nicholas, trying to make sense of what had happened. 'I would be lying dead in that street now if they had wanted to kill me. No, they were after something else.'

'Your purse?'

'They left that, Anne. What they stole was my satchel.'

'With your prompt book in it?' she gasped.

'Yes. That is what they wanted – *Gloriana Triumphant*.'

Anne Hendrik saw the implications at once and she blenched. The one complete copy of the play had now disappeared and there was no way that Nicholas could control the performance without it.

'This is terrible!' she exclaimed. 'You will have to cancel the play tomorrow.'

'That is their intention, Anne.'

'But why?'

'I can only guess,' he said. 'Malice, spite, envy, revenge . . . There are many possible reasons. We work in a jealous profession.'

'Who would *do* such a thing?'

'I will not rest until I have found out,' he pledged. 'One thing is clear. Redbeard has an accomplice. I could not understand how he could have gained entry to The Cardinal's Hat without being recognised. The answer must be that he did not go back there after that poor creature. It was the other man who slit Alice's throat.'

'To prevent her helping you?'

'I believe so. Redbeard knows that I am after him.'

Anne Hendrik gave a little shiver and finished tying the bandage around his head. The blood had discoloured his fair hair and there was an ugly bruise on his temple from his fall on to the cobbles. Tears of love and compassion trickled down her cheeks. She grabbed at his arm as he stood up.

'You are in no condition to go out again, Nick.'

'I have no choice.'

'Let me come with you,' she volunteered.

'No, Anne. I can manage alone. Besides, it will be a long night. Do not expect me back until morning.'

'Where will you be?' she said, following him to the door.

'Writing a play.'

Edmund Hoode had an author's gift for happy invention. Desperate to fall in love again, he had settled on Rose Marwood and he persuaded himself that she was the most divine member of her sex. Her deficiencies were quickly remedied by his burgeoning imagination and she emerged as the girl of his dreams – a magical compound of beauty, wit, charm and understanding. Without realising it, Rose Marwood had tripped across the innyard and been transformed. Hoode made no allowance for the fact that he had hardly spoken to her. He was in love and romance knows no reason.

An hour of reflection upon her virtues confirmed him in his plan to send her the sonnet. Having written it out again in a fair hand, he appended the phrase 'Every Happiness', picking out the *E* and the *H* with such flourishes of his pen that he felt sure she would identify the initials of her swain.

Further indulgence was cut short by a banging on the door. Nicholas Bracewell was soon invited in to explain his head wound and tell his story. Panic all but throttled Hoode when he heard that his play had been stolen. It was like losing a child.

'What can we do, Nicholas?' he wailed.

'Start again.'

'From what? You had the only complete copy.'

'We will patch it together somehow,' promised the other. 'I have roused George Dart and sent him to fetch what sides he can get from the players. I have been back to The Curtain and retrieved my copy of the Plot. Then there is your knowledge of writing the play and my memory of rehearsing it. If we put all that together, we should be part of the way towards making another prompt book.'

'It will take us all night, Nicholas!'

'Would you rather cancel the performance?'

The thought of it was enough to make Hoode tremble. He needed only a few seconds to come to his decision. Fourteen lines to Rose Marwood were put aside in favour of a few thousand for the audience at The Curtain.

As soon as the scrivener arrived, they got to work as fast as was compatible with accuracy. The copious detail of the Plot which Nicholas had prepared was an enormous help and it stimulated Hoode's memory at once.

Lawrence Firethorn was the next to appear, fulminating against the Earl of Banbury's men whom he had already identified as the villains. His towering rage, however, was tinged with relief. Appalling as the theft of the prompt book was, it had rescued him from interrogation by Margery.

Since his own part was the leading one, the copy which he brought gave the scrivener ample material to work on. Most of the gaps were filled in when the panting George Dart came on the scene with the individual sides from some of the players. While the stagekeeper got his breath back,

Nicholas sifted through them and put them in order. One particular copy was missing.

'Did you call on Creech?' asked Nicholas.

'He was not at his lodging, Master Bracewell,' said Dart.

'The nearest tavern is his lodging!' sighed Firethorn.

'I tried there as well, sir.'

'Thank you, George,' said Nicholas.

'Can I go now?'

'Yes,' ordered Firethorn. 'Find Creech. There is one scene involving him and two mariners that we do not seem to have here. Root him out from his drinking hole, George.'

'Must I, sir?' moaned Dart.

'Indeed, you must!'

'But I've been running about for hours.'

'Run some more, sir. This is the theatre!'

Cowed into submission, George Dart went off into the night in search of the hired man. Hoode, Firethorn and Nicholas carried on reassembling the play while the scrivener's quill fluttered busily. Shortly before midnight, the first stoup of wine was served. They would need plenty more to get them through their arduous task.

Dawn was plucking at the windows by the time that a fair copy was ready. Matthew Lipton, the scrivener, was groaning with exhaustion and his writing arm lay limp across his lap. Nicholas now took over. Using his Plot and calling on his phenomenal memory for detail, he annotated the prompt book so that he had every call, cue, entrance, exit and hand property listed in the appropriate place. Seven hours of frantic labour had restored their text to them but it had taxed their strength.

'I need some sleep,' said Hoode with a yawn.

'It's too late for that,' decided Firethorn. 'We should have breakfast together instead then make an early start for The Curtain.' He turned to Nicholas. 'We will stay beside you as bodyguards every step of the way, dear fellow.'

'You will not need to, Master Firethorn. I will be much more wary now. They took me unawares in Bankside.'

'Banbury's Men!' said Firethorn. 'I know it.'

'Would they stoop to this?' doubted Hoode.

'If they employ Randolph, they'll stoop to anything!'

'They certainly timed their strike well,' admitted Nicholas.

'On the eve of a performance,' noted Hoode. 'It would have crippled any other company.'

'But not Westfield's Men,' said Firethorn proudly. 'We have done famously this night, gentlemen – and that includes you, Master Lipton. We have stared defeat in the face and frightened it away. Nick, here, acted with great presence of mind in raising the alarm so quickly. I'm eternally grateful.'

'So am I,' echoed Hoode.

'It was the least I could do,' replied Nicholas with embarrassment. 'I felt so responsible for the theft of the prompt book that I had to do something.'

'You must not blame yourself,' said Firethorn kindly.

'My job was to safeguard that book.'

'When two ruffians set upon a man without warning, he is entitled to feel outrage and not guilt.' He stood up and made a sweeping gesture. 'It's monstrous! Piracy is something we have come to accept in our profession but this is a crime of a very different order. It's a treachery against the whole spirit of the theatre. Banbury's Men must pay!'

'If they did it,' said Nicholas sceptically.

'Of that there is no question, sir! Who else has so much to gain from our humiliation? Giles Randolph and that pack of knaves he calls an acting company! They are definitely behind it.'

'Will you tax them about it, Lawrence?' asked Hoode.

'Oh, no. We must make our enquiries by stealth first.'

'And my play?'

'We simply carry on as if nothing had happened, Edmund. We show these varlets that it will take more than violence and theft to stop Westfield's Men. We are adamantine proof!'

There was a pathetic knocking on the door. Nicholas went to open it and George Dart crept in, collapsing from fatigue but bearing what he had been sent to fetch. He held it up to Firethorn and waited for a word of congratulations that never came.

'You're late, sir,' complained the other.

'I'm sorry, Master Firethorn.'

'Where have you been?'

'Running, sir. To and fro.'

'Did you find Creech?'

'Just after midnight,' said the stagekeeper with a yawn.

'Then what has kept you?'

'He would not wake up, master. As soon as he did, we went back to his lodging and he gave me what I needed.'

He wanted some sort of recognition for his efforts. 'Have I done well, sir?'

'No,' said Firethorn.

'Very well, George,' corrected Nicholas.

'I'll say aye to that,' supported Hoode.

George Dart smiled for the first time in a week. He handed the sheets to Firethorn then closed his eyes tightly.

'Good night, sirs!'

Nicholas caught him as he slumped forward.

Shoreditch was as busy as ever next morning and the crowds were restive in the hot sun. By midday, people began to converge on The Curtain for the afternoon's entertainment. One of the first to arrive was a short, intense, studious young man in dark attire and hat. He paid a penny to gain entry to the playhouse then a further twopence for the privilege of a cushioned seat in the front row of the second gallery. It was the ideal spot for his purposes.

As he stared down at the empty stage, he was at once excited and repelled. His work belonged there but it had been viciously flung aside by an uncaring profession. The time had come for him to make his protest and he would do so in the most dramatic fashion that he could devise.

Roger Bartholomew wanted his revenge.

Chapter Ten

The atmosphere backstage at The Curtain was as tense as a lute-string. Keyed up already by the occasion, the company was one large collection of taut nerves when it heard the full story of the missing prompt book. The idea of a direct and vicious attack upon Lord Westfield's Men was deeply unsettling and speculation was rife as to whom the perpetrators could be. It did not put them in the best frame of mind to tackle their new play.

Superstition weighed heavily with many people and Barnaby Gill voiced the fears of a substantial number.

'What will be next, I wonder?'

'How say you?' asked Hoode, already reduced to a shambling wreck by the events of the night.

'Disasters come in threes, Edmund.'

'Do they?'

'We had Dick Honeydew's accident. Then the theft of the book.' His voice explored a lower octave. 'Now – what is to be the third catastrophe?'

'Your performance!' said Samuel Ruff under his breath and set up a few sniggers around him.

In seeking to dispel the tension, Lawrence Firethorn merely increased it. Summoning the whole company together in the tiring-house, he gave them a short speech about the need to fight back at their enemies by raising the level of their performance. His exhortations united them all in a common purpose but disseminated an unease that was strangely akin to stagefright. Only the more experienced actors were immune from it.

'Samuel . . .'

'Yes, lad?'

'I feel sick.'

'Take some deep breaths, Martin.'

'This dress is suffocating me.'

'Drink some water.'

'I'll never be able to stand still on stage.'

'Of course, you will,' assured the hired man. 'The moment you step out there, all your worries will disappear. It's the same before a battle when everyone – no matter how brave – feels afraid and unready. As soon as things start, they get carried away by the thrill and the emotion of it all. Theatre is a form of battle, Martin. You'll fight well, I know.'

The very fact that Martin Yeo could turn to Samuel

Ruff showed the extent of the boy's discomfort. Three full years with the company had given him a confidence that sometimes spilled over into arrogance, but he was now bereft of all that. With long faces and dry throats all around him, Yeo had sought out a man whom he had always disliked before. Ruff's composure set him apart from most of the others and the boy drew strength from it. He was even ready to confide a secret.

'Do you know something, Samuel?'

'What?'

'I never thought I'd say this but . . .'

'You wish Dick was here to play Gloriana.'

'Yes! How did you guess?'

'It was not difficult, lad,' said Ruff with mild amusement. 'Shall I tell you something now?'

'What?'

'If Dick were in that costume, he'd be wishing that *you* were taking on the role instead.'

Nicholas Bracewell was grateful for someone like Ruff to act as a calming influence. Cold panic showed in most eyes and Edmund Hoode was a prime victim. After his sterling work throughout the night, he was now in danger of losing his nerve completely. Doubts about his play became uncertainties about himself and widened into questions about the whole validity of the playhouse. Here was creative suffering of a kind that nobody else could understand. Hoode therefore stalked the perimeter of the tiring-house on his own, finding more and more phantoms to assail him.

It was Nicholas himself who was the main antidote to the general hysteria. With his head still swathed in bandages, he exerted his usual cool control in a way that instilled peace. As long as the book holder was there, the company had a solid framework in which to operate. It heartened them. Nicholas went out of his way to pass a remark or two with those most in need of moral support. As people swirled to and fro in the tiring-house, he was there with friendly comments.

'The music was excellent yesterday, Peter.'

'Thank you.'

'It could not be improved upon . . . Thomas . . .'

'Yes, master?'

'We'll need to rely on you heavily today.'

'Oh, dear,' muttered the old stagekeeper.

'Your experience will be a rock.'

'I hope so.'

'Hugh . . .'

'Aye?' called the tireman, fluffing out petticoats for John Tallis.

'Those costume changes will need to be quick.'

'We can manage.'

'Especially Gloriana in the last act.'

'Two of us will be standing by.'

'George . . .'

'Here, master,' said Dart through a spectacular yawn.

'You were a Trojan last night.'

'Did Trojans run their legs off as well, then?'

'Try not to fall asleep too often.'

'How am I supposed to stay awake, Master Bracewell?'

'Gregory . . .'

'Not here!'

'Where is he?'

'Where do you think?'

'*Again?*'

The general laughter eased the tension. Everybody knew where the jangled Gregory was and it was his fourth visit. Like every other part of the playhouse, the privy made a significant contribution to the performance.

Nicholas fought off his fatigue and looked around the company. Nerve ends were still raw, mouths were still dry and faces were still lack-lustre; but he sensed that the worst was past. They were professionals. The ordeal of the wait would evanesce into the excitement of the performance, and nobody would let himself down. Lord Westfield's Men would survive with honour. He actually began to look forward to it.

Resplendent in his Italian doublet and Spanish cape, Lawrence Firethorn sidled over to whisper in his ear.

'Should I do it again, Nick?'

'What?'

'Speak to the troops.'

'Oh, no.'

'Have I done enough to lift them already?'

'More than enough,' said Nicholas tactfully.

'Good, good.'

'Lead by example now.'

It was, as ever, sound advice and Firethorn would take

it. He walked away and went through his first speech in a hissed gabble. His book holder had just prevented him from causing even further disarray. The fragile calm which had now descended on the tiring-house would be preserved.

Sunshine gilded the tall, cylindrical structure of the playhouse and turned the arena into a chequered arrangement of light and shadow. The warmth of the sun produced more sweat and smell among the penny stinkards in the pit, and promoted the sale of beer, wine and water. By the same token, it caused mild discomfort in the galleries among the over-dressed gallants and the corseted ladies. There was no breeze to alleviate the heat. George Dart would be needed as the west wind.

It was a glittering occasion. In noise, bustle, eagerness, vulgarity, style, colour, character and high fashion, it even outdid *God Speed the Fleet*. On a glorious afternoon in an English summer, The Curtain was truly a microcosm of the capital. All classes were accounted for, all tastes included. Courtiers displayed themselves above while criminals concealed themselves below. The middling sort were there in profusion. Accents varied, timbres differed. Wit, repartee, banter and foul abuse were in play. High intelligence and bovine illiteracy shared the same space. The wooden circumference enclosed a veritable city.

Lord Westfield was there to enjoy the reflected glory of his company and to toss down patronising smiles and waves to the actors. Dark, stocky and of medium height, he wore a doublet that accentuated his paunch and a hat that prevented anyone behind him from seeing the stage. There was a wilful extravagance about Westfield that showed itself in the excesses of his apparel and the size of his entourage. A cup of wine seemed always in his hand, a smile upon his lips. He was a middle-aged sybarite with all the defects that that implied, but his love of the theatre was genuine and his knowledge of its workings was close.

Sitting diametrically opposite him in another of the lords' rooms was the Earl of Banbury, there to mock and denigrate rather than to be entertained. He picked fussily at his goatee beard and passed disparaging remarks about the players. His own company was going through a comparatively lean patch and envy was never far away. Catching Westfield's eye across the playhouse, he gave a dismissive wave with his fingers and turned away, thus missing the expressive scowl on the other's face.

Lady Rosamund Varley made a startling entrance. As soon as she settled in her seat, necks craned and eyes popped. She was a rich blend of blues and whites and yellows, and there was no dress to match her. Happily conscious of the attention she was getting, she bestowed a radiant smile on the world.

Roger Bartholomew remained stonily silent amid the gathering tumult. Everything he saw fed his hate, everything he heard served to swell his rage. Instead of being a celebrated poet with the acclaim he deserved, he was an unsung nonentity with cruel wounds he did not merit. Something darker than envy, and deeper than vengeance, had wormed its way into his brain. It caused a persistent throb in his veined forehead.

Exiled from the stage that he coveted, he would make his bid for attention. They would all take note of him this time. His plan had the riveting simplicity of its own desperation. It was a searing drama in one unforgettable line. The throbbing in his head got worse. Bartholomew would soon cure it.

Applause greeted the arrival of the trumpeter and the hoisting of the flag. This was no routine performance. Gossip had been at work. Danger lay at the heart of the enterprise. Lord Westfield's Men had been dogged by fate. A hired man was murdered, a young apprentice was injured, a book holder was attacked, and valuable property was stolen. It all added to the sublime feeling of dread, the possibility that something extraordinary was about to happen.

When the Prologue had introduced the play, *Gloriana Triumphant* took a grip on the audience that it never relinquished. Its secret lay in its relevance. Everyone could find themselves and their lives in it. The ancient domain of Albion was such an accurate portrait of the England they knew that some of the lines and conceits made them start. Edmund Hoode had found a rare blend. His play had a soaring purpose with a common touch.

Nicholas Bracewell's hand was much in evidence, and not just in the smooth stage management of the afternoon. He had been involved in the creation of the play and had supplied Hoode with endless details about the navy, its ships, its language, its traditions. Again, Nicholas had suggested a number of scenes which involved ordinary English seamen and the privations they suffered. It not only gave Hoode an opportunity for low comedy, it threw the world of admirals and captains into sharp relief.

One of the Armada myths of the day was that scarcely a hundred English lives were lost in the engagement. Though technically true, it did not take account of the immediate consequences of the battle. Despite widespread illness from rough seas and stale beer, the English seamen had served bravely. Then their water ran out and they were forced to drink their own urine. Typhus began to kill them like flies and some ships lacked enough men to weigh anchor.

Gloriana Triumphant did not dwell on all this but it was not ignored. A fuller, rounder, more honest picture of life at sea began to emerge. Samuel Ruff and Benjamin Creech were ideal seamen, tough, comic, long-suffering and endlessly loyal. The standees in the pit connected with the men at once.

But the real hero of the play and the afternoon was Lawrence Firethorn in a part that enabled him to use all his wolfish energy and all his technical tricks. He was by turns rough, romantic, outspoken, tongue-tied, base and noble. His wooing of the Queen was a mixture of subtle comedy and surging passion, and it was at this point that his performance was directed up at Lady Rosamund Varley. It was quite hypnotic.

Lady Rosamund was enthralled and Lord Westfield was enraptured. Even the Earl of Banbury was reduced to impotent silence. Roger Bartholomew was captivated in another way. The sight of Firethorn at once sharpened his urge to act and delayed the moment. It was as if Bartholomew wanted to build up maximum fury before he moved. His chance came in the fifth act.

Nicholas Bracewell had spent a long time devising the sea battle and it had a whole battery of complex effects. Agile stagekeepers were kept running around to provide various effects and George Dart was the western wind on a blustery day. Firethorn stood on the poop deck and yelled his orders. Ruff, Creech and the other seamen sweated on the gun deck below. The mast was secured by the ropes. The cannons were positioned on both sides of the vessel.

Through the open trap door in the middle of the stage could be heard the swishing of water. As the battle intensified, water was thrown up on stage to splash and soak and run. One of the seamen, apparently hit by a cannon ball, was knocked through the trap door and into the sea. It was a simple device but it pleased the audience and worked well.

Action became more frenetic as the play moved towards its climax. Firethorn shouted and bellowed to fine effect as his vessel came under intense bombardment. At the pull of a rope, half the rigging on the mast came adrift and fell to the stage. Explosions, fireworks, drums, cymbals, gongs and trumpets were used to augment the sound and din the ears. Metal trays of fire were slid onstage to suggest areas of the deck that had been hit. Buckets of water filled from the trap door were thrown over the flames to douse them.

Firethorn now gave the command and the cannon went off, not one as in the earlier play, but four in ascending order of volume. Even this effect was topped. As the booming echoed and reverberated around the playhouse, the figure of a small man in black climbed on to the balcony of the second gallery and launched himself off with a wild cry of despair.

Misjudging his leap, he landed in the folds of the sail, which broke his fall before hurtling him to the stage with sufficient force to knock him unconscious. It was a breathtaking moment and the audience had never seen anything like it. Neither had Lawrence Firethorn but he coped with the situation magnificently. Everyone believed it was part of the play and he did not break faith with them. With two extempore lines, he ordered his men to gather up the body of the Spanish dog and throw it overboard. Roger Bartholomew was lowered unceremoniously through the trap door.

In trying to ruin the play and achieve immortality by his public act of suicide, the tormented poet had enhanced the drama and simply given himself a worse headache.

Martin Yeo came on to knight her faithful sea dog then the piece ended to sustained applause and cheering. The whole company had been superb and overcome all their problems.

Nobody noticed that Bartholomew missed his bow.

Lady Rosamund Varley waited with friends in a private room and marvelled afresh at the remarkable stunt they had seen. *Gloriana Triumphant* was well-named. It had consigned *God Speed the Fleet* to a watery grave. Edmund Hoode's play would rule the waves.

Refreshments were served while the chat continued, then Lord Westfield brought in Lawrence Firethorn. He began with an elegant bow to Lady Rosamund and her radiant smile shone for him alone. Though he was introduced to the others in the room, he hardly heard their names. Only one person existed for him.

She extended a gloved hand for him to kiss.

'You were superb, Master Firethorn,' she congratulated.

'I was inspired by your presence, Lady Varley.'

'You know how to flatter, sir.'

'Truth needs no embellishment.'

Her brittle laugh rang out then she moved in closer.

'What is your next play to be?' she asked.

'Whatever you wish, Lady Varley.'

'Me, sir?'

'We have a large repertory. How would you care to see me?'

'As Hector.'

Their eyes were conversing freely and they talked with a pleasing directness. Firethorn was entranced by her coquettish manner and she was fascinated by his boldness.

'When would you have me play, Lady Varley?'

'As soon as it may suit you, sir.'

'The performance will be dedicated to you.'

'I would regard that as a signal honour, Master Firethorn.'

'Shall I send word when a date has been set?'

'I will be mortified if you do not.'

'Then it will be soon, that I can promise you.'

'Good,' she said evenly. 'I'll hold you to that, sir.'

'And I will hold you, Lady Varley.'

The assignation was made. In a crowded room, and at the first time of meeting, they had agreed to a tryst. He was quite transported. The afternoon had blessed him. It is not given to many men to defeat the Spanish Armada and conquer Lady Rosamund Varley within the space of a few hours.

Benjamin Creech left the playhouse with some of his fellows but he soon left them to head off on his own. Like the rest of the company, he had enjoyed the exhilaration of performance and it had left him with the same feeling of release. In his case, however, that feeling was tempered by something else. A man with divided loyalties finds it difficult to rejoice.

Nobody knew the taverns of London as intimately and as comprehensively as he did, so he had no difficulty in finding the one to which he had been summoned. A stroll along Eastcheap, a left turn, then a right, and he was there. At the sign of the Beetle and Wedge. Feeling his thirst deepen, he went in through the door and ducked beneath the low beam.

'Hello, Ben. Thank you for coming.'

'Aye.'

'Let me buy you a drink, old fellow. Wine or beer?'

'Beer.'

'You haven't changed, I see. Come and sit down.'

'Aye.'

Creech lowered himself into a chair opposite his host and looked up into the dark, satanic features. When the drinks were served, they raised their cups and clinked them together.

'To the future!' said his companion.

'That's as may be, sir.'

'You are in a position to help us a great deal, Ben.'

'Aye.'

'We are grateful.'

Creech watched him carefully and waited for him to make the first move. They had known each other for some years now. The man was clever, persuasive and resourceful with a dark streak in his nature that commended him to Creech. It gave the two of them something in common. He liked Giles Randolph.

Anne Hendrik was dining at home with her lodger and hearing about the extraordinary events at The Curtain that afternoon. She put her cutlery aside in astonishment when she heard about the dive that Roger Bartholomew had made from the second gallery.

'Was he badly hurt?' she said with concern.

'The surgeon recovered him,' explained Nicholas. 'He was taken back to his lodging to rest.'

'Why on earth did he do such a thing?'

'As a means of revenge against the company.'

'Because you rejected his play?'

'Master Bartholomew could not live with the disappointment. It preyed on his mind until his wits turned. The theatre can drive people to extremes at times, Anne.'

'I know that,' she said meaningfully.

'He was greatly vexed that his suicide jump failed,' Nicholas went on. 'Nothing he has done in a theatre has succeeded.'

'Poor fellow! He has been sorely tried.'

'Yes, Anne. But he did solve one mystery for us.'

'Mystery?'

'Those playbills that George Dart put up for us.'

'Master Bartholomew tore them down?' she said in amazement.

'Desperate men are pushed into desperate actions.'

Anne sighed and picked up her cutlery again. Then her eye went back to the bloodstained bandage around Nicholas's head. Her worries converged upon him once more.

'How is your own wound, Nick?' she said.

'My head is still attached to my body,' he joked lightly.

'Did you ask the surgeon to examine it?'

'Do not distress yourself about it, Anne. I am in good health now.' He raised a finger to touch the bandage. 'I wear this simply to excite your sympathy.'

'What of that man with the red beard?'

His manner changed at once and he became much more earnest.

'I have even more cause to find the rogue now,' he said with his jaw tightening. 'Redbeard and his accomplice have a lot to answer for and I mean to bring them to account.'

'But how?' she asked. 'In a city of over a hundred thousand people two men can easily stay hidden. How will you seek them out, Nick?'

'I may not have to do that,' he suggested.

'What do you mean?'

'Instead of going after them, I can wait till they come to me. For they will surely strike again.'

'Oh, Nick!' she sighed, fearing for him once more.

'*I* am not their intended victim,' he assured her. 'They had their chance to dispose of me last night and they did not take it. No, Anne, they are working to some complex plan.'

'I do not follow you.'

'It all started with the death of Will Fowler.'

'But that was an accident,' she argued. 'He lost his temper and was drawn into a quarrel. It was a random brawl.'

'That is what I thought,' he admitted, 'but I have grave doubts now. I believe that Will was deliberately murdered and that everything else which has happened – including the theft of our prompt book – is linked together.'

'What are you saying, Nick?'

'The real target is Lord Westfield's Men,' he said with conviction. 'Someone is trying to destroy the company.'

Chapter Eleven

Having found a rose in full bloom, Edmund Hoode lost his heart to her completely. He loved her ardently with a reckless disregard of her unsuitability for this honour. Rose Marwood was a goddess in an apron to him. Her blithe presence in his life gave it new hope and purpose. The agonies surrounding the performance of his play had left him even more in need of the heady consolations of romance, and he was driven by one desire. She must be his.

Alexander Marwood was a serious hindrance to his wishes. The landlord's vigorous melancholy drew much of its strength from his fears for his daughter. Obsessed with the notion that Rose would be debauched at any moment, he rarely let her out of his sight. One of the penalties of giving hospitality to a dramatic company at The Queen's Head was that every female on the premises was put at risk. To the harrowed landlord, all actors were promiscuous lechers without a moral scruple between them and the fact that two of his serving-wenches were with child confirmed this view.

Edmund Hoode was therefore baulked time and again. Whenever he stole upon the girl, her father appeared from nowhere with an errand which sent her running off. On the one occasion that Marwood himself did not prevent a casual meeting between the lover and his lass, it was the girl's mother who intervened. Tall, big-boned and generously plump, she had a hawk-eyed watchfulness that put Hoode to flight in seconds.

His chance eventually came, however, and he was equal to it. From the window of the rehearsal room, he saw his beloved stroll into the yard with her young brother. Hoode had already bribed one of the stagekeepers to assist him and he now signalled the fellow over. George Dart – the most loveless member of the company – had been chosen to bear Cupid's arrow.

'Yes, master?'

'Come with me, George.'

'Where are we going, sir?' asked the other, as he was hustled out and down a flight of stairs. 'Am I to perform that service for you now?'

'God willing!'

They reached the yard and Hoode glanced in through the open door of the taproom. Delighted that both Marwood and his wife were busy within, he gave Dart his orders.

'She talks over there with her brother.' He handed over a small scroll. 'Give this to her privily.'

'How, sir? The young fellow will see me.'

'Distract him in some way.'

'By what device?'

'Do your office and be quick about it.'

'I will try, sir.'

'You will succeed, George,' warned Hoode ominously. 'That missive is for her eyes only. Away!'

'Yes, master.'

Hoode stepped into the taproom and loitered near the door. Keeping one eye on the girl's parents, he watched the diminutive stagekeeper skip across the yard. George Dart excelled himself. He reached the couple, stepped between them and relayed a message to the boy before guiding him firmly away. Rose Marwood was left alone, wondering how the scroll had got into her hand.

When she studied the seal, a look of pleasant surprise lit up her whole face. Edmund Hoode positively glowed.

'Open it, my love,' he whispered. 'Open it.'

She obeyed his command as if she had heard it, breaking the seal and unrolling the parchment. Her surprise now gave way to bewilderment. With a frown of concentration, she stared at the sonnet for a few moments then turned it upside down to regard it anew from a different angle.

Hoode was aghast. He had expected his fourteen lines to wing their way straight to her heart and make her melt with passion. It had never even crossed his mind that this paragon, this ethereal beauty, this image of perfection could have any flaw. The truth was forced upon him with brutal suddenness. Rose Marwood could not read.

It had been going on for several days before a pattern began to emerge. Hugh Wegges noted that a few small items were missing from the tiring-house, Peter Digby was irritated by the disappearance of some sheet music, Thomas Skillen lost his favourite broom, and John Tallis could not find his cap. Other instances of petty pilfering went unreported. The next victim was Samuel Ruff.

He and Nicholas Bracewell had enjoyed a drink together after a day's rehearsal at The Queen's Head. They were seated in the taproom and Ruff made to pay the reckoning. When he opened his purse, however, it was empty.

'My money has been stolen!'

'How much was in the purse?' asked Nicholas.

'No more than a few groats but they were honestly earned.'

'And dishonestly taken, it would seem.'

'When could it have happened?' said Ruff, as baffled as he was annoyed. 'I've not been in crowds where pickpockets could easily set on me. My whole day has been spent here among my fellows.'

Nicholas sighed. 'We have a thief in our midst.'

'Here?'

'You are not the only victim, Sam. I have had complaints all week. Someone has a wandering hand.'

'Hunt the villain down!'

'We will. But do not trouble yourself about the reckoning. I will settle it this time.'

'Only until I am paid,' insisted Ruff. 'I will owe you the money until then, Nick. I always pay my debts.'

'It is such a small amount, Sam. Hardly a debt.'

'I felt nothing,' admitted Ruff, staring in dismay at his empty purse. 'He is a light-fingered rascal, whosoever he is.'

'When did you last take coins out yourself?'

'At noon. To pay for my food and drink.'

'And since then?'

'The purse has been at my waist ever since.' A memory nudged him. 'Except for a few minutes when Hugh Wegges made me try on a new costume. There were a dozen or more of us in the tiring-house.'

'Can you recall who they were?'

'No. I had no call to pay heed. Why?'

'One of them is the thief.'

Samuel Ruff was deeply upset by it all. It had been some time since he had earned a regular wage and he had learned to husband his money carefully. The thought that one of his own fellows might have robbed him hurt badly. He plunged into gloom.

'This is an omen,' he decided.

'Of what?'

'The tide is turning against me. It had to come.' A sigh of regret was followed by a helpless shrug. 'I was happy to belong to the company until this.'

'We are happy to have you, Sam.'

'It has meant everything to me, Nick, and I cannot

thank you enough for your part in it all.' Embarrassment made him lower his head. 'You met me at . . . a difficult time . . . when I was . . .'

'You do not have to explain,' said Nicholas kindly to spare him any further discomfort. 'I understand.'

Samuel Ruff had been brought back from the dead as an actor. Having resigned himself to leaving the profession, he had been given one last chance to redeem himself and had done so admirably. The tiny spark inside him had been fanned into flame again and he had revelled in the world that he loved. Nicholas had watched it with pleasure. Samuel Ruff had been given back his dignity.

'And now it is all over,' said the actor sadly.

'That is not so, Sam.'

'But Master Gill is adamant. He will not tolerate me.'

'He is only one of the sharers,' Nicholas pointed out. 'The others know your true value, Sam.'

'They would still rather let me go than Master Gill.'

'It may not come to that.'

'Please try to help me!' begged Ruff, clutching at the other's wrist. 'I am desperate to stay with Westfield's Men. No other company would take me now. Please, Nick, use what influence you have on my behalf.'

'I will,' promised Nicholas. 'Take heart.'

'And what of Master Gill?'

'We must study to persuade him.'

'Will he submit, think you?'

'Every man can have his mind changed.'

'I truly hope so!' He released Nicholas's wrist and

sat back with a tired smile. 'Such a change in my life! When we two first met in that tavern, I was minded to go home.'

'You did go home, Sam.'

'I did?'

'To the theatre.'

Ruff acknowledged the remark with a nod then his smile became more confidential. He leaned across the table.

'Shall I make confession to you, Nick?'

'Of what?'

'I hate cows. I cannot abide the beasts.'

'We saved you from that,' said Nicholas with a grin.

'Oh, you did so much more, my friend!'

When Marwood had been paid for the ale, they went out together into the yard. Evening was starting to close in on what had been a fine, clear day. They reached the main gate and paused at the archway. Ruff's emotion showed through again.

'I could not bear to lose this, Nick!'

He shook the book holder's hand warmly then strode off through the archway to head towards his lodging. Nicholas cast one more glance around the yard and would have gone out into Gracechurch Street himself if his attention had not been caught by a sign of movement at a window. It was the tiring-house.

Nicholas was troubled. Everyone else from the company had gone home and the room had been locked up to protect the valuable costumes that were stored there. His first instinct was to cross to the window and peer in but that might alert whoever was inside. He decided instead to go back into the taproom to confront Marwood.

'Could I have the key to the tiring-house, please?'

'It has not been returned, Master Bracewell.'

'Then who has it?'

'I have no idea, sir.'

'Give me the key to the adjacent room.'

'What is amiss?' asked the worried landlord.

'Oh, nothing,' said Nicholas casually, trying to make light of it. 'I daresay that Hugh Wegges is working late on a costume.' He took the proffered key. 'Thank you, Master Marwood. I will return it very soon.'

Nicholas hurried off to the tiring-house and tried the door. It was locked. He went around to the door of the adjacent room and let himself quietly in. Crossing the floorboards with a gentle tread, he reached the door that connected with the tiring-house and put his ear to it. Muffled sounds came from within and he thought he heard a costume swish. He had no doubt what was happening. The thief was at work again.

Lifting the latch with painful slowness, he eased the door wide enough open to look into the tiring-house. He was so startled by what he saw that he had to blink. It was the most unexpected discovery of all and he could not at first believe it.

In the corner of the room, Barnaby Gill was kissing a young woman. They were locked in a tender embrace and the actor was behaving with almost knightly courtesy, taking his pleasure softly and with evident respect for his lady. If it had not been so astonishing, the sight would have touched Nicholas.

He opened the door further and it creaked on its hinges. The couple immediately sprang guiltily apart and swung round to face him. He was given another severe jolt. The woman wore the costume and auburn wig that would be used in the next play.

It was Stephen Judd.

The apprentice turned red and Barnaby Gill blustered.

'What business have you here, sir?' he demanded.

'I saw something through the window.'

'It is nothing that need concern you. I was giving the boy some instruction, that is all. We are done now.'

'Yes, Master Gill,' said Nicholas evenly.

'You may leave us,' added the other loftily.

'I will see Stephen safe home first.'

'Get out!'

There was an expressive venom in the command but Nicholas held his ground and met the other's glare. Barnaby Gill gradually backed off as cold reason searched him out. If the book holder reported what he had witnessed, the sharer would be placed in a very awkward predicament. Firethorn and the others were well aware of Gill's preference for boys but it was mutually understood that he would not pursue or corrupt the apprentices. His brief moment with Stephen Judd could be fatal.

Nicholas stared him out. In those long, silent minutes, a bargain was struck between the two men. In return for saying nothing of what he had seen, Nicholas would keep

Samuel Ruff in the company. It was an uneasy compromise but Gill yielded to it.

Stephen Judd was still flushed with guilt, which suggested that this had been the first time that he had succumbed to the actor's blandishments. Nicholas was determined that it would also be the last time. A serious talk with the boy was now due.

'Get changed, Stephen,' he said.

Nervous and confused, the apprentice turned to Gill for guidance. The actor made a vain attempt to take control of the situation and waved a dismissive hand at the book holder.

'You need not wait for him, sir,' he said fussily. '*I* will take the lad back to his lodging. We bid you adieu.'

'Get changed,' repeated Nicholas quietly.

After a long pause, Gill gave the boy a curt nod and the latter began to remove the costume and wig. Nicholas opened the door fully and stepped to one side. Barnaby Gill took his cue. Without a backward glance, he marched quickly away from the scene of his latest disappointment. Another conquest had been lost.

Sunday morning found Lawrence Firethorn in his accustomed place in the parish church of St Leonard's, Shoreditch, with his wife, children, apprentices and servants. He sang lustily, prayed zealously and stayed awake throughout a long and wayward sermon on a text from the Gospel According to St Mark. To all outward appearances, he was a contented family man at his regular devotions, and nobody in the full pews would have guessed that the matronly woman who stood, sat or knelt beside him was harbouring such murderous thoughts about her husband.

The Spanish Armada had served to strengthen the Protestant church immeasurably and to extend its hold over some of its less devout souls. Fear of invasion sent everyone hurrying to matins and vespers to pray for deliverance, and the English victory was celebrated in every pulpit in the land before a packed and grateful congregation. During that summer and autumn of 1588, churchwardens in town and country alike had far less cause to tax any feckless parishioners with poor attendance. Armada fever and its association with Rome swelled the flocks of even the most undeserving shepherds, and banished any nostalgia for the glories of the old religion.

Lawrence Firethorn had never been lax in attending to his spiritual needs. Old enough to remember the Latin liturgy that was restored during Mary's reign, he had been pleased when Elizabeth's accession brought a return to the Protestant service. He had quickly fallen under the spell of the Books of Common Prayer and the beauty of its language was a gift to an actor of his stature. The colour and ritual of the church had a theatricality which appealed to him and he was always ready to learn something from a priest who brought histrionic skills into the pulpit.

As he went down on his knees once more at the end of the service, his eyes did not close in prayer. They were fixed on the altar and a beatific smile covered his face. Margery Firethorn took a sidelong glance at him and wondered if he had been transfigured, such was the light that shone from him. But her husband was not suffused with the joy of Christian worship. What mesmerised him was the colour of the altar cloth – a royal blue embroidered with gold. It precisely matched the hue of the bodice that Lady Rosamund Varley had worn to The Curtain.

The text of the sermon wafted back into his ears.

'Behold, I send my messenger before thy face . . .'

Nicholas Bracewell wasted no time in passing on the good news to Samuel Ruff. Though concealing the circumstances in which it had occurred, he told the actor about Barnaby Gill's change of mind. Ruff was so delighted that he gave the book holder a spontaneous hug that crushed the breath out of him.

'This gladdens my heart, Nick!'

'They are happy tidings for us all.'

'You must have a persuasive tongue in your head.'

'I used reason and art. No more.'

'Should I speak with Master Gill on the matter?'

'That would not be wise,' said Nicholas hurriedly. 'Put your past differences behind you, Sam. I am sure that Master Gill will not wish to raise the issue again.'

They had arrived at The Queen's Head to start a morning rehearsal and they were standing outside the tiring-house. Nicholas could not have given his friend a more welcome present than the intelligence that he would remain with Westfield's Men. Ruff's normally serious face was alive with pleasure.

A booming voice interrupted their conversation.

'Nicholas, dear heart!'

'Good morning, master.'

'Good morning, sir,' muttered Ruff, withdrawing a few paces.

Lawrence Firethorn bestowed an amiable grin on the hired man then turned to Nicholas. The latter knew exactly what to expect.

'You wish me to carry a message for you?'

'Without delay, Nick.'

'Could not George Dart do the office?'

'No!' thundered Firethorn. 'I could not insult the recipient of my missive by sending such a mean bearer. This is a man's work, Nick, and must not be left to some squirrel-faced youth.'

'But I am needed here,' argued the other.

'Someone else will hold the book in your absence, dear fellow. You are called to a higher duty.'

Firethorn took a letter from beneath his doublet and planted a resounding kiss on it before handing it over.

'See it delivered.'

'Yes, master.'

'Wait for an answer.'

'I will.'

The actor adopted the pose which the vicar of St Leonard's had favoured in the pulpit on the previous day, and he spoke with holy resonance.

'"Behold, I send my messenger before thy face . . ."'

Breaking into irreverent laughter, he clapped Nicholas

on the back and went off into the tiring-house to spread his feeling of joy more liberally among the company.

Samuel Ruff stepped forward with raised eyebrows.

'Am I right in guessing who the lady is?' he said.

'Yes, Sam.'

'Does Master Firethorn *know* her reputation?'

'It is one of the snares that leads him on.'

'He might be less enthralled by her, if he knew what I do, Nick. Lady Rosamund Varley has been very free with her favours.'

'That is no secret.'

'This may be,' suggested Ruff, lowering his voice. 'Is he aware that she was once the mistress of Lord Banbury?'

Cheapside was the largest and noisiest of the London markets, with scores of country people standing shoulder to shoulder behind their trestle tables, exhibiting their wares in baskets on the ground or holding them up in their hands. Opened early in the morning by the tolling of a bell, the market was a swirling mass of humanity in a cauldron of sound and smell. The best poultry and milk was sold in Leadenhall Street, and those in search of fish would go to Fish Street Hill or to the quays of Queenshythe and Billingsgate, but it was Cheapside that offered the widest choice and brought in the greatest crowds.

As he made his way past the endless stalls, Nicholas Bracewell had much to occupy his mind. He was uncomfortable about his role as an intermediary between Lawrence Firethorn and his latest inamorata. Apart from his fondness for the actor's wife, he was never happy when he was brought in to help stage manage Firethorn's private life. A new and disturbing element had now been added. If Lady Rosamund Varley had had such an intimate relationship with Lord Banbury, it was conceivable that she was being used by him as a way of attacking a rival company. By distracting Lawrence Firethorn, she could do a lot of harm to Westfield's Men.

Nicholas walked on towards the Gothic bulk of St Paul's. Even though lightning had deprived it of its tower, the building still dominated the skyline and acted as a magnet for the citizens of London. Houses and shops crowded the precinct walls, and an army of criminals found their richest pickings both inside and outside the cathedral. Absorbed as he was in thought, Nicholas kept a careful watch for nips and foists who might try to take his purse.

By the time he reached Ludgate, he was having deep misgivings about his part in promoting an amour which might damage the whole company. The sight of the Bel Savage Inn nearby stirred Nicholas. It figured prominently in his life because it was there that he first fell in love with the mystique of the theatre during an exhilarating outdoor performance given by the Queen's Men. On a cold afternoon in April, the Bel Savage had determined his future and directed him to Lord Westfield's Men. With all its glaring faults, he loved the company and was ready to defend it from any threat. As he gazed affectionately at the inn, he came to a decision. He would somehow scupper the new romance. In the interests of the company, Lawrence

Firethorn had to be saved from the consequences of his rising lust.

Nicholas hurried out past the City walls and along Fleet Street to the Strand. When he reached the looming opulence of Varley House, he delivered the letter but was told by a maid-in-waiting that her mistress was not at home. He was glad that there was no reply to carry back with him.

As he set off towards the City again, his mind turned once more to his quest. Will Fowler had begged him to pursue the murderer and not a day had passed when Nicholas did not renew his pledge. Redbeard would be found.

He was striding along Fleet Street when an idea brought him to a dead halt. The battered girl at the Hope and Anchor had talked about the raw wounds on her client's back, and Nicholas had wondered if the man had been dragged through the streets at a cart's tail and whipped for some minor offence. He now realised that Redbeard may have gained his scars elsewhere.

Swinging off to the right, he headed at speed in the direction of Bridewell. Built as a royal palace by Henry VIII on the banks of the Fleet River, it was a huge, rambling structure of dark red brick set around three courtyards. Members of the royal family had lived there, visiting dignitaries from abroad had stayed there, and the place had been leased to the French Ambassador for some eight years. Since the time of Edward, however, its inhabitants had been of more common stock.

Bridewell was a hospital and a prison.

Orphans, vagrants, petty offenders and disorderly

women now stayed at the former palace and its regimen was strict. When Nicholas reached the building, he was given a vivid demonstration of its methods of discipline. A crowd of vagrants had just arrived at Bridewell and they were being whipped in public by the City beadles. The adults were each given a dozen strokes of the whip while the younger ones received half a dozen. With their backs bare, they whined and howled as the savage punishment was enforced.

Several onlookers had gathered to enjoy the spectacle of human suffering, but Nicholas had to turn away. It gave him no pleasure to see flesh sliced open and blood spurt out. During his time at sea, he had been forced to witness many floggings and the cruelty of it all had always turned his stomach. The short, wiry man standing beside Nicholas did not share his qualms. He roared on the beadles and cheered as each stroke landed.

'They should give a taste of the whip to *them* as well,' he averred. 'A hundred lashes for each one!'

'Who do you mean, sir?' asked Nicholas.

'Them!' retorted the man. 'The Spanish prisoners. Captives from the Armada. They should be flogged every morning!'

'Why, sir?'

'For speaking such a scurvy tongue!'

The man emitted a harsh cackle before turning back to his sport. He was soon reviling the victims again, exhorting the beadles to strike harder and revelling in each cry of anguish that was beaten from the shredded bodies. Nicholas despised him with all his soul yet he was grateful to him. The man had reminded him that Bridewell was being used to house captured Spaniards and Catholic prisoners.

Without quite knowing why, Nicholas Bracewell felt that he had just made an important discovery.

He walked away with growing excitement.

Chapter Twelve

Firmness of purpose had always been Margery Firethorn's hallmark. When she committed herself to a course of action, she held to it with single-minded determination. Her husband did everything in his power to coax and soften her but his most cunning wiles yielded no fruit. He was treated with such cold disdain, then lashed with such a hot tongue, that his domestic life seemed to consist entirely of fire and ice. Margery would not relent until he confessed the truth to her and there was no way that he could bring himself to do that. Stalemate therefore prevailed at the house in Shoreditch.

'Good morning to you, my angel.'

'Be silent, sir.'

'Leave off these jests, Margery. Let us be friends.'

'Is that your desire?'

'Nothing would please me more, my love.'

'Then satisfy my wishes, Lawrence.'

'I prostrate myself before you.'

'Who *is* she?'

He lapsed into his usual silence and she clambered out of the four-poster to carry her bitterness through a new day. There had been a time when Martin Yeo, John Tallis and Stephen Judd had crept along at night to the bedchamber of their host, and sniggered together in the dark as they heard the rhythmical thump of the mattress within. Such nocturnal bliss was a thing of the past for the couple – and for the apprentices – and Firethorn knew that he would need an armed escort and a pack of dogs if he were ever to mount his wife in her present mood. Only the thought of Lady Rosamund Varley sustained him.

Estranged from her husband, Margery dedicated her energies to running the household. She tackled her chores more eagerly, nurtured her children more lovingly, upbraided the servants more often, and kept the apprentices under even closer surveillance.

'How is that ankle now, Dick?'

'I am recovered, mistress.'

'There is no more pain?'

'Not from my foot,' said Richard Honeydew. 'But I still hurt when I think of what I missed at The Curtain.'

'It was an act of God.'

'My accident?'

'A perfect case of divine intervention, I warrant.'

'To what end, mistress?' he asked. 'Was God so displeased with my performance as Gloriana that he prevented it?'

'No, child. He wished to bring something to my attention.'

'What was it?'

'A trifling piece of jewellery.'

They were in the garden and Margery was gathering up herbs to put into a stone pot. The autumnal sky was overcast with dark clouds weighting down the heavens. Margery took some fennel between her fingers and crushed it to sniff its aroma. She moved on in search of other herbs, speaking over her shoulder as she did so.

'Do you have anything to report to me?'

'About what, mistress?'

'Those three rascals. Have they been up to their tricks?'

'No.'

'Do not be afraid to tell me, Dick. They will not harm you.'

'There is nothing to tell.'

It was true. The others now left him alone. Martin Yeo felt he had reaffirmed his position with *Gloriana Triumphant*, Stephen Judd had withdrawn, and John Tallis, the lantern-jawed juvenile, had neither the wit nor the bravado to act without the support of his co-mates. They still did not befriend Richard but the persecution had ceased.

'They are jealous of you,' said Margery.

'I have done so little compared with them.'

'You will do so much more in time,' she prophesied.

'That is what they fear. Your talent.' She turned round to face him. 'Do you have ambitions, Dick?'

'Yes, mistress.'

'What are they?'

'To be a good actor.'

'Not a great one?'

'I could never be as great as Master Firethorn,' he said with humility, not noticing the way that her expression froze at the mention of her husband. 'But I can study to be good. My other ambition is to play at court.'

'That opportunity may not be too far away, Dick.'

'Nothing could compare with that!' he announced with joyful sincerity. 'I was cheated out of my chance to play the role of Her Majesty. I could ask for no greater recompense than to act before her. That is ambition enough for anyone!'

His young face glowed with innocent hope.

Anne Hendrik was grateful for his company at Southwark Market. Not only was Nicholas able to carry what she bought from the stalls, his muscular presence cleared a path through the crowd and spared her the attentions of many undesirables. She was always happy to be in public with him, and felt that their friendship took on a new meaning when they engaged in simple chores together. Anne examined some fruit with a knowing eye, but her mind was on other matters.

'It is a blessing that the child was safely delivered,' she said. 'I feared that she might miscarry.'

'Because of the shock of Will's death?'

'Less tragedies have altered the course of nature.'

'Not in Susan's case, thank God,' he said with a smile.

'No, mother and daughter are both well.'

Nicholas sighed. 'The pity of it is that Will Fowler never lived to see his bonny child.'

A letter had arrived from St Albans the previous day to tell them of the birth of a daughter to Susan Fowler. Since neither she nor her parents could write, the missive had been penned by the parish priest. Nicholas and Anne had been delighted to hear the news but they were puzzled by one item in the letter. Susan Fowler had thanked them for a gift of a crib.

'We sent no crib,' said Anne. 'Why did she think we did?'

'It must have been left for her to find,' he suggested. 'A secret offering with the sender unnamed. We should feel flattered that she thought of us, Anne. Susan must believe us capable of such kindness.'

'If only we had been. I will send another present for the child. It has many needs, I am sure, and few enough of us to care.'

She bought some apples, pears and plums and put them in the already overflowing basket that Nicholas was holding. It was time to head back. As they turned their steps toward home, Anne Hendrik tucked herself in beside him and puzzled over something.

'Nick . . .'

'Yes?'

'If *we* did not send that gift – then who did?'

It was a problem which exercised them all the way back.

239

Because they had set out so early, it was still well before eight when they reached the house. Nicholas took the basket inside and helped her to unload it, then he had a frugal breakfast before going out again. His working day would be another long one.

Taking a boat across the river, he alighted on the north bank and struck off towards Gracechurch Street. There was a performance at The Queen's Head that afternoon and they were due to rehearse *Marriage and Mischief* – a seasoned comedy from their repertoire – until noon. Barnaby Gill would take the central role of a jealous husband who is driven into a demonic rage by the apparent infidelity of his wife. Stephen Judd was cast as his spouse.

In view of what he had seen them doing in the tiring-house, Nicholas felt that the drama would have extra piquancy for him. The actor and the apprentice would act out intimacies in public which would be abhorrent in private. The audience who would laugh and mock the old husband's plight would have no inkling of the poignancy that lay behind it.

Nicholas was still meditating on the layered irony of the situation when something claimed his attention with a stunning immediacy. Benjamin Creech was standing in a shop doorway near the inn, deep in conversation with a tall, hulking man.

It was Redbeard.

'Hold the villain!'

The shout burst forth from his lips as he broke into a run.

240

'Stop him!'

Alerted by the yells, Redbeard looked up to see Nicholas tearing towards him. He reacted swiftly, spinning on his heel and haring off towards Fenchurch Street in a wild panic. Shoppers were scattered, vendors knocked aside, stalls overturned, and dogs sent howling as the tall figure charged recklessly on through the press. Nicholas chased him at full pelt, oblivious to the irate cries and loud protests he left in his wake. The whole street was now in an uproar.

Redbeard was moving fast but Nicholas found additional speed to close on him. He got within ten yards of his quarry before he came to grief. Sensing that the pursuit was closing in, Redbeard suddenly stopped to grab a low cart and swung it around himself into Nicholas's path. Before he could stop himself, the book holder had gone headfirst over the obstacle and landed on the ground in a huge pool of cracked shells and egg yolk. The owner of the cart immediately grappled with him and demanded compensation for his ruined produce. By the time that Nicholas shook him off, it was too late. Redbeard had vanished in the crowd.

Trudging back to The Queen's Head with disconsolate steps, Nicholas threw apologies right and left to the baying multitude. It was only when he reached the inn that he remembered Benjamin Creech. He straightened up and went quickly in through the main gate. Creech was on the far side of the yard, chatting with one of the journeymen. Nicholas hurried over to him, took him aside and pinned him up against a wall.

'Who was that man?' he demanded.

'Take your hands off me!' growled Creech.

'Who *was* he?' pressed Nicholas, tightening his grip.

'I have never seen the fellow before.'

'That is an arrant lie, Ben!'

'You wrong me, Master Bracewell.'

'I saw you talking with the man even now.'

'He stopped me in the street and asked directions to Islington.' Creech struggled to escape. 'Leave go of me!'

'You *know* him!' accused Nicholas.

'He was a stranger to me until this day.'

'Well, he is no stranger to me, Ben. I have seen that cur before. He is the man who murdered Will Fowler.'

'Then I wish I had shaken the fellow's hand.'

The smirk on Creech's face made Nicholas explode with anger. He banged the actor hard against the wall then hurled him to the ground. Creech slowly picked himself up. All his resentment and bile came bubbling to the surface now and his lip curled in contempt. Lowering his shoulder, he charged into Nicholas and knocked him back several yards. Creech was a powerful man and he would fight to the finish.

But Nicholas was roused now. The insult to Will Fowler made something snap inside him. He closed with Creech again and the two of them wrestled violently, watched by a small knot of people who came running over. Creech got his adversary in a bear hug but Nicholas was strong enough to break it and send the other reeling backwards. As Creech lunged at him again, he met a flurry of punches that stopped him in his tracks. Shaking his head to clear it, Creech swung wild punches of his own but Nicholas eluded them with ease.

Panting hard, the actor stopped for a moment to gather his strength then he charged in again with fists flying. Nicholas was ready for him. Throwing Creech off balance with a clever feint, he sank a punch into the man's solar plexus which took all his breath away. As his opponent doubled up with pain, Nicholas despatched him with a blow to the chin. Creech slumped to the ground in a heap and a few cheers went up from the spectators.

Nicholas rubbed the raw knuckles on his right hand and gazed down at Creech. The man had deserved his drubbing for his callous remark about Will Fowler but he clearly did not know Redbeard. Annoyed with himself for losing his temper, Nicholas stooped down to help the fallen man up.

'Keep off!' snarled Creech, pushing him away.

Staggering to his feet, the actor wiped some of the blood away from his mouth and shot Nicholas a look of malevolent hatred. Benjamin Creech then lumbered out through the main gate of the yard. Lord Westfield's Men had just lost a member of the company.

The performance that afternoon passed in a kind of blur for Nicholas Bracewell. Though he held the book for *Marriage and Mischief* and discharged his duties with his customary efficiency, his mind was elsewhere. The image of Redbeard stayed before him. He was galled that he had come so close to the man then let him get away.

Creech's absence had caused no major problems because he was only playing two small parts. Samuel Ruff took over one of them and the other was excised altogether. Barnaby Gill kept the audience rocking with mirth at his comic rages and Stephen Judd brought a willing competence to the role of the wife. In the small but telling part of a maidservant, Richard Honeydew showed real flair and his pert banter caused much amusement. Edmund Hoode, as a doddering old man, equipped his character with gout, deafness and a pronounced stutter in order to reap his laughs.

Lawrence Firethorn took the romantic lead. Though not as long a role as Gill's, it was equally effective and it glittered through the afternoon. Barnaby Gill held sway over the coarser appetites of the groundlings but it was Firethorn who appealed to the more sensitive palates in the galleries. He made his speeches ring with passion and vibrate with subtle innuendo. When he delivered the Epilogue in rhyming couplets, he addressed each honeyed word to Lady Rosamund Varley, who was gracing the occasion with another of her spectacular dresses. Delighted yet again with his performance, she threw something down to him as he came out to take his bow.

Nicholas was relieved that it was all over and that he had not made any blunders through lack of concentration. He now braced himself for the reproaches that were to come. Because of him, Benjamin Creech stalked out of the company on the day of a performance. Part of the book holder's job was to prevent violence, not to provoke it. Firethorn would certainly take him to task now that *Marriage and Mischief* could be put safely back in the playchest again. Fighting in the company was something that the actor would not tolerate. It was possible that Nicholas's own future with Westfield's Men was at risk.

'Ah! There you are, you varlet!'

Lawrence Firethorn came sweeping into the tiring-house like an avenging angel. He made straight for the book holder and lifted him bodily from his stool.

'Come with me, Nick!'

'Why, master?'

'We must have private conference.'

Firethorn dragged him off to the room at the rear, banished its occupants with a peremptory wave, then shut the door firmly behind them. Alone with the book holder, he regarded him seriously from beneath curling eyebrows.

'The day of judgement has arrived, sir,' he began.

'It was my fault,' apologised Nicholas frankly. 'I should not have let Creech put me to choler like that.'

'Creech?'

'His loss may yet be a gain, master. I believe that Creech may have been responsible for all our recent thefts.'

'Forget Creech,' said Firethorn irritably. 'I came to speak on a mightier theme.'

With a sinking sensation, Nicholas understood what he meant.

'Lady Rosamund Varley?'

'She has replied to my entreaty, Nick.' He produced the red rose which she had thrown to him on stage. 'With this.'

'Oh.'

Firethorn sniffed the rose and savoured its fragrance. A huge grin split his face in two like a sliced melon. He slapped his thigh with glee.

'She is mine!' he exclaimed. 'The day of judgement has come and I have not been found wanting. This is the appointed night for our tryst. We will need your assistance, Nick.'

'What must I do?' asked the other, hesitantly.

'Smooth the wrinkled path to love, dear heart!'

'How, master?'

Firethorn gave him instructions. He was to repair with all speed to the Bel Savage Inn on Ludgate Hill and hire their best rooms for the night. Supper was to be served at a stipulated hour and there were precise details of the menu. Even the nature of the lighting was specified. When he had finalised all these arrangements, Nicholas was to return to The Queen's Head and convey a message of confirmation to Lady Rosamund Varley, who would still be with Lord Westfield and his entourage in their private room.

'May I ask one question?' said Nicholas.

'Ask away, dear fellow.'

'Why have you chosen the Bel Savage?'

'Because,' replied the other, letting his chest swell with pride, 'it was there that I first gave the world my Hector!'

He bowed extravagantly to imagined applause then left the room with a flourish. Nicholas gave a wan smile. At a time when much more urgent concerns pressed upon him, he was being used to promote Firethorn's adultery. He did not forget Lady Varley's old association with Lord Banbury and his earlier decision stood. He would emulate the play which had been staged that afternoon.

Nicholas would cause mischief in a marriage.

The injustice of it all gnawed at the very entrails of Edmund Hoode. A sonnet which achieved its desired objective for another man had signally faded for its author. The mellifluous verse which helped to enchant Lady Rosamund Varley had been wasted on Rose Marwood. The landlord's daughter was beyond the reach of poetry.

The poet was devastated but there was worse to come yet. When he changed out of his costume after the performance, he went to the taproom for some refreshment. Alexander Marwood pounced. The landlord's twitch was in full operation.

'A word with you, Master Hoode.'

'What ails you, sir?'

'A most grave matter. There is lechery abroad.'

'Indeed?'

'Read the sinful document for yourself.'

He thrust a small scroll at the other and Hoode found himself staring down at his own sonnet. It had not been handled with kindness. The parchment was creased and covered with crude fingerprints. It was symbolic.

'Well, sir?' demanded Marwood.

'It is . . . moderately well-written,' said Hoode, pretending to read the lines for the first time. 'How came this into your hands, sir?'

'It was given to my daughter by some scoundrel.'

'Who was he?'

'Rose could not say. It happened so quickly.'

'Then how may I help you?'

'By finding the author of this vile stuff,' insisted the landlord. 'I tried to speak to Master Firethorn about it but he brushed me off. I turn to you instead. We must root out this fiend.'

'Why, sir?'

'Why, sir? Because my daughter's virtue is in danger as long as this lascivious knave remains in your company. My wife is resolved, Master Hoode. The man must go.'

'Go?'

'We will not lie easy in our beds until he is unmasked. The villain means to ravish our daughter.'

'I see nothing of that in the sonnet.'

'It is between the lines,' hissed Marwood. He controlled his twitch long enough to deliver an ultimatum. 'My wife and I are agreed, sir. Unless he is driven out, we must henceforth close our doors to Westfield's Men.'

'But how do you know he belongs to the company?'

'We know,' said the other darkly.

Edmund Hoode felt his heart constrict. Instead of winning the favours of Rose Marwood, his sonnet had brought the full weight of her parents down upon him. The relationship between landlord and company was always uneasy. His poem had thrown it into jeopardy.

'Rose fetched it to us,' explained Marwood. 'She does not read. No more do I with any great skill, but my wife is educated. She read its bold message clear enough. My wife has a quick mind. You may have noticed.'

'Yes, yes,' agreed Hoode.

'She thinks that scroll might have a clue.'

'Clue?'

'At the bottom there,' said the landlord, jabbing a bony finger at the poem. 'Two letters are picked out, sir. *E* and *H*. Might they not be his initials?'

'Oh, I think not,' replied the poet, trying to put him off the scent. 'That is too obvious a device for the fellow. He works in deeper ways.' He stared at the sonnet and invention came to his aid. 'I think I have it, Master Marwood!'

'You know the villain's hand?'

'No, but I can guess at his name. There *is* a clue here if we can but unravel it. Read the opening lines.'

'Do it for me, sir. I am no scholar.'

'"Be mine, sweet creature, come unto thy love, O rarest rose, wilt not upon thy stem . . ."'

'Lechery in every word!' wailed the landlord.

'You see how the first letter is writ large?' said Hoode, thrusting the scroll under his nose. 'That *B* stands for Ben, I'll wager.'

'Ben who?'

'Look to that "sweet creature". There is our clue. Hidden in that "creature", I dare swear, is a certain Creech.'

'Ben Creech?'

'One of the hired men in the company.'

'I know him. A surly fellow who cannot hold his ale.'

'He is our man, sir.'

'Could such a man as that write *poetry*?'

'He paid some scribbler to write it for him,' argued Hoode. 'Creech has been eyeing your daughter, Master Marwood, and it comes as no surprise to me. We had trouble with the fellow when we played at The Saracen's Head in Islington. It was a serving-wench on that occasion. Creech is a hot-blooded rogue.'

'He must be sent on his way!' yelled Marwood vengefully.

'He already has been. Ben Creech is no longer with us.'

'Is this true?'

'It is an accident that heaven provides,' said the other easily. 'Danger has passed and your daughter is safe.'

'This news brings much relief, sir.'

'To me as well!' muttered Hoode with feeling. 'Tell me, Master Marwood. Did anyone read the sonnet to your daughter?'

'My wife did,' answered the landlord, twitching merrily. 'That was part of our concern, sir. Rose liked it. She is a fanciful girl and easily led astray. The poem touched her.'

Marwood went off across the room and Edmund Hoode wiped some of the perspiration from his lip. Agility of mind had saved both him and the company. Benjamin Creech had been palmed off as the lovelorn swain. Hoode's own hopes had been dashed for ever but there was one consolation. Rose Marwood did respond to a poet's lute, after all. She would think fondly of her admirer.

Needing some fresh air after the encounter with the landlord, Hoode went out into the yard where the stage was being taken down. It was a scene he had witnessed many times but it was to hold a cruel element for him now.

George Dart was as busy as always, carrying trestles away under the eaves that ringed the yard. The little stagekeeper paused to catch his breath and caught more. Rose Marwood popped out of her hiding place near the stables and kissed him on the cheek before racing away again. Since he had given her the poem, she clearly thought that he was its author.

Edmund Hoode's misery was complete. He went home.

The Bel Savage Inn supplied all his needs. He was given a large, low, well-furnished room with an adjacent bedchamber which featured rich hangings around its four-poster. Nicholas Bracewell had been as reliable as always. Walking around the room, Lawrence Firethorn gave silent thanks for his book holder. Everything was as it should be, even down to the number and position of the candles. As night began to draw its curtains, the whole place was bathed in a soft, bewitching glow.

His patience was at last rewarded. When Lady Rosamund arrived, they would share an exquisite repast and drink the finest Canary wine. Musicians had been hired to play for them. He would then woo her ardently and they would glide together into the bedchamber to consummate their love on a four-postered paradise. Life could hold nothing sweeter for him.

He heard a sound on the landing outside and came out of his reverie. There was a tap on the door. He cleared his throat.

'Come in.'

The door opened and Nicholas Bracewell looked in.

'The lady is below, master.'

'Show her up, sir.'

'She will be with you presently.'

Nicholas closed the door behind him and Firethorn moved to the mirror to check his appearance for the last time. Because Lady Rosamund had expressed a wish to see his Hector, he had thought of dressing up in the costume that he had worn while playing the role, but he decided that that would be gilding the lily. Looking spruce and gallant in his doublet and hose, he adjusted his hat slightly then smiled at himself in the mirror.

Footsteps sounded outside. He took up his stance and cleared his throat again. There was another tap on the door, it swung open and she was conducted in to him. The whole room was filled with her presence and he swooned as he inhaled her luscious perfume. Nicholas withdrew and closed the door, leaving them alone together for the first time in their lives.

Lady Rosamund Varley stood in the shadows and smiled tenderly at him. A long gown covered her dress, a hood concealed her face. She had come to the assignation with as much eagerness as he had and he sensed her breathless urgency.

Firethorn had the speech to fit the occasion.

Now shall great Hector lay aside his sword,
Put off the garlands of a warrior
And, talking terms of love, embrace defeat,
Surrender to his mistress all he hath!

He removed his hat to make his bow. Her gloved hands applauded softly as she stepped forward into the light. It was exactly as he had imagined it would be.

'I have waited for this moment a long time,' he said.

With courteous boldness, he moved towards her and gently eased back her hood so that he could taste the honey of her lips. The kiss was brief and light and oddly familiar. He pulled back and looked her in the face. His amorous inclination fell stone dead. It was not Lady Rosamund Varley at all. It was his wife.

'And have you done all this for *me*, Lawrence?' she asked.

'For whom else, my dove?'

His actor's training saved him once again.

It was well past midnight and a sudden downpour was washing the streets of London and carrying away their refuse in busy rivulets. Splashing through the puddles, Benjamin Creech lurched his way home from the tavern and cursed the weather. It had been a bad day for him. His anger had made him walk out of Westfield's Men and he now saw what a mistake it had been. He was no longer of use. Giles Randolph wanted him where he could do harm.

By the time that he reached his lodging, he was soaked to the skin. He let himself in and blundered his way upstairs. Belching loudly, he went into his tiny room and tottered towards the mattress, ready to drop on to it as he was to sleep off his inebriation. As he leaned forwards, however, strong arms grabbed him and thrust him into the only chair.

'Sit down, sir!'

'Who are you?' grunted Creech, totally bewildered.

'An old friend has come calling.'

Too drunk to get up and too weak to protest, Creech had to sit there while the tallow was lighted. The yellow flame helped him to identify his visitor.

'Master Bracewell!'

'You left before we had finished our dealings, Ben.'

'I've no dealings with *you*, sir!'

'No,' replied Nicholas. 'Your dealings have been with Banbury's Men.' He held up some gloves. 'These were stolen from Hugh Wegges. That music there was taken from Peter Digby. I found John Tallis's cap here and George Dart's shoes and much else that you sneaked off with.' He threw a glance of disgust around the miserable lodging. 'It is a pity you did not bring Thomas Skillen's broom back here and put it to some use.'

'Get out!' said Creech drowsily.

'Not until we have had a talk, Ben.'

'I've nothing to say to you.'

'Did you steal this?' demanded Nicholas, thrusting a tabor at him. When Creech remained silent, he grabbed him by the throat and squeezed. 'Answer me, sir!

'I cannot . . . breathe . . .'

'Did you steal it?' said Nicholas, exerting more pressure.

'Aye.'

'And the rest of the things?'

'Aye.'

'Did you try to cripple Dick Honeydew?'

'You will choke me!'

'*Did* you, Ben?'

'Aye.'

'And was it to help Banbury's Men?'

Fearing that he would be strangled, Creech nodded his admission of guilt. Nicholas released him and took a step back to reach for something from the table. Starting to retch, the other man rubbed at his sore neck. When Nicholas put his face in close, he could smell the stink on Creech's breath.

'There is more you have to tell me, Ben.'

'No.'

'You did know Redbeard. You were his accomplice.'

'As God's my witness, I never saw the man before.'

'You set on me that night in Bankside,' said Nicholas with subdued fury. 'The two of you worked together.'

'That is not true!' howled Creech.

'Then how did you come by this?'

Nicholas dropped something into his lap and his companion stared at it with blurred, uncomprehending eyes. The object had been lying with the rest of Creech's spoils.

It was the prompt book for *Gloriana Triumphant*.

Chapter Thirteen

Lord Westfield's Men had grown accustomed to the idiosyncrasies of their leading actor but he could still surprise them from time to time. When Lawrence Firethorn summoned a meeting of the full company they all expected that it would follow its normal course. He would first harangue them for what he felt were gross lapses in standards then he would commend anything praiseworthy that he had noted in their recent work. Finally, he would remind them of the intense rivalry they faced from other dramatic companies and urge them on to greater efforts to enhance the reputation of Westfield's Men.

It was different that morning. He did not even look like the same man. In place of the usual alert and spirited personality was a rather dull, jaded, weary human being.

Jokes immediately circulated about the exhausting effects of his supposed night with Lady Rosamund Varley and many sniggers had to be held back. Barnaby Gill was on hand with a characteristically tart comment.

'No wonder he cannot walk straight,' he said to Edmund Hoode in a whispered aside. 'The lady has broken his middle leg!'

'What is amiss with him?' wondered the other.

'Lust, Edmund. Over-satisfied lust.'

They were gathered in the tiring-house at The Queen's Head. Instead of attacking them with a barrage of words, Firethorn spoke quietly and almost without interest. There was no condemnation, no praise and no inspiration. He supported himself with one hand against the door jamb.

'Good morning to you one and all, gentlemen.'

There was a murmured response from the whole company.

'I speak of our future,' he began, suppressing a yawn. 'Over the next six weeks, we shall be playing here, principally, at the Red Lion in Stepney, the Boar's Head near Algate, The Curtain, The Theatre and at Newington Butts. We will also make our debut at The Rose.' Another yawn was threatened. 'Our repertoire will be *Love and Fortune*, *The Two Maids of Milchester*, *Cupid's Folly*, *The Queen of Carthage*, *Marriage and Mischief* and . . .' The pause brought the slightest twinkle to his eye. 'And *Hector of Troy*.' There was a buzz of interest. 'That is all, gentlemen.'

The buzz became a mild hubbub and the meeting started to break up. Lawrence Firethorn quelled all movement with a raised voice that flew to the back of the room like a spear.

'One thing more!'

Silence fell instantly. He was in no hurry.

'One thing more, gentlemen,' he repeated casually, as if passing on some minor piece of gossip. 'Westfield's Men have been invited to appear at Court this Christmas.'

Joy and amazement greeted the announcement and Firethorn watched it all with a beaming smile. His energy now seemed fully restored and he shared in general happiness. Performance at Court would bring no great financial advantage but it was a signal honour and it conferred status on the company. The previous year, it had been Banbury's Men who had played before the Queen during the Christmas Festivities. Firethorn's company had now supplanted them and there was a special pleasure in that.

Nicholas Bracewell watched it all with wry amusement. The leading actor could not simply pass on the good tidings to his fellows. He had to give them a performance and his air of fatigued indifference had fooled them all. The actor had set the place ablaze. Nicholas gazed round the faces in the tiring-house and saw the impact that the news had made.

Barnaby Gill wore a look of smug satisfaction as if he had just been accorded his just deserts. Edmund Hoode seemed a trifle overwhelmed. Richard Honeydew was ecstatic and almost in tears. Martin Yeo grinned, Stephen Judd giggled and the lantern jaw of John Tallis was dropped in awe. But it was Samuel Ruff whose reaction interested Nicholas the most. He sat in the corner with his eyes glistening, a man whose dream had just been fulfilled. Here was a faded actor, outlawed from the profession, then rescued from obscurity. Instead of milking cows in Norwich over Christmas, he would be playing before Queen Elizabeth. Nicholas was very pleased for him.

Lawrence Firethorn now swooped down on him.

'Come here, you knave, you Satan!'

'Was everything to your satisfaction last night, master?'

The actor's rich chuckle cut through the tumult. With an arm around Nicholas, he led him out on to the stage which had already been erected in the yard. There were a few people about but there was an illusion of privacy.

'Why did you not tell me it was Margery?' asked Firethorn.

'It would have spoiled the moment of discovery.'

'Indeed, it would.'

'Mistress Firethorn is an astute woman,' argued Nick. 'She would have to be to marry you, master.'

'How came she to the Bel Savage?' demanded Firethorn.

'I brought her there.'

'Why?'

'Because she learned of your tryst,' lied Nicholas with convincing sincerity. 'Do not ask me how. Some gossip in the company may have told her. Mistress Firethorn purposed to come to the inn herself last night.'

'Heaven forfend!'

'I took your part in the matter and swore that you were faithful to her. The proof of which, I said, was that it was

260

she who was bidden to supper at the Bel Savage.' He gave a discreet smile. 'The rest, I believe, you know.'

'I do, Nick,' said Firethorn nostalgically.

'Everything was to your taste?'

'Margery was a changed woman,' recalled her husband fondly. 'I played Hector once again and sheathed my sword for lack of argument.' He massaged the other's shoulder. 'Marriage has many pains, Nick, but it has its pleasures, too.'

Nicholas nodded sagely. One night of marital bliss had altered the case considerably. The fever of passion that Lady Rosamund Varley had excited had broken in the arms of Margery Firethorn. He was no longer besotted.

'How did you dispose of my other guest?' said the actor.

'By making your excuses. I told her that you had been struck down by a mysterious illness and that you would not be able to meet her. She was not too pleased, master.'

There was a long, ruminative pause. Firethorn chuckled.

'No matter. There are other ladies in London.'

Barnaby Gill and Edmund Hoode came out of the tiring-house in search of their colleague. Nicholas detached himself and left the three sharers alone on stage.

'Why was I not told first?' said Gill petulantly.

'But you were,' reminded Firethorn. 'No man heard the news before you, Barnaby.'

'What are we to play, Lawrence?' wondered Hoode.

'That is a question we must address with all speed.'

'Why not *Marriage and Mischief*?' suggested Gill, choosing a drama that gave prominence to his talents.

261

'Parts of it are too base,' complained Hoode.

'Only those in which Barnaby is involved,' teased Firethorn.

'It has held the stage these three years for us,' argued Gill hotly. 'It has proven its worth.'

'So have many other plays,' countered Hoode.

'My vote is for *Marriage and Mischief*,' insisted Gill.

'And mine is not,' added Firethorn. 'Tried and tested it may be, Barnaby, but we cannot offer such a tired piece to the Court. Novelty is in request, sir. That is why I will commission a new play for the occasion.'

'By whom?' asked Edmund Hoode cautiously.

The look in Firethorn's eye made him quiver.

Outdoor performances were less comfortable as the days got colder and the nights started to draw in. Nicholas Bracewell found that the journeys home were now much quicker as he was hurrying to get in out of the chill. As he made his way back after another day at The Queen's Head, he was conscious of winter's swift approach. The wind bit more hungrily and the flurry of rain stung his face. He pulled his hat down over his brow and lengthened his stride. Bankside was not far away now.

Nicholas was as thrilled as anyone by the invitation to play at Court. It would bring kudos to Westfield's Men. It also gave them an opportunity to perform in conditions which were unique and which would force them to modify their outdoor techniques. Most important of all, it lifted the morale of the company after a succession of setbacks and enabled them to look forward instead of glancing back.

The past still obsessed Nicholas, however. Will Fowler's death had not been avenged and he was still dogged by the memory of the slit throat of Alice at The Cardinal's Hat. He was constantly reminded of the savagery of the men he sought. Creech may have been removed but the company was threatened by more malign forces. He had to be vigilant.

His walk through Bankside took him past the Hope and Anchor and a wash of noise slopped out as he went by the tavern. He thought of the last time he had seen Will Fowler alive, enjoying the company of his two friends, crackling with good humour and infused with a kind of truculent benevolence. Danger had attracted him to his profession and it was danger which had brought him down when he was off guard.

Nicholas determined that he would never be taken unawares. After the earlier attack on him, he was excessively careful when out alone at night. His increased watchfulness now came to his aid. He was no more than twenty yards from the house when he saw the man. The tall figure was lurking in the shadows behind the angle of the house. Nicholas would not make any rash move this time. He had learned his lesson.

Pretending to have noticed nothing, he went up to the front door and fumbled for his key. Out of the corner of his eye, he watched for movement but none came. Yet the man was still there, still waiting, still exuding a profound menace. Nicholas prepared for attack. Inserting his key in the lock, he suddenly turned away from the door and flung himself at the figure in the darkness.

He met no resistance. The moment he hit the body, it went limp and collapsed against him. He lowered the man carefully to the ground so that he was face down. Between his shoulder blades was the handle of a long dagger.

Nicholas was totally confused.

The dead man was Redbeard.

Anne Hendrik was torn between relief at his safety and horror at the murder which had taken place on her doorstep. When officers had been summoned and the body removed, she drew Nicholas into her bed once more for comfort and reassurance.

Afterwards, they lay in each other's arms.

'Who *was* he?' asked Anne.

'There was no clue to his identity upon his person,' he said. 'We may never know his true name.'

'And was he working with Benjamin Creech?'

'No,' replied Nicholas. 'I am certain of that now. Ben never met him until that day. Redbeard contrived to be seen with him for my benefit.'

'Why?' she wondered.

'To throw suspicion upon Ben. I was meant to come upon them as I did. Redbeard knew that he could escape in that crowd.'

Anne considered the notion then sat up in surprise.

'Then it was all part of some deep plot?'

'I believe so.'

'What about the prompt book?' she reminded him. 'It was in Creech's lodging with some of the other things he stole.'

'I was deceived by that at first,' he admitted. 'It was intended that I should be. I would hazard a guess that Redbeard placed the book at the lodging for me to find. It linked Ben with the attack on me and with the killing of Will Fowler.' He shook his head. 'No, Anne. This is not the work of Ben Creech. We are up against a much more cunning adversary. He has been clever enough to hide his trail and ruthless enough to murder his own accomplice.'

'Redbeard?'

'My belief is that he was killed by his friend.'

She was aghast. 'His *friend*?'

'Yes,' he argued. 'Who else would get close enough to a man like that to stab him in the back? Redbeard lived in foul dens and dark alleys. That was his world. Nobody would ever gain an advantage over him there.'

'Unless it was someone he trusted.'

'His accomplice. The man who hit me from behind.'

'Oh, Nick!'

The memory of the assault made her cling to him for a long time. He had to soothe her with kisses and caresses. Three people had now been murdered in gruesome circumstances and she was convinced that he would be the next victim. Nicholas was equally persuaded that he was quite safe. His life had already been spared once and he now realised why.

'He will not kill me, Anne,' he decided.

265

'How can you be so sure?'

'Because he needs me alive. He needs me in the company.'

'For what reason?'

'I have not fully divined it yet,' he confessed. 'But it has something to do with our appearance at Court. Perhaps that was the desired end all along. Once it had been achieved, Redbeard had served his purpose. He could be cast aside with a dagger in his back.'

'But why *here*? Outside my house?'

'So that I would be aware of his death. So that I would be misled even further. So that I would think all danger had passed.'

'I cannot make sense of this, Nick,' she complained.

He pulled her down to him and embraced her warmly. Then there was a long silence as he tried to puzzle it all out. She began to think that he was dozing off but his mind was racing as he evolved a plan.

'Who is your best hatmaker, Anne?' he said abruptly.

'What?'

'At the shop. Who is your most skilful craftsman?'

'Preben van Loew.'

'Can he make other things than hats?'

'Preben can make anything,' she said confidently.

'Could he make a dress?'

'Of course.'

'This would be a very special and elaborate costume.'

'You have your own tiremen in the company,' she pointed out. 'Could not they handle this commission?'

'It would not be politic,' he said. 'This is a secret that must be shared by as few people as possible. Master Firethorn will have to be involved but the rest of the company must be kept in ignorance. Apart from the boy, that is.'

'The boy?'

'It will all become clear in time,' he promised.

'Nick, what *are* you talking about?'

He pulled her closer and whispered in her ear.

'Play-acting.'

When he got to The Queen's Head next morning, the first person he sought out was Samuel Ruff. They went off to a corner of the yard to be alone together. Nicholas told him what had happened the previous night. The actor was astonished to hear about Redbeard's death, but that astonishment quickly converted to anger.

'Where is he, Nick?'

'He was taken away by the officers.'

'Find out where. I wish to see him.'

'Why?' asked Nicholas.

'Because I want to look on the face of the cur who killed Will Fowler.' Sarcasm took over. 'I want to pay my respects!'

'Stay well away, Sam. That is my advice.'

Ruff punched the palm of his left hand.

'If only *I* had got to him first!' he said ruefully. 'I hoped to avenge Will's death myself. Redbeard escaped me.'

'He came to a deserved end.'

'*I* wanted to plunge the dagger into him!'

'It is too late for that now,' observed Nicholas.

Samuel Ruff inhaled deeply and fought to control his

temper. When he calmed down, he nodded sagely.

'You are right,' he agreed. 'I suppose that we should just be grateful that his wretched life is now over. At least we have no more to fear from the villain.'

'Not from him, Sam. But we still have a mortal enemy.'

'Who?'

'The man who struck Redbeard down. His accomplice.'

'Accomplice?' echoed the other in disbelief. 'That cannot be, surely? Why would he kill a friend?'

'Because that friend was no longer of any use,' suggested Nicholas. 'Indeed, he was starting to become a problem.'

'In what way?'

'Redbeard was too intemperate – we saw evidence enough of that in Bankside. If he was given free rein, there was always the chance that his wildness would lead him to make a serious mistake. And that would endanger the whole enterprise.'

'What enterprise?' asked Ruff with interest.

'The destruction of Westfield's Men.'

The actor pondered. He found much that was plausible in Nicholas's line of reasoning. A name eased itself into his mind.

'Ben Creech!'

'What of him, Sam?'

'*He* was Redbeard's accomplice.'

'I think not.'

'He was, Nick,' argued the other. 'Ben stabbed him in the back. He paid Redbeard off.'

'No,' countered Nicholas. 'Ben Creech has much to

answer for but he is not a murderer. He could never devise the sort of plan that lies behind all this. Ben is not shrewd enough. He had nothing whatsoever to do with Redbeard.'

'How do you know?'

'Because he could never control someone like that. Still less could he kill him off when the time was ripe.'

'I am not so sure,' murmured Ruff.

'Ben was working for Banbury's Men,' continued Nicholas. 'He was responsible for all the thieving. His task was to unsettle the company but he could only do that while he was a member of it. Now that he is gone, that threat has vanished.'

'Yet we still have an enemy, you say?'

'We do, Sam.'

'Inside the company?'

'No. He attacked from outside. With Redbeard.'

'Do you have any idea who the man is?'

'None,' said Nicholas. 'All I know is that he will be more dangerous than ever now.'

'Why?'

'Because he failed in what he set out to do. His intention was to cripple Westfield's Men and Will's murder was his first blow against us. But we survived.'

'Instead of being laid low, the company has prospered.'

'Exactly, Sam. Our appearance at Court is proof of that. But it is bound to stir up his envy even more. I believe that he will do his best to snatch that honour away from us.'

'Not while *I* have breath in my body!' vowed Ruff.

'We must be Vigilence itself,' insisted Nicholas. 'He will strike when it is least expected.'

'We must be armed against him!'

'I shall say as much to Master Firethorn. The whole company must be on guard from now on. Nothing must be allowed to rob us of our appearance at Court.'

'Nothing will,' said Ruff grimly.

Nicholas patted him on the shoulder and they strolled across the yard together. The book holder remembered someone.

'This news might be welcome in St Albans,' he mused.

'St Albans?'

'I was thinking of Susan Fowler. She will be interested to learn that her husband's killer has met his own death.'

'Interested and gratified, too.'

'Oh, Susan will take no pleasure from it,' said Nicholas. 'Hers is not a vengeful nature. But I hope she may draw some modicum of comfort from it. Poor girl! She will need all the comfort she can get in the days that lie ahead. Susan will have to bring up her daughter without the love and support of a husband.'

'God protect them both!' added Ruff.

'Amen!'

Lord Westfield's Men continued their regular round of performances but it was their visit to Court which dominated their thoughts and their conversation. December came and Christmas hove into sight. Their excitement increased with each day that passed.

Goaded into creation once more, Edmund Hoode worked hard on the new play and delivered it for comment. *The Loyal Subject* was the inspiration of Lawrence Firethorn and it was tailored to the generous dimensions of his talent. He suggested a number of changes himself then disputed those that were offered by Barnaby Gill. The author reached for his pen again. When the final draft was ready, it was sent off to the Master of the Revels with the usual fee. It came back with the seal of approval.

The company committed itself wholeheartedly to the new piece. The prime advantage of a Court performance was that they were given excellent rehearsal facilities and a longer period in which to perfect their work. After the hectic compromise of their normal hand-to-mouth existence, the new dispensation came as a luxury. They were indoors, they were warm, and, moreover, they were about to cut a dash at Court.

The Loyal Subject was set in a part of Italy that was quintessentially English in every detail. Edmund Hoode had made his Duchess of Milan remarkably like his own sovereign and his play was a celebration of loyalty to the Crown. In the opening scene, the hero was arraigned on a charge of treason and condemned on false evidence. He went to the block but his loyalty was so great that it outlived him. In the person of his ghost, the loyal subject controlled the action of the whole realm for the benefit of his monarch, even crushing a threatened rebellion.

Richard Honeydew was overjoyed to be given the part of the Duchess of Milan. It more than made up for his disappointment over losing the opportunity to play Gloriana. The Duchess was another version of Gloriana and there was the additional thrill this time of portraying the character in front of its mirror image, Queen Elizabeth herself. The boy was determined to prove his worth. He brought willingness and enthusiasm to every rehearsal.

Nicholas watched it all with calm satisfaction. After one of the rehearsals, he chose the moment to take Richard aside. He smiled his congratulations at the boy.

'You are excelling yourself, Dick.'

'Thank you, Master Bracewell.'

'Everyone is delighted with your work.'

'I am very anxious to please.'

'That is good.'

'I want my appearance at Court to be a success in every way.'

Nicholas nodded then he became more confidential.

'Dick . . .'

'Yes, master?'

'I have a favour to ask of you.'

'It is granted before it is asked,' said the boy amiably.

'Hear what it is first,' advised Nicholas. 'It is a very big favour, Dick.'

'No matter.'

'It will mean sacrifice and it will call upon your loyalty.'

'Loyalty? To whom?'

'To me. To the company. And to your Queen.'

Richard Honeydew listened with fascination.

* * *

Lawrence Firethorn did not believe in treating the text of a play as holy writ. He was compelled to modify and refine at every turn. Adjustment was a continuous process. *The Loyal Subject* would not reach its finished version until the day of performance.

The person who suffered most as a result of all this was Edmund Hoode. He became more and more embattled. While accepting that a new work could always be improved, he rejected Firethorn's glib assertion that daily tinkering with a play kept it fresh and alive. It merely kept Hoode busy when he should have been devoting his energies to the playing of Marsilius, the decrepit old judge in the opening scene.

Firethorn would not relent. As the two men dined together one day, therefore, Hoode braced himself for the inevitable. The actor-manager waited until they had eaten their meal before he broached the subject. Poets responded best on a full stomach.

'Did you enjoy the Westphalian ham?' he asked.

'I will *not* change the trial scene again,' said Hoode.

'Nobody is suggesting that you should, dear fellow.'

'As long as that is understood, Lawrence.'

'Perfectly.'

'I regard the trial scene as sacrosanct now,' affirmed the poet. 'We have altered it so many times that I have no heart left for further changes.'

'I would not amend a single word of it, Edmund.'

'I am relieved to hear it.'

'However . . .'

Feeling that he needed liquid fortification, Hoode reached for his cup and drained it. He suspected another veiled attack.

'However,' repeated Firethorn, 'we must always be looking to extract the full dramatic value out of each scene. A performance at Court is a special occasion. Nothing less than our best will suffice. We must bear that in mind.'

'Come to the point, Lawrence.'

'My soliloquy in prison.'

'I feared as much!' groaned Hoode.

'It is a truly magnificent speech,' praised Firethorn, 'but I believe we can add to its lustre.'

'We have added to its lustre almost every day.'

'This is my final comment.'

'I pray that it is!'

Firethorn leaned across the table with a knowing smile.

'Lorenzo must have more passion.'

'Passion?' Hoode was taken aback.

'Yes, Edmund.'

'On the eve of his execution?'

'You misunderstand me, sir,' explained Firethorn. 'I wish to introduce a more personal note into the speech. Lorenzo bewails his fate and then extols the virtue of loyalty. He talks about honour, duty and patriotism.' The smile returned. 'He should also talk about love.'

'For whom? For what?'

'For his sovereign and for his country. The two should be wedded together in his mind. He would not dare to betray either because it would be an act of infidelity. A lover

274

being unfaithful to his lady.' Firethorn sat back in his chair. 'Six lines will be enough. Eight, at most. Show Lorenzo in a more passionate vein.'

'I will try, Lawrence.'

'Pursue that theme. A loyalty that is rooted in a deep love. Let him woo the Duchess in choice phrases. Ten lines are all that I require. A dozen would make that speech eternally memorable.'

'Leave it with me,' sighed the other.

'I knew that you would listen to reason, Edmund.'

'Is that what I did?'

The reckoning was paid and the two men rose to go.

'One thing more,' said Firethorn easily.

'Yes?'

'The execution.'

'What about it?'

'It will now take place on stage.'

Hoode gulped. 'But that is impossible!'

'Theatre is the art of the impossible,' reminded Firethorn.

'An execution . . . in full view of the audience?'

'Why not, sir? It will be far more effective than the present device, where the executioner appears with Lorenzo's gory head in his hand. I will perish before their eyes.'

'*How?*'

'Nicholas has the way of it. Let him explain it to you.'

Respect for the book holder at least made Hoode consider the idea properly, but he could not imagine how the effect would be achieved. He shrugged his shoulders.

'I am prepared to try it,' he conceded.

'It is not a question of trying it,' said Firethorn seriously. '*That* is the way it will be done during the performance. I am resolved upon it.'

Samuel Ruff was as pleased as anybody that Richard Honeydew had secured the female lead in the play. He was genuinely fond of the boy and appreciative of his talent. He was both hurt and puzzled, therefore, when things began to go wrong. Richard's attitude slowly changed. His eagerness faded and he became almost timid. He faltered badly. The apprentice was clearly unhappy.

Ruff took the opportunity of a private word with him.

'What is it, lad?' he asked solicitously.

'It is nothing, Master Ruff.'

'I am not blind, Dick. Something ails you.'

'It will pass, sir.'

'Is it the other boys?'

Richard gave a noncommittal grunt.

Martin Yeo was annoyed that he had not been offered the role of the Duchess of Milan but he had done nothing beyond some mild verbal sniping at Richard. Stephen Judd and John Tallis likewise mocked their young colleague without taking any more drastic action against him.

'I watched you rehearsing just now,' said Ruff with concern. 'You stumbled over lines that you knew well a few days ago.'

'My mind becomes a blank.'

'Let me help.'

'You cannot, sir.'

'But I could teach you your part.'

'That is not the help I need.'

'Then what is, lad?'

Richard tried to tell him but the words would not come. He was evidently in some distress. Biting his lip, he turned on his heel and ran out of the room. Samuel Ruff was mystified. He took his problem to Nicholas who was poring over a sketch with one of the carpenters. Ruff spoke of his anxiety about the boy.

'Leave him be,' suggested Nicholas.

'What has happened to him? Why has he lost his way?'

'It is not his way that he has lost, Sam.'

'How so?'

'The lad is scared. He has lost his nerve.'

'With such an opportunity before him?'

'That is the cause of it all,' said Nicholas. 'The occasion is too much for him. Dick is still very young and raw. This will be his first leading role and he has to play it before the Queen of England and the whole Court. That is a lot to ask from such an inexperienced actor.'

'He is equal to it, Nick.'

'Let us hope so for all our sakes.'

'What can we do for him?' asked Ruff.

'Give him time,' advised Nicholas. 'He needs our care and understanding. I have spoken to Master Firethorn and told him not to browbeat the boy if he stumbles. That could be fatal.'

'How do you mean?'

'You have seen him, Sam. He is in a delicate state and can only take so much. If Dick Honeydew is pushed too far, he will crack.'

Queen Elizabeth was spending Christmas at Richmond that year. For some months now, she had been sad and withdrawn, shattered by the death in September of her old favourite, the Earl of Leicester, and shrinking from public appearances. Instead of rejoicing in the defeat of the Armada, she mourned the loss of a loved one.

The Queen chose the splendid Richmond Palace for the Christmas festivities and it was hoped that they would bring some cheer into a royal life which had narrowed considerably throughout the autumn. A full programme of music, dance and drama had been arranged for her. *The Loyal Subject* was the first play she would see and it was due to be given on the day after Christmas. Its theme had a particular relevance in Armada year.

The rehearsal period approached its climax.

'Place your head in the middle of the block, lad!'

'I am trying to, Master Firethorn.'

'Hurry, you knave, or I will use the axe myself!'

Lawrence Firethorn was working on his own execution. Nicholas Bracewell had devised the effect and he was there to supervise it. Edmund Hoode watched nervously from the corner of the room. He still had reservations about the whole thing.

The Loyal Subject opened with the trial scene in which the noble hero, Lorenzo, was condemned to death. Taken off to await his unjust fate, he delivered his long soliloquy in the prison cell. Gaolers then entered to prepare him for his final hour. Brave to the last, he was led out.

The block was brought on stage and the executioner stood beside it with his axe. When the condemned man reappeared, however, it was not Firethorn. A clever substitution had taken place. John Tallis, much shorter than the actor-manager, came in wearing an identical costume, except that his own head was below the neck of the doublet. A false head had been made, painted and covered with a wig. It bore a striking resemblance to Lorenzo.

When the head was on the block, it was chopped off.

'Remain quite still, you young rascal!'

'Will it hurt, Master Firethorn?' whimpered Tallis.

'That depends what we decide to cut off!'

'Take care, sirs!' wailed the boy.

'Silence!'

'Have no fear, John,' said Nicholas, bending down to position the apprentice behind the block. 'You will not feel a thing.'

'But it is a real axe, Master Bracewell!'

'The weapon is in safe hands, I assure you.'

He turned to the sturdy actor who held the axe ready.

'I'll not hurt you, lad,' promised Ruff.

'But *I* will!' threatened Firethorn. 'If you dare to move.'

'There is no danger,' continued Nicholas, trying to calm the boy. 'Sam has been practising with that axe for days. We chose him because he is so reliable. Stay exactly where you are, John, and it will be over in a matter of seconds.'

Nicholas stood back and gave the signal. Ruff raised the blade high in the air. When it swished down, it sliced clean through the wax neck and embedded itself in the block. The false head went rolling across the floor with stunning effect.

John Tallis howled from inside the doublet.

'Am I still alive?'

Christmas Day began early in London and all the bells of the city tolled out their message of joy. Margery Firethorn was up well before dawn to take charge of the multifarious chores that fell to her and still find time to accompany her family to church for matins. There was great excitement in the house at Shoreditch. Her children were up to savour the wonder of the special day, and they were soon joined by Martin Yeo, John Tallis and Stephen Judd.

Margery could not understand why Richard Honeydew was so tardy. It was his first Christmas with the company and she had done what she could to ensure that he would enjoy it. Troubled by his absence, she went off to find him herself.

'Dick! Wake up, boy! It's Christmas Day!'

Now that the beams in the attic had been replaced, Richard had moved back in there. She puffed up the stairs as fast as she could. Overflowing with seasonal benevolence, she cooed and called all the way to his door.

'Don't lie abed in there, Dick! It's Christmas! Come and see what we have for you! Get up!'

Margery knocked, entered and reacted with horror.

'Lord help us!' she exclaimed.

The bed was empty and the window was wide open.

Richmond Place was a sumptuous Gothic residence that was well situated between Richmond Green and the River Thames. Its skyline of turrets and gilded weather-vanes gave it a romantic image, and it was flanked by gardens and orchards that were painted with hundreds of fruit trees. The palace covered some ten acres in all and had a regular layout round a series of spacious courtyards.

The birthplace of her father, it had not been one of Elizabeth's favourite homes in the early part of her reign. Now, however, she was coming to appreciate the singular charms of a place that she called her warm winterbox. Descending upon it with her household, the Queen filled it with light and noise and colour. She even began to look forward to the Christmas festivities.

Lawrence Firethorn did not share her anticipatory pleasure. Deserted by his female lead on the day before the performance, he rushed around in a frenzy to try to repair the damage. Martin Yeo was once again promoted to royal status in place of the youngest apprentice and Hugh Wegges had to make hasty alterations to the costumes to accommodate Yeo's greater bulk. A dark shadow had been cast over the long-awaited appearance at Court. The early carefree excitement had now gone out of the event.

The afternoon of December 26th found the company at Richmond for a last rehearsal. There was much anger over Richard Honeydew's disappearance and the upheaval it had caused. But one person at least tried to see it from the boy's point of view.

'I feel sorry for him,' said Ruff sadly.

'So do I,' agreed Nicholas.

'He must have been very unhappy to do this.'

'He was.'

'Yet I never thought he would run away like that.'

'I am not sure that he has, Sam.'

'What do you mean?'

'Look at the evidence,' said Nicholas. 'His room was empty. Dick and his belongings had gone. There was a ladder outside the open window.'

'How else can you explain it?'

'People go up ladders as well as down them.'

'So?'

'Dick may have fled,' conceded Nicholas, 'but it is equally possible that someone came in through the window to take him away. I think that he has been abducted.'

'By whom?'

'Redbeard's accomplice. The man who has dogged us for months now. I said he would strike when least expected. What better way to hurt us than by kidnapping Dick on the eve of performance?'

Samuel Ruff was bewildered but he had no time to speculate on what might have happened. Lawrence Firethorn called them to order. They were in a crisis once more. It was time to assert his leadership and lift sagging spirits.

'Gentlemen,' he began, 'I do not need to remind you

how important this occasion is for Westfield's Men. We have the honour to play before our beloved Queen and the opportunity to enhance our reputation with the highest in the realm. What occurs here this evening will have a bearing on our whole future so we must not be distracted by a minor upset. The loss of Dick Honeydew is unfortunate but it is no more than that. It is but a trifle. With hard work this afternoon, we will make up any leeway and give our new play the performance it deserves!' He raised a fist in a gesture of pride. 'Let us show our true mettle here. Let us prove we are lusty fellows, loyal subjects and the finest actors in London!'

Amid the hubbub, they all raced to their positions.

The play was being presented in the hall, which was a hundred feet long and some forty feet wide. It had an elaborate timber roof with hanging pendants. There was a lantern in the roof over a charcoal fire. The upper parts of the walls had large perpendicular windows with paintings in between of those kings of England who had distinguished themselves on the battlefield. If they had been able to study it, they would have seen that the whole apartment was an architectural wonder.

As it was, they were so preoccupied with their rehearsal that they took little stock of their luxurious surroundings. They performed on a raised platform at one end of the hall. Seating was arranged in tiers on three sides and the royal throne was set up on a dais in front of the stage.

The rehearsal was an amalgam of professional calm and frantic improvisation. Several mistakes were made but they were quickly retrieved. Martin Yeo was not as fine a Duchess as Richard Honeydew but he was more than competent. The other players adapted their performances around his. Morale was slowly boosted. The play achieved its own momentum and carried them along.

When it was all over, they rested in the adjacent room that was being used as their tiring-house. The tensions of the last twenty-four hours had sapped them mentally and physically but recovery was imminent. With Firethorn at the helm, they now believed that they could distinguish themselves with *The Loyal Subject*. A wounded optimism spread.

John Tallis did not share it. Nothing could quiet his urgent pessimism. He was still highly apprehensive about the execution scene. Though it went exactly to plan, with the axe doing its work some inches away from the top of his skull, the boy was not reassured. What if Samuel Ruff's aim was wayward during the performance? How could the lad defend himself?

Execution was not a precise art. The most famous headsman of the day, Bud, was notorious for his errors. When he officiated in the grim tragedy at Fotheringhay Castle, he needed three attempts to behead Mary Queen of Scots. Yet Bud was heralded as a master of his trade. Why should Ruff be any more reliable? He was an untrained novice with a murderous weapon in his hands.

Tallis took his problem to Firethorn once more.

'Find someone else to double as Lorenzo,' he pleaded.

'There *is* nobody else,' replied the actor-manager.

'What about George Dart? He is short enough.'

'Short enough, yes,' conceded the other. 'But is he brave enough? Is he clever enough? Is he good enough? Never, sir! He is no actor. George Dart is a willing imbecile. He does simple things well in his own simple way. Lorenzo is a heroic figure in the ancient mould. I will not be doubled by a half-wit!'

'Release me from this ordeal!' implored Tallis.

'It will help to form your character.'

'But I am afraid, master.'

'Control your fears like every other player.'

'*Please!*'

'You will honour your commitment.'

'It grieves me, sir.'

'Cease this complaint.'

'But why *me*?'

Lawrence Firethorn produced his most disarming grin.

'Because you do it so well, John,' he flattered.

He moved away before the boy could protest any further. Tallis was trapped in the matching doublet. He looked across at Samuel Ruff. The latter was as relaxed and composed as ever but the boy's qualms remained. If the executioner's hand slipped, the career of John Tallis could be sliced in two. It was a devastating thought.

A muted excitement pervaded the room. Everyone else was savouring the experience of playing at Court. What the play offered them was a brief moment at the very pinnacle of their profession. *The Loyal Subject* was about duty and patriotism and love. It was the perfect Christmas gift for their Queen.

John Tallis viewed it differently. The execution scene was paramount for him. He had no concern for the themes of the drama or for its wider values. Only one thing mattered.

Where would the axe fall?

It was a pertinent question.

Queen Elizabeth and her Court supped in splendour that night. Fresh from their banquet and mellowed by their wine, the lords and ladies took up their appointed places in the hall at Richmond Palace. Caught in the flickering light of a thousand candles, they were an august and colourful assembly. A good-humoured atmosphere prevailed. Behind the posing and the posturing and the brittle repartee was a fund of genuine warmth. They were a receptive audience.

Every one of the tiered seats was taken but the throne stayed empty. While her guests waited for the entertainment, the Queen herself caused a delay. It was unaccountable. The longer she stayed away, the greater became the speculation. In no time at all, the whole place was a buzz of rumour.

The delay brought grave disquiet backstage. Keyed up for their performance, the actors were distressed by the unexpected wait. They were all on edge. Lawrence Firethorn paced uneasily up and down. Edmund Hoode's throat went dry and Barnaby Gill fidgeted nervously with his costume. Martin Yeo's bladder seemed to be on the point of bursting and John Tallis felt a prickly sensation around his neck. As he stood ready to set the furniture for the opening scene, George Dart was shaking like an aspen.

Even Samuel Ruff was disconcerted. His anxiety steadily

increased. Perspiration broke out all over him and his naked arms and shoulders were glistening. As the delay stretched on and on, he fondled the handle of the axe with sweaty palms.

'Where is her Majesty?' whispered Gill.

'Exercising the privilege of royalty,' returned Firethorn.

'Making her players suffer?'

'Taking her time, Barnaby.'

A trumpet fanfare told them that the Queen had at last arrived. The comfortable din in the hall fell to a murmur. The tension among the players increased. Their moment was at hand.

Lawrence Firethorn applied his eye to a narrow gap in the curtain at the rear of the stage. He described what he saw in a low, reverential voice.

Surrounded by her guard, Queen Elizabeth sailed down the hall and ascended the dais to take up her seat on the throne. Resplendent in a billowing dress of red velvet, she acknowledged all those around her with a condescending wave. Her hair was encircled with pearls and surmounted by a tiny gold crown that was encrusted with diamonds. Her jewelled opulence filled the hall. Time had been considerate to her handsome features and her regal demeanour was unimpaired. Flames from the candles and from the huge fire made her finery dance with zest.

The actor-manager concluded with an awed whisper.

'Gentlemen, we are in the presence of royalty!'

Nicholas Bracewell took over the watch. When the Queen was settled, she motioned to Sir Edmund Tilney, the

Master of the Revels, and he in turn signalled to the book holder. On a call from Nicholas, the command performance began.

Music wafted down from the gallery where Peter Digby and his musicians were placed. The prologue was delivered and the trial scene commenced. From his first line, Firethorn exerted his power over the audience. He went on to bewitch them with his voice, to thrill them with his spirited honesty and to move them with his anguish. By the end of the scene, he had touched all their hearts and prompted the first few tears.

When sentence of death was passed, the judge vacated the stage and Lorenzo was led away by two gaolers. Music played as the others processed off. George Dart came on to set a stool in position and to remove the bench he had brought out earlier for the trial. He skipped hurriedly off.

Assuming a look of wistful integrity, Firethorn was led on stage again by his gaolers. He sat on the stool in his cell. The two men departed, Lorenzo stared at the manacles on his wrists then he looked up with supplication in his eyes.

> O Loyalty! Thy name Lorenzo is!
> For twenty faithful years I have been true
> To my fair Duchess, angel from above,
> Descended here to capture all our hearts
> And turn our Milan into paradise.
> Could I betray such sovereign beauty
> For ugly coins of foul conspiracy?
> Rather would I live in cruel exile

Or kill myself upon a dagger's point.
Fidelity has always been my cry
And constant will I be until I die!

While Firethorn declaimed his soliloquy, the players in the tiring-house got ready for their next entrance. As Nicholas lined them up in order, he kept a wary eye on Ruff. The executioner was more nervous than ever. One of the most experienced actors in the company seemed to be unsettled by the occasion. Sweat still poured out of him and he moved from foot to foot.

'Do please take care, Master Ruff!'

'What?' he replied with a start.

'My safety lies with you, sir.'

The voice came from inside the doublet of the figure standing beside him. Equipped with a false head, John Tallis was about to double as Lorenzo during the execution.

'Use me kindly,' said the boy plaintively.

'I will, John,' promised the other.

'Let the axe fall in its rightful place.'

'Oh, it will,' said Ruff grimly. 'It will.'

As Lorenzo finished his speech, the gaolers went on to bring the condemned man out of his cell. The trembling George Dart now replaced the stool with the block. Drums rolled and the procession made its way solemnly on stage.

Edmund Hoode was first in his role as the judge. Courtiers and guards followed him. The chaplain came next, holding his prayer book tightly. Lorenzo was guided to the centre of the stage by the two gaolers. Ruff brought up the rear as the executioner.

When the tableau had been formed, the chaplain turned to admonish the prisoner sternly.

'Settle Christ Jesus in your heart and confess.'

Lorenzo remained silent but Tallis's teeth chattered.

'Join in prayer with me,' continued the chaplain, 'for the salvation of your soul. Go to your Maker with a contrite heart.'

He began to recite prayers at the hapless Lorenzo.

Samuel Ruff only half-listened to the words. Dressed in the traditional black garb of an executioner, he stood beside the block with the head of the axe resting between his feet. Through the slits in the mask, he stole a glance at the Queen of England. She was a serene and majestic figure no more than a dozen yards from him. Though guards flanked her, they were caught up in the action on the stage.

Closing his eyes for an instant, Ruff offered up his own prayer. His opportunity had been heaven-sent. It was up to him to seize it with eagerness. The significance of it all was brought home to him and extra pressure was imposed. His arms and shoulders were now awash with sweat and his palms were pools of moisture. He schooled himself to wait just a little longer. To buttress his determination, he recalled other executions that Queen Elizabeth had witnessed. The blood was soon pulsing in his temples.

Anxiety was turning its hunger on Nicholas Bracewell. From a vantage point at the rear of the stage, he watched the proceedings with mounting concern. He was more fully aware than anyone of the extent of the danger. As the moment of truth approached, he wondered if he had made the right decision or if he had delivered up an innocent life to the stroke of death. Nicholas had an impulse to rush on stage and intervene but he resisted it. The chance had to be taken. Peril had to be faced.

The chaplain intoned the last words of his prayer.

'And may God have mercy on your soul . . . Amen!'

Having completed the spiritual offices, he stood back so that the rigour of the law could be enforced. The loyal subject was about to be executed for his supposed disloyalty. On the command of the judge, the gaolers took Lorenzo to the block, made him kneel in front of it and position his false head carefully over the timber.

The drums rolled more loudly. Nicholas was on tenterhooks.

Samuel Ruff now took over. He was no mock executioner in a play. He was a gleaming figure of vengeance with murder in his heart. A last fleeting look at the Queen showed him that Her Majesty was totally captivated by the performance. Everyone was off guard. Ruff swallowed hard, tightened his jaw then wiped his palms dry on his hips. It was now or never.

He took a firm grip on the glittering axe.

Nicholas fought off another urge to interrupt. Teeth clenched and fists bunched, he was tormented by the helplessness of his situation. Whatever the cost, he must hold back.

The drums beat out their tattoo, the judge nodded

and the executioner lifted the axe high in the air. Its blade shimmered in the candlelight. Its menace was real. But it did not arc towards John Tallis. Another victim had been selected for execution. Jumping down from the stage, Ruff charged towards the throne with a wild cry of revenge.

'Death to all tyrants!'

His weapon was aimed at the head of the Queen.

Yet somehow she was prepared for the attack and ducked out of the way with great dexterity. The guards, too, were ready and they closed in upon Ruff to grapple with him. Instead of scything through the royal neck, the axe thudded into the back of the throne and almost split it asunder.

'Seize the villain!'

'Hold him!'

Shouts and screams rent the air. A large space was cleared around the throne as terrified nobles scampered out of the way. The Court was horrified that the sovereign had been so close to a grisly death and the suddenness of it all bewildered them.

Overpowered by the guards, Ruff was held tight. The glare of hatred that he directed at the Queen soon turned to a look of utter amazement. Removing crown, wig and pearls she gazed back at him with the hurt expression of someone who feels she has been betrayed by a close friend.

It was not the Queen of England at all.

It was Richard Honeydew.

Waves of astonishment rolled across the hall. Sir Edmund Tilney, a spruce figure in almost garish apparel, climbed on to the stage and raised his hands to quell the noise.

'You will not be deprived of your entertainment,' he told them. 'There will be a short intermission then Her Majesty will join us. What you have just witnessed requires some explanation . . .'

Ruff was not allowed to hear it. He was hustled out of the room without ceremony. Richard Honeydew went with him. They found Lawrence Firethorn and Nicholas Bracewell waiting for them in the corridor.

The book holder's immediate concern was for the boy. He was relieved to see that Richard was quite unharmed. The actor-manager looked at Ruff and gave a dark chuckle.

'Caught like a rat in a trap!' he noted. 'You were right, Nick. This was indeed the way to draw his hand.'

The stunned Ruff turned on the book holder.

'How did you know?'

'There were many things,' explained Nicholas. 'They all pointed towards religion. You were so true to the old faith that you were prepared to kill for it.'

'And to die for it!' said Ruff defiantly.

'Will Fowler was a devout Roman Catholic as well but he renounced his religion. You could not forgive him for that, Sam. Nor could you rest easy while your days in the theatre came to an end and Will's talent flourished. Your bitterness went deep.'

'Will betrayed us!' argued Ruff.

'Out of love for his young wife,' reminded Nicholas.

'I did not know of her,' said the other quietly. 'It is perhaps as well. Susan would have weighed on my conscience.'

'What conscience?' sneered Firethorn, pointing a finger at him. 'You're a traitor, sir!'

'I am loyal to the old religion!'

Richard Honeydew was baffled by an important detail.

'But why was Will Fowler murdered?' he asked.

'So that Sam could take his place,' said Nicholas. 'Most of us cheered when the Armada was defeated but it was a crippling blow to those of the Romish persuasion. Sam wanted to strike back on their behalf in the most terrible way he could imagine – by killing Her Majesty. The only chance he had of getting close enough to her was during a performance at Court.'

'With Westfield's Men,' added Firethorn. 'Our company was the most likely to be invited to play here. This rogue sought to hide himself behind our reputation.'

Nicholas smiled and patted the boy on the back.

'As it happened, *you* gave the outstanding performance, Dick. You not only deceived an assassin, you convinced the whole Court.' He turned to Ruff. 'A true actor will never desert his audience. The lad did not run away on Christmas Day. He stayed with me at my lodging and rehearsed his new part. This dress of his was made by a Dutch hatmaker. It was worthy of a Queen.'

'You have been very brave, Dick,' observed Firethorn.

'I was a little afraid, sir,' confessed the boy.

'As were we all,' said Nicholas.

Samuel Ruff was embittered but chastened. He recognised just how cleverly the book holder had misled him. Nicholas had evidently suspected him for a long time. As the guards tried to move him away, he held his ground to make a last admission.

'*I* gave that crib to Susan Fowler.'

'She would rather you spared her husband,' said Nicholas.

'I know.'

'You should have gone to that farm in Norwich, Sam. You would have been far better off working with your brother.'

Ruff shook his head sadly and gave a smile of regret.

'There was no farm and I *did* work with my brother.'

'Redbeard?' Nicholas was shocked.

'He was my half-brother. For all his wild ways, Dominic was as committed to the true faith as I am. They imprisoned him in Bridewell for it and gave him those scars on his back. When Dominic was released, he was ready to do anything to help me.'

'So you repaid him with a sly dagger.'

'No!' denied Ruff vehemently. 'I could never murder my own kin. That was not my doing.' Pain contorted his face and his chin dropped to his chest. 'We both knew that it would cost us our lives in the end. Dominic was getting out of hand. The plan was in jeopardy while he lived. I did not want him killed but . . . it was in some ways a necessary despatch. He had done all that was required of him.'

'Who stabbed him, then?' pressed Firethorn.

Samuel Ruff met his gaze with dignity and defiance.

'That is something you will never know.'

'Someone has suborned you and set you on!' accused the other. 'The rack will get the truth out of you. Take him away!'

As the guards dragged their captive off, Ruff lapsed back into Latin to proclaim his faith.

'*In manus tuas, Domine, confide spiritum meum.*'

They were the last words spoken by Mary Queen of Scots as she laid her head upon the block. In trying to behead another Queen, he had delivered himself up to execution. Interrogation would be followed by a slow agonising death.

Nicholas was not entirely surprised to learn that Ruff was part of a wider conspiracy. He and Redbeard had been the active partners in the scheme while others lurked in the shadows. Their names would doubtless emerge in conversation in the privacy of the torture chamber.

One revelation, however, had rocked the book holder.

'I had no idea that Redbeard was his brother,' he said. 'I guessed that he was a fellow Catholic when he attacked the inn sign at The Cardinal's Hat. It mocked his faith. But I did not realise that he and Sam were related.'

'Two yoke-devils!' snarled Firethorn.

'There is no madness worse than religion,' murmured Nicholas.

Richard Honeydew was troubled by feelings of regret.

'But Master Ruff was such a kind and friendly man.'

'He was a fine actor,' said the book holder. 'He was even ready to receive a wound in order to play his part effectively. It was his bout with Master Gill that set me thinking.'

'In what way?' asked the boy.

'Sam tried to avoid it in order to hide his fencing skills. But he was forced into the bout and we saw his true merit. A swordsman as expert as that could easily have rehearsed the brawl in the Hope and Anchor. Will Fowler was murdered to plan.'

Edmund Hoode came scurrying along the corridor to join them. Confused by the speed of events, he only half-understood why his play had been halted in such dramatic fashion.

'What is going on, I pray?'

'Retribution!' declared Firethorn. 'We have unmasked an assassin and brought him to justice.'

'Samuel Ruff?'

'Villainy incarnate,' said the other. 'The man was deep and cunning but he met his match in our book holder. Ruff stage-managed things so cleverly that we were all fooled by him at first. Nick alone was equal to him.'

'I did what was needful,' said Nicholas modestly.

'You were magnificent!' insisted Firethorn. 'You won the villain's confidence and made him believe that you feared a threat from outside the company. Ruff thought that he was undiscovered. It then remained to show him in his true light.'

'Yes,' agreed Nicholas. 'By creating the very opportunity that he sought.'

'I begin to see,' said Hoode. 'When you asked me to put the execution on stage, you had a definite purpose in mind.'

'We did. Edmund.' explained the book holder. 'By casting Sam in the role of executioner, we knew exactly when and how he would strike. With the aid of Dick here, we were able to prepare an irresistible trap for him.'

Slightly peeved that he had not been party to it all, Hoode nevertheless congratulated them warmly. There was one particular point that he wanted clarified.

'What of the theft of *Gloriana Triumphant*?' he asked.

'That puzzled me, too,' said Nicholas. 'When the book was stolen from me, I thought it was another blow at Westfield's Men. Yet why should Ruff and his accomplice seek to wound the company? It was in their interests to ensure that it thrived.'

'So what lay behind it?' wondered Hoode.

'Religion. Your play was a celebration of the victory over the Spanish Armada and the defeat of Roman Catholicism. It offended them and their faith. That is why they tried to stop the performance.'

'Nobody can stop a performance by Westfield's Men!' asserted Firethorn grandly. 'We have foiled a plot to kill our own dear Queen and we have rendered our country a sterling service. But we still have unfinished business here. Gentlemen, we play before our sovereign this night. Let us prepare ourselves for this supreme moment in our history. Dick Honeydew has shown us the way. Onward to another royal triumph!'

The Loyal Subject was staged at midnight with reverberating success. Its themes gained extra resonance from the thwarted assassination attempt and it caught the mood of the hour to perfection. The whole Court surrendered itself to a unique and stirring experience. Richmond Palace was alive with unstinted praise.

Presiding over it all was Queen Elizabeth herself, who occupied her throne in a spirit of happy gratitude. She was ostentation itself. She wore a dress in the Spanish fashion with a round stiff-laced collar above a dark bodice with satin sleeves which were richly decorated with ribbons, pearls and gems. A veritable waterfall of pearls flowed from her neck and threatened to cascade down on to the dais. As befitted a sovereign, her radiance outshone the entire Court.

To repair the absence of Ruff – and to assauge Tallis's rampant fears – Nicholas Bracewell took over the small role of the executioner himself. With a measured sweep of the axe, he severed the wax head and sent the head spinning across the floor. The effect was breathtaking. Deathly silence held sway for a full minute before applause broke out. After exhibiting the head of the traitor, Nicholas went off to take up his book again.

Richard Honeydew had played his part already. He now stayed in the tiring-house with the others and sneaked an occasional look at the action on stage. Westfield's Men were at their best. The music was excellent, the costumes superb and the performances quite remarkable. Martin Yeo won plaudits for his youthful brilliance as the Duchess of Milan, Barnaby Gill supplied some stately comedy as a wrinkled retainer and Edmund Hoode was a suitably judicious judge.

Lawrence Firethorn was charismatic as Lorenzo and he caused many a flutter among the ladies. Constrained by the presence of her husband, Lady Rosamund Varley could only watch and sigh. Her erstwhile swain was no longer aiming his performance at her. It was directed to a higher station. Lorenzo was patently acting for his Queen and country.

At Firethorn's request, Hoode had written a new couplet to end the play. It related the capture of Samuel Ruff to the action of the drama. Firethorn made the two lines ring with conviction as he laid them proudly at the feet of his sovereign.

> For I alone have turned aside the traitor's baneful
> blade
> And now his spotted soul for aye will wander
> Hades' shade.

An ovation ensued.

Lord Westfield himself basked in the approval of the Court. The company had markedly improved the standing of their patron with the Queen. By the same token, the earl of Banbury sat in sour-faced discomfort as he touched his palms together in reluctant applause. Westfield's Men had carried the day in every sense. His own company was obliterated from the memory.

After taking several bows, the players adjourned to the tiring-house. A communal ecstasy seized them. They had succeeded beyond all expectation. It was a fitting climax to the year's work.

Firethorn swooped down on his book holder.

'Stop hiding away in that corner, Nick!'

'I was merely reflecting on events, master.'

'There is no time for that, dear heart,' urged the other, pummelling his arm. 'Her Majesty wishes to favour us. She has asked to meet the principal members of the company.'

'Who else is there but you?' teased Nicholas gently.

'How profoundly true!' agreed Firethorn without a trace of irony. 'Take charge, Nick. Be swift, sir.'

'Whom should I call?'

'Use your discretion. It has always served us well.'

Nicholas organised a line-up of the principal artistes, making sure that Richard Honeydew was given pride of place. Queen Elizabeth was conducted up on to the stage to be introduced to each one of them in turn by the fawning actor-manager. She praised Edmund Hoode for his play and she congratulated Barnaby Gill on his amusing antics.

When she showered her personal thanks upon Richard, the boy was duly overwhelmed. Being so close to the royal person reduced him to open-mouthed wonder. His performance had helped to save the Queen from the attack yet it now seemed a gross impertinence even to try to impersonate her.

With a becoming lack of modesty, Lawrence Firethorn claimed much of the credit for himself and wished to be remembered as her loyal subject in thought, word and deed. He gave the impression that he alone was responsible for keeping the Queen's head firmly on her shoulders.

Nicholas Bracewell stayed quietly behind the scenes.

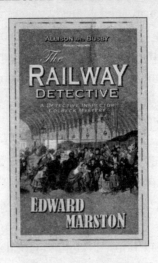

THE RESTORATION SERIES

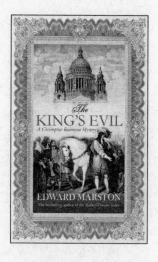

The King's Evil
The Amorous Nightingale
The Repentant Rake
The Frost Fair
The Parliament House
The Painted Lady

⋈

To discover more great historical crime and to
place an order visit our website at
www.allisonandbusby.com
or call us on
020 7580 1080